Every Month Original Novels, Stories, and Articles

USA Today Bestselling Writer
Dean Wesley Smith

TABLE OF CONTENTS

SHORT STORIES

FULL NOVEL

SERIAL BOOK

NONFICTION

Smith's Monthly Issue #27

All Contents copyright © 2015 Dean Wesley Smith
Published by WMG Publishing
Cover and interior design copyright © 2015 WMG Publishing
Cover art copyright © by Adrenalinapura/Dreamstime

"Introduction: Another Thunder Mountain Novel" copyright © 2015 Dean Wesley Smith

"The Smoke that Doesn't Bark" copyright © 2015 Dean Wesley Smith, cover design copyright © 2015 WMG Publishing.

"The Call of the Track Ahead" copyright © 2015 Dean Wesley Smith, cover design copyright © 2015 WMG Publishing.

Writing into the Dark copyright © 2015 Dean Wesley Smith, cover design copyright © 2015 WMG Publishing.

"Growing Pains of the Dead" copyright © 2015 Dean Wesley Smith, cover design copyright © 2015 WMG Publishing.

"The Case of the Dead Lady Blues" copyright © 2015 Dean Wesley Smith, cover design copyright © 2015 WMG Publishing.

Grapevine Springs: A Thunder Mountain Novel copyright © 2015 Dean Wesley Smith, cover design copyright © 2015 WMG Publishing.

This book is licensed for your personal enjoyment only. All rights reserved.
This is a work of fiction. All characters and events portrayed in the fiction in this book are fictional, and any resemblance to real people or incidents is purely coincidental.
This book, or parts thereof, may not be reproduced in any form without permission.

The Writings and Opinions of

Dean Wesley Smith

Introduction
ANOTHER THUNDER MOUNTAIN NOVEL

I can't begin to say how happy I am about having another Thunder Mountain novel in this issue. I love the series and the entire idea of being able to go back into other timelines and live in the Old West.

Some of you might know that my family members, on both sides, were pioneers into Idaho. And my grandparents on the Smith side worked in old mining towns, some of which I write about.

My grandfather worked in the mines, my grandmother cooked for the miners. And when a mine shut down, they moved on to another mining town. Some of the stories I heard from my grandparents when I was young were amazing.

And in the 1950s, when I was old enough to remember, they even showed me some of the towns and places. It was magical for a young kid.

It was their stories and those trips with them into the wilderness that gave me my intense interest in the Old West.

As an adult, I also tried to spend some time in the area I write about now. I have been in the Thunder Mountain region three times and it really is the most remote, rugged, and inaccessible area in the lower 48 states. It is designated a primitive area and only accessible by walking or horse.

I even have a story of being airlifted out of the area on my last try going in there. (I only tell the story in person. Much sadder and funnier that way.)

After seeing the area my grandparents worked and lived, I have a massive amount of respect for them and what they managed to survive.

And for all the pioneers in the Old West.

So writing about the area and the wonderful pioneers who lived there is wonderful fun for me. I sure hope you enjoy this new Thunder Mountain story.

Thanks for the Support

Dean Wesley Smith

I have another story set in the same region in this issue. It is called "Growing Pains of the Dead" and is set on the very trail and in the valley where I have set a number of Thunder Mountain novels. But from a very different perspective.

Next month a new novel serial will start in these pages. Actually not a newly written novel, but my first novel published in 1988 from Warner Books. It is also set in the same mountains, in the same valley as Thunder Mountain is set, but again with a very, very different perspective.

It is clear that even thirty plus years ago, my interest was in writing about the Thunder Mountain region in the Idaho Primitive Area.

There is just something about that remote valley with an old mining town on the bottom of a lake that can catch an imagination.

And the lodge on the top of the Monumental Summit that no one can find the remains of. I only know it even actually existed by reading newspapers from that time that advertised the lodge.

The novel in this book only visits the lodge at the top of Monumental Summit above the Thunder Mountain Valley, but the idea of remoteness and inaccessibility of the entire area comes through in this book just fine.

And when you get to the point in the novel where the characters are crossing a rock slope, I hope I portrayed the terror through the characters that I felt when I had to cross one of those.

Enjoy.

—Dean Wesley Smith
December 15th, 2015

Don't Miss an Issue!
Subscribe
Electronic Subscription:
6 Issues... $29.99
12 Issues... $49.99
Paper Subscription:
6 Issues... $59.99
12 Issues... $99.99
For Full Subscription Information
Go To:

www.SmithsMonthly.com
All Issue Also Available
at Your Favorite Bookstore

Coming Next Issue in Smith's Monthly
AN EASY SHOT
A Golf Thriller

Smith's

NUMBER TWENTY-EIGHT
JANUARY, 2016

MONTHLY

Original Stories,
Novels, and Articles

DEAN WESLEY SMITH

AN EASY SHOT
A Golf Thriller

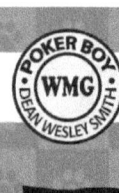

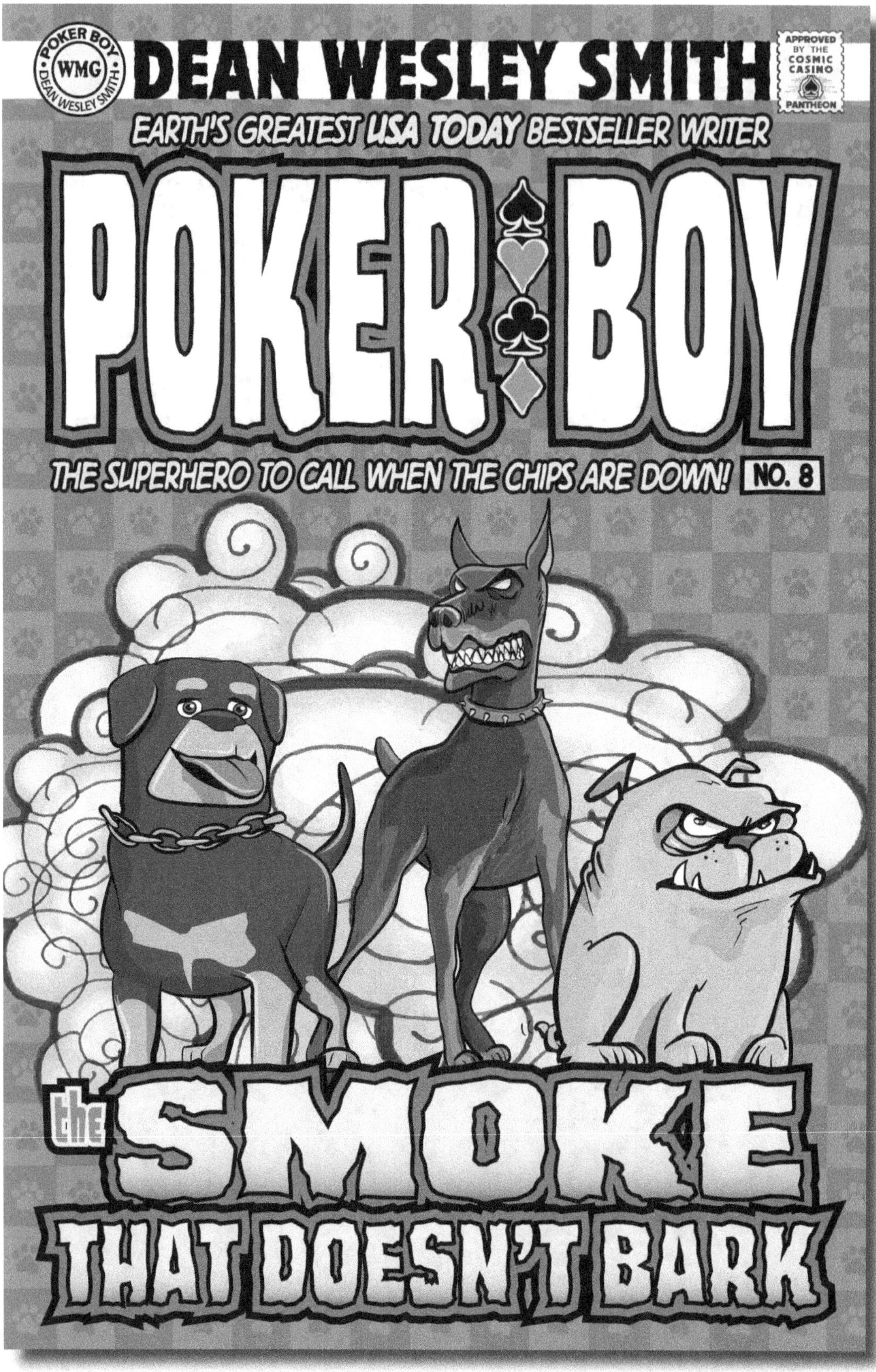
POKER BOY
WMG
DEAN WESLEY SMITH
DEAN WESLEY SMITH
APPROVED BY THE COSMIC CASINO
PANTHEON
EARTH'S GREATEST USA TODAY BESTSELLER WRITER
POKER BOY
THE SUPERHERO TO CALL WHEN THE CHIPS ARE DOWN!
NO. 8
the SMOKE
THAT DOESN'T BARK

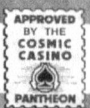

Gambling universe superhero Poker Boy loves saving dogs, even though that's not part of his duty in the gambling universe. He sometimes thinks he saves more dogs than he does people.

Now he and his team must use every skill they have to save not just one dog, but all dogs from a force that can't be stopped.

Or can it?

THE SMOKE THAT DOESN'T BARK
A Poker Boy Story

ONE

AS A SUPERHERO in the gambling universe, I have no idea why I always end up saving dogs. It sure seems that every time there is a person for me to save there is also a dog that needs my help. Not always, but my sidekick, Patty Ledgerwood, aka Front Desk Girl, thought it funny because it happens so often. And as she said, "It's kinda sweet."

Sometimes the person who needs the help owns the dog, other times the dog is not related in any way to the person I'm trying to help. I asked my boss, Stan, the God of Poker, about it once and he just thought I was kidding. It seems that animals have their own gods that take care of them.

Stan told me that over the years there has been very little reason for the Gambling Gods to associate with the Gods of Animals and Reptiles. That made sense to me considering animals are not known for placing bets.

But sometimes the lines between the different branches of gods are not as clear as some people make them out to be.

It was New Year's Eve, or more accurately, two in the morning on New Year's Day. One of my favorite things to do on New Year's Eve was to play a tournament at the MGM Grand on the strip in Vegas. Granted, that is a long way from my double-wide mobile home near a large Indian casino in Oregon, but Patty lives and works in Vegas, so I look for any reason to visit her as often as I can.

I must confess that Patty and I have a relationship. Sometimes that isn't smart between superhero and sidekick. But she's actually a superhero as well, working under the God of Hospitality. And we aren't serious enough yet for me to move from Oregon to Vegas. We have talked about it, sure, just not there yet.

By Vegas standards, the New Year's Eve tournament wasn't a big event, not like others around town, but for the past ten years I had made the little tournament at the MGM Grand on New Year's Eve a tradition, and I like tradition. And since half the people playing in the tournament were drunk tourists, and most of the professional poker players were at the bigger tournaments at other casinos, it made getting into the money fairly easy. In fact, I had made the final table and the money every year.

Besides, I love the sounds of a casino alive with people laughing and talking and machine bells going off, and on New Year's Eve, all that seemed to be more in focus, sharper, and if possible, louder.

The money was always nice as well, since the MGM Grand also kicked in a few grand added money. I have nothing against making some money in a decent poker game. After all, superheroes have to make a living to pay for chasing after the bad guys. Most people thought the gods paid for the superheroes working for

them, but they sure don't. We are expected to make a living and solve everyone's problems at the same time.

Considering that I make my living playing poker, I'm not complaining.

But Patty had to work tonight on her new job at the front desk of the MGM Grand, and she wouldn't be off until 3 a.m., at which time we would head to her wonderful apartment and enjoy the first day of the New Year together.

So I still had an hour, and had made the final table of the tournament. In fact, I was chip leader, and planned on using my chip advantage over the other eight players at the table to eventually take all their chips. In less than an hour, I hoped.

Suddenly, the dealer froze in the middle of her deal, the card suspended in midair, her nose scrunched up in concentration. All the loud noise of the casino and the laughing and talking cut off like I had been transported to an empty desert without any wind.

Around the table the players' faces were frozen in the moment. I had learned over the years that when you freeze a person in a moment, they seldom look good. A person's looks are dependent on movement. If you don't believe me, just randomly stop your DVD player with an attractive person on screen. Chances are their eyes will be rolled into their head slightly, their mouths open in a doofy fashion, and their expression twisted. The eight other players at the table and the dealer were no exceptions to the "frozen uglies" as I liked to call what they looked like.

Someone had taken me out of time and I only knew of a few people beside me that had that power, so I glanced around. Stan, the God of Poker, was winding his way through the frozen-in-time players,

Now Available
from all your favorite booksellers in trade paper and electronic editions.

clearly headed my way. Another silver-haired man was walking a few steps behind him.

The guy had large and slanted dark eyes, set far enough apart that, for a second, I wondered if he could see in two directions at once. He was dressed in a dark silk suit and matching tie that shouted money and power. He moved so smoothly behind Stan I wasn't sure he was even walking.

"Poker Boy," Stan said as I stood and stepped toward them, "meet The Smoke."

The Smoke just nodded and didn't bother to step close enough to shake my hand, so I didn't offer. I had a very odd feeling about the guy, but couldn't place it, which made me even more uncomfortable. As a poker player, my greatest strength was easily summing up a person and figuring them out. This guy would be tough across a poker table.

Now understand I didn't dislike the guy. I just couldn't get a read on him.

"I'm assuming there's a problem," I said to Stan, adjusting my superhero costume, which consisted of a black leather coat and black Fedora-like hat. My six-foot height made me about five inches taller than the compact frame of The Smoke. For some reason that pleased me.

"Let's walk," Stan said. "We need to meet Patty."

If Stan was putting both of us on a case, something really important had gone wrong.

Really important.

I pointed at my stack of tournament chips on the table. "Release the room and I'll tell them to blind me off. I'll follow you in a moment."

Blinding off a stack meant that a player in a tournament still had to pay the blinds every round, even if they weren't in the chair. So my chip stack would dwindle slowly until gone while all my hands would be folded.

Stan nodded and turned to leave. I sat back down just as he released the freeze and let me drop back into normal time. The sounds of the casino came crashing back in like a hammer and every face around the table returned to normal.

I quickly stood again and nodded to the dealer. "Blind me off until I get back."

She nodded and I turned and headed out of the poker room. Unless I got back quickly, I wouldn't win the tournament, but with the size of my stack, just being blinded off slowly might get me third or fourth as other players knocked themselves out. Still a decent payday for my New Year's tradition.

I was about halfway to the lobby of the casino when everything around me froze again and the noise vanished once more. Stan and Patty and The Smoke were standing in the middle of the wide aisle near the huge, open hotel lobby, talking.

Patty looked better than ever. I had first met her five years back when she worked downtown at the Horseshoe, the last year the World Series of Poker was held there. Tonight the white blouse and dark pants accented her perfectly trim body in a way I very much liked. Her long brown hair was tied back and up, giving her a serious look.

I know it sounds corny, but every time I saw her, my heart sort of raced, and this time was no exception, even though I had talked to her just an hour ago during one of the tournament breaks.

Patty glanced over at me with her large brown eyes and smiled a smile that could melt anyone into a puddle on the ornate tile floor. "You winning?"

"Of course," I said, laughing. "Chip leader. Final table just got started."

"Sorry," Stan said.

I just shrugged. "Work needs to come first. So what's the problem?"

Stan glanced at The Smoke, then said simply, "About two hours ago, someone placed a number of very large bets with a number of bookmakers around town that all the dogs in North America would be killed at exactly twelve noon on the first day of the year, Vegas time."

Patty gasped and I tried to understand what Stan had just said. "All the dogs? Why?"

"No one knows," Stan said.

"That's just sick," Patty said.

The Smoke seemed to be showing no emotion at all. He just stood there, his thin, dark, wide-set eyes seeming to observe everything around him.

The silence of the frozen casino seemed to grow as Patty and I tried to take in what we had been told.

I turned to face The Smoke directly. "I assume you work for the animal gods."

The Smoke nodded. "We are aware of your ability to save dogs," he said, his voice deep and low. "Since this involves a bet, my boss went to Laverne and we asked for your help."

Laverne was Lady Luck herself. I hoped she had a lot more than me and Patty and Stan on this problem.

I nodded and turned to Stan. "I assume you are looking for the guy who placed the bet."

"Oh, we know who it was. He has nothing to do with the coming deaths. He's just trying to make some huge money on it to rebuild his house."

"The Bookkeeper!" both Patty and I said at the same time.

Stan nodded and we all went back to being silent. Three months ago the Bookkeeper, while trying to prove to the world that there was no luck, had mathematically trapped Lady Luck herself.

Don't Miss an Issue!

Subscribe

Electronic Subscription:

6 Issues... $29.99

12 Issues... $49.99

Paper Subscription:

6 Issues... $59.99

12 Issues... $99.99

For Full Subscription Information
Go To:

www.SmithsMonthly.com

Patty and I and Screamer, the third member of my team, had barely rescued her in time. But in the process, the Bookkeeper's home had been completely destroyed, along with all of his super computers and about three bedrooms and a living room full of very smelly trash.

The Bookkeeper had an uncanny ability to predict future events with just math.

"We'll need to talk to him," I said.

Stan nodded. "I'll bring him to you. Where?"

"Does he still smell?" Patty asked about a half-second before I did.

"He smells like a field of lilacs now," Stan said. "Something one of his bosses did to him."

"A small field I hope," I said.

Stan shook his head. "Not so small."

"Oh, wonderful," Patty said.

"Our normal place in fifteen minutes," I told Stan.

Stan nodded.

Our normal place was a small restaurant, open 24 hours a day, called The Diner. It pretended to be an old 1960s diner, and was tucked into a hole on a side street near the old Horseshoe Casino downtown. When the team of Patty and Screamer and I first formed, that's where we met, and it's become our normal meeting site for any case we were working together.

Besides, it had great milkshakes, and right now I could use one.

Stan released the "out of time bubble" on us and Patty and I headed across the lobby toward the exit to the parking area out back, with her explaining how she managed to get off an hour early on her shift tonight. We were most of the way across the hotel lobby when I realized that The Smoke was following us about five feet back, walking as silently as anyone I had ever met.

"Where's Stan?" I asked, turning to him.

"He said I was to help you," The Smoke said, again his voice low and rough and at the same time very smooth. "He said he had a few other leads to check out and would catch up."

I nodded and said, "Sounds fine. More help the better."

I turned back to Patty, who handed me her cell phone as we walked, with The Shadow following a few feet behind us. When I put it to my ear the phone was already ringing.

"Patty," Screamer said as he answered, clearly seeing his caller id. "What's up?" His voice was chipper and I could hear music and laughter behind him.

"Sorry to bother you tonight," I said, "We've got a pretty nasty one."

"Hey, Poker Boy. Great hearing your voice again. When?"

"Fifteen minutes," I said.

"I'll be there," he said and hung up.

I handed Patty back her phone, then said. "The old gang is back together again. I just hope we can pull off another miracle."

"So do I," The Smoke said softly behind us.

TWO

IT TOOK US exactly sixteen minutes to get to The Diner downtown from the MGM Grand on the Strip. Screamer was already there and he was sitting in our normal booth, but I indicated we should move to the big table in the corner. The idea of sitting next to the Bookkeeper in a tight booth was nightmarish at best.

Madge, the slightly overweight waitress with far, far too tight slacks walked up, popped her gum, and said, "Well, looks like the Weird Bunch is back in town. And with a new member as well."

"Great seeing you again, Madge," I said. I didn't blame her for being sort of curt with us. Over the years some strange things had happened in this restaurant around us, and we had left unfinished more meals than we had eaten here.

"Milkshakes around?" Madge asked, her gum popping again.

Screamer, Patty and I nodded. The Smoke simply said, "Water. Hamburger very rare, no onion or pickles or anything green on it. Hold the mustard and any other sauce."

Madge took it all down and glanced at The Smoke. "You fit right in with this group. Anyone else?"

We all shook our heads and after Madge left, I introduced The Smoke to Screamer. They didn't shake hands, just nodded at each other.

"I've heard of you," Screamer said, sitting back in his chair. You've rescued more animals than Poker Boy here, and that's going some."

"And I've heard of your ability to get inside someone's head," The Smoke said, nodding in respect. "It is a pleasure to meet you."

The Smoke was talking about Screamer's superpower. He could transfer what one person was thinking to another or read their minds just by a touch. He got his nickname by making a serial killer scream in horror by digging up his worst fears and making him see and live them to get him to confess. His methods never would stand up in court, but it gets the really bad guys off the streets.

Screamer turned to me. "I assume we're dealing with a problem with animals if The Smoke is joining us."

I nodded and quickly outlined what we already knew. I had just finished when the sounds of the restaurant vanished and Stan and The Bookkeeper appeared.

Across the small restaurant, Madge was frozen bending over to pick something off the floor near the cash register. Luckily for all of us, she was slightly behind the counter so we didn't have to see frozen all that her tight outfit exposed.

Suddenly a wave of purple smell hit us. Intensely purple lilac smell.

The Smoke got up and moved quickly to the other side of the table away from Stan and The Bookkeeper, while the three of us instantly covered our noses. I wasn't sure which was worse: the intense smell of rotting food and trash The Bookkeeper used to smell like, or this intense perfume smell of lilacs, so thick I wasn't sure I would ever taste anything but purple again.

"Hey, Poker Boy, Patty, Screamer," the Bookkeeper said. "I never did get to thank you for saving my ass with Lady Luck."

"No problem," I said, then started to say something else and choked on the smell and couldn't speak.

"We'll make this quick," Stan said. "Screamer, would you touch the Bookkeeper and then connect him with Poker Boy." He glanced at Patty and The Smoke. "You two touch Poker Boy so you all get what he knows exactly."

I'd been inside the Bookkeeper's mind once before and I wasn't looking forward to doing it again. I could tell that neither were Patty and Screamer. I had no idea what The Smoke was feeling.

Stan faced the Bookkeeper. "Focus on everything you know about the coming death of the dogs, including how you worked it out."

The Bookkeeper nodded and Screamer touched his shoulder and then my arm as Patty and The Smoke both touched my shoulders, one on each side.

Like a movie run in fast forward, I could instantly see the Bookkeeper sitting at a computer, his fingers flying as he worked out some sort of equation that I didn't understand. I tried to focus on what facts he was plugging into the equations, but none of it made any sense to me.

At the same time I could sense Patty's mind and Screamer's. Both of them I was used to, but The Smoke was like a dark place in the connection, his mind not really part of the group for some reason or another.

Screamer broke the connection and I shuddered, glad to be out of the Bookkeeper's head once again.

The Bookkeeper looked at Screamer. "That's just so weird."

"Come on," Stan said, and an instant later he and the Bookkeeper were gone and the noise of the restaurant and the street outside flooded back into the silence.

I took a napkin and blew my nose, trying to clear some of the smell without success. I could taste lilacs, and it felt like my skin was coated in the smell, like someone had dumped an entire bottle of cheap perfume over me.

"Anyone get anything out of that?" I asked, "Besides the need for a shower?"

The Smoke came back around the table and sat down again as we all tried to piece together the thing we had seen in fast motion from the Bookkeeper's mind.

"He seemed to only be working with probability equations," Screamer said.

Patty nodded.

"So what in the world made him even start on those equations?" I asked. "A person like the Bookkeeper just doesn't come up with 'all dogs dying' out of the blue."

We all sat in silence trying to dig back through the wave of information we had all gotten from the connection with the Bookkeeper's mind. It was like trying to sort through a library of information. The closer you looked, if you looked in the wrong spot, the deeper you got into the wrong details.

Like rewinding a DVD, I ran back over the Bookkeeper working on the problem until the moment he first sat down at a computer with the idea. Then I slowed down what I was seeing, still in reverse, until I finally got to the trigger point.

"Oh, no," The Smoke said softly.

He must have gotten to the same point I had managed to get to in the information in our minds.

"How is that possible?" I asked The Smoke.

"What possible?" Patty and Screamer asked at the same moment.

"Please," Patty said. "I don't want to play around in that guy's mind anymore than I have to."

"Basically," I said, glancing at The Smoke, "At noon today all dogs are going to become human. Sort of."

He nodded. "That's what it looks like."

Before I could ask him the dozen questions I had for him, Marge said, "What's that smell?"

She was waving her hand in front of her face while carrying a tray of milkshakes with the other.

"Sorry," I said. "A little perfume bottle accident."

She half-dropped the milkshakes and tray on our table. "Smells more like a perfume factory disaster," she said, heading for the door at full speed. She opened it and blocked it open, then headed for the back room. "Got to get a cross-breeze in here."

I glanced at the milkshake in front of me, but had no desire to drink it at the moment. Not only would it just taste like purple lilacs, but with what we had discovered by putting all the pieces together, the Bookkeeper was going to win his bet.

"Is it possible for a dog to become human?" Screamer asked. "Isn't that something like being a werewolf?"

"Wolves become human, yes," The Smoke said. "I am a werewolf, actually."

I was so startled, I just opened my mouth and then closed it again with no words coming out.

Patty just stared at him.

"Full moon stuff and all?" Screamer asked.

The Smoke, smiled, sort of, without showing his teeth. "No, I can turn at will and have complete control over both forms."

"So is that what's going to happen to all the dogs?" Patty asked. "Are they suddenly going to have your power?"

The Smoke shook his head sadly. "I was a human first before my power came about. Dogs have much smaller brains and would not understand their new form or how to live as humans. They would still have the minds and actions of dogs."

"This is a disaster," Screamer said. "Millions of new humans are suddenly going to appear. Humans that need help and can't take care of themselves as humans. This is going to crash our entire economy."

"So what's causing this?" Patty asked. "Or who? And why?"

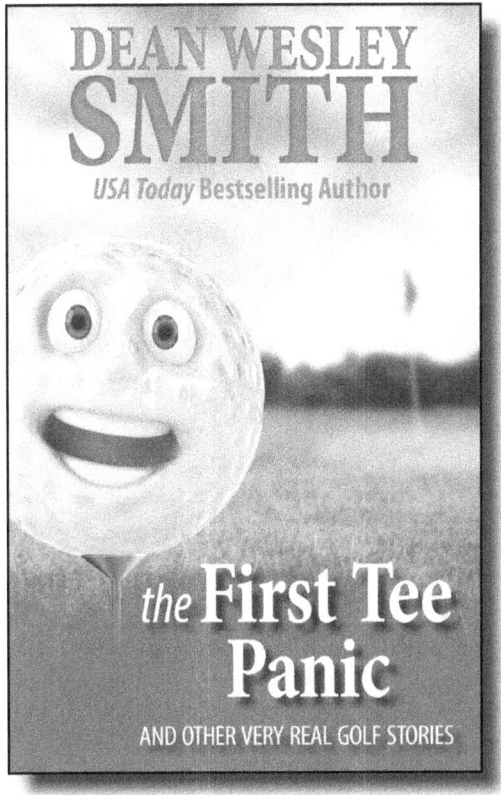

Former PGA Golf Professional and USA Today *bestselling writer Dean Wesley Smith walks you step-by-step, club-by-club from your car to the first tee and beyond in a laugh-out-loud style that not only teaches, but entertains.*

A perfect gift for the golfer in your family.

Now Available
from all your favorite booksellers in trade paper and electronic editions.

"Back to what triggered the Bookkeeper to figure it out," Screamer said.

"No one is causing this. We have no villains," I said and The Smoke nodded.

"Radiation spike," I said. I could see clearly how the Bookkeeper had read a study on a coming short, intense burst of radiation from a cloud in space that the Earth would pass through.

The focus of the hit would be the North American continent and it would only last for a fraction of a second exactly at noon Vegas time. Scientists believed it would be harmless and were just planning on studying the coming burst. But when the Bookkeeper learned of the exact frequency of the burst, he started to work the probability equations.

The Smoke just nodded. "The Bookkeeper somehow knew a secret very closely guarded among the animal gods on how to turn an animal human."

"Are more than just dogs going to be changed?" Screamer said. "I'm having a hard time imaging mouse-sized humans running around."

"Luckily, no," The Smoke said. "If the Bookkeeper is correct on the information he has on the frequency and duration of the burst, it will be only dogs. All dogs."

"So what are we going to do?" Patty asked.

I knew exactly what needed to be done. I didn't think it was possible, but I sure hoped it would be.

"We're going to call in the big guns," I said, smiling, remembering what had happened outside of the Bookkeeper's home when it blew up.

"Big Guns?" Screamer asked, looking at me with puzzlement.

I turned to The Smoke. "What level are you over in your world of deities?"

"I'm a superhero like you three," he said. "I can change my shape at will into a dozen different animals, pass through walls like a ghost, and hear and smell things from a great distance."

"And your bosses?" I asked. "What can they do?"

The Smoke made a poor imitation of a shrug in his expensive suit. "I do not know. They are gods, they can do about anything as far as I know."

"And they are working on this as well?" I asked.

"They are," he said.

I nodded, then turned to Patty and Screamer. "Seems we need a God Summit to fix this problem."

"A what?" Screamer asked.

Patty just laughed. "You're not thinking what I think you're thinking, are you?"

I smiled. "I am." Then I turned and shouted into the lilac-smelling air, "Stan!"

THREE

ONE HOUR LATER the four of us, with Stan, were standing in front of Lady Luck's huge oak desk. As best as I could tell from the faint light starting to fill the winter sky over Vegas, her office was floating a few thousand feet in the air. It looked like any other corporate president's office except for the large pair of white dice sitting on the corner of her desk, and the fact that there were windows on all four sides of the room and no building under us.

Lady Luck was dressed in a business power-suit of dark silk, with a white blouse under the vest. Today her hair was brown and pulled back tightly, giving her a serious look that would scare just about anyone, since her features were classic Greek with the sharp, pointed nose and high cheekbones.

I hated standing near or even being around Lady Luck. As a professional poker player, if she got mad at me I could go on a very long and very dry spell of bad cards. Sure, poker was a game of skill, but without a little luck at times, losing would happen much more often.

I had just finished explaining to her what we had found and my suggestion to stop the problem. She was just staring at me with the best poker face I had ever seen.

I just stared back, keeping my own poker face in complete control as well.

"This will take a lot of power to cover the entire continent with a shield like you are suggesting," Laverne said. "I do not have that much power. In fact, all of the gods under my control don't have that kind of power, even for the fraction of a second it will need to be in place."

"I was afraid of that," I said. "But if you combined forces with the animal gods and some of the others, as many others as would be possible, then there might be enough. Right?"

I honestly had no idea if I was correct or not, but I sure hoped I was. Otherwise the world was in for a very tough time with millions of more humans showing up suddenly, all in need of care just as dogs had needed.

I couldn't even imagine just the toilet training issues alone.

She stared at me and then laughed. Having Lady Luck herself laugh at you is not something I had ever imagined happening. Her laugh was sharp and high and it cut.

"You are suggesting something that has never been done before," she said. "All the gods working together. We've never even been in the same time zone or area of the planet at the same time before, let alone work together on anything."

I nodded and said nothing.

Lady Luck walked to the window of her office and stared down at the lights of the Strip below. Then she said "Burt!"

The round, red-faced God of Casino Operations, and second in command of all the gambling universe under Laverne, appeared beside Stan and close to Laverne.

"What do you think of what Poker Boy and his crew are suggesting?" Laverne asked Burt.

"We might get enough of the gods to help if we called in a few chits and asked for a few favors," Burt said. He turned to The Smoke. "What about your bosses?"

"I have already conferred with them and they will follow whatever decision Laverne makes on this. Only a few of them have the power of the shield that will be needed, but they will add what they can."

I didn't say anything, but it was just another example of how Laverne had grown in power over the centuries to become one of the most powerful gods of them all. She only answered to the Fates, and I doubted she even talked to them much these days.

She nodded. "The gods that will help will meet back here in one hour. We have a lot of invitations to send out and little time to do it."

Laverne then nodded to me. "Be prepared to state your case in one hour."

I was about to ask just what she meant by that when the four of us found ourselves back at our normal booth in The Diner.

The front door was still open and the place smelled much better. None of us had drunk our milkshakes, and The Smoke hadn't even gotten his hamburger when we had vanished from the place an hour before. But we had left Madge more than enough money to cover everything before Stan jumped us away to Laverne's office.

"The Weird Bunch is back again," Madge said, coming out from the back room. "What would you like to order this time that you won't eat?"

I was too stunned at what Laverne had said before we jumped back here to even order, so Patty had Madge bring me a vanilla milkshake again. I doubted I would drink it.

What did Lady Luck mean that I needed to be prepared to state my case? After I sat for a moment with that question going over and over through my mind, I turned to Patty.

"What did Laverne mean by 'me stating the case'?"

Patty smiled, but it was the smile I had seen her use on me a number of times when she was humoring me.

Screamer laughed an uneasy laugh. "Laverne is going to pull in as many gods from around the planet as she can and have you explain to them what everyone needs to do."

I opened my mouth, then shut it. I had enough trouble talking to just Stan and Laverne and Burt. How in the world was I going to talk to dozens of different gods all at once? And with so much at stake?

I couldn't do it. I just couldn't. And that meant that very shortly the average IQ of the human race was going to drop dramatically.

FOUR

AFTER A HALF HOUR of talking with my friends, I was starting to calm down. Finally, with Patty's hand resting on my arm to give me strength, I started to focus on the real problem. If I could get past the stage fright, I had to have an exact plan.

I sipped my vanilla milkshake and then turned to The Smoke. "Do you have the exact frequency needed to change dogs into humans?"

"I do," he said.

"So, are there other frequencies of radiation we need to worry about that change other animals into humans or frogs into cats or things like that?"

He nodded. "There are a few. But the frequency that is due to hit here is exact, and harmless for the most part except for this problem we are facing. All we have to do is block it exactly and we will be fine."

"Better," I said. I turned to the air and shouted "Stan!"

A moment later the restaurant froze with Madge behind the cash register ringing up the money we had given her for our current batch of food and drinks.

"Need a little help," I said to the Poker God now pulling up a chair on the end of the booth. "When you and Burt stopped that explosion at the Bookkeeper's house from spreading anywhere but upward, what kind of field was that? And how did you generate it?"

"You all have one form or another of the same power," Stan said. He looked directly at me. "When you take people out of time, as I have done here now, you simply imagine them slipping between the molecules, right?"

I had to admit he was right. I did it that way. I nodded.

Stan turned to Patty. "When you are working with an upset customer, how do you calm them?"

She nodded. "I change some hormone molecules in their minds to a calming substance that makes them feel good and happy."

Stan turned to The Smoke, who was already nodding. "When I go through walls, I simply imagine the molecules very wide apart so that I can slip through them, like turning the structure of the wall into a gas for an instant."

"Exactly," Stan said, turning back to face me. "All Burt and I did was harden the air around the explosion so nothing could get through for the brief moment of the explosion."

"And that's exactly what we need to do," I said, "for the few seconds the radiation is hitting North America. We need to harden the air enough to block an exact frequency."

"It will work," Stan said. "If we have enough power to generate the hardening field for long enough and at the right time."

"So how many gods are coming to help?" I asked.

Stan stared up at the ceiling for a moment, clearly somewhere else, then said, "Six hundred and twelve."

"There are six hundred and twelve gods?" Screamer asked as I sat back, stunned.

Stan smiled. "Oh, there are far more than that. But only six hundred and twelve have accepted Laverne's invitation to help."

"How in the world is she going to co-ordinate all of them?" Screamer asked.

"She's not," I said, closing my eyes and trying not to panic. "That's what she wants us to do."

"I'm afraid so," Stan said. "I'll be back in a half hour. She's got a mess with the seating chart that needs all of us working on it. We gods, you know, have egos."

Suddenly the noise of the café and the street outside flooded back in and all I could do was lean back in the booth and try not to panic.

Unsuccessfully.

FIVE

AFTER ABOUT five minutes, with Patty's gentle touch on my arm, I was calm enough again to work on the problem.

We all four talked for a few minutes, then Screamer said exactly the conclusion I had been coming to. "There's just no way to get over six hundred gods with different levels of powers to cover everywhere completely."

I nodded. "To do that would take years of math and someone like the Bookkeeper to figure it out, and that's if we knew exactly the level of every god's powers. And we don't and never will."

"So how do we do this?" Patty asked. "Are we going to be happy with saving only some dogs and not all?"

I hated that thought. I hated it every time I couldn't save a single dog.

"No," I said, "we need all the power to go through one source and out over the entire continent, to form a complete dome of hardened air for a second or two."

"And who's going to do that?" The Smoke said.

"We are," I said. "All four of us together, linked."

Screamer opened his mouth, then shut it again. Patty just shook her head slowly. The Smoke seemed frozen.

But for the first time in a couple of hours I was starting to feel more confident.

"With the four of us linked, The Smoke can form the dome and make sure we are blocking the right frequency, Screamer can hold us together and add energy, and Patty and I can control and funnel the energy to the shield that The Smoke forms."

"That's going to be a lot of power," Screamer said.

"I don't think we'll survive it," Patty said. "We're not gods."

"And that's why we can do it," I said. "We're the workers, the superheroes who get our hands dirty every day saving lives. We don't need to touch the power, just like a fireman with a powerful hose of water doesn't touch the water. We just aim it."

"I hope you're right, Poker Boy," The Smoke said.

"If I'm not," I said, "we'll be dead and a lot of dogs will be human."

I glanced at the clock on the wall. "We only have a few minutes. We need to practice this a few times."

Screamer nodded for The Smoke to touch his shoulder and then reached for Patty and my hands.

It took us a moment, but then we each settled into our spots in the bigger mind we had created with Screamer's connection.

I thought directly at The Smoke that he should imagine hardening the air over the booth next to ours in a way that would only block a certain frequency.

He did, and then Patty and I formed an imaginary hose and connected it to the shield to power it. We ran through it twice, then Screamer let us go.

"I want to practice that with Stan feeding us some light energy just before we go."

Everyone nodded, so once again I called for Stan.

"Almost time," he said as he appeared, taking us out of time at the same moment.

"One quick practice session," I said. I quickly explained what we were doing. Stan nodded. "Might just work."

For Stan, that was as encouraging as he ever got.

Screamer linked the four of us up and we could hear Stan ask, "Ready?"

"Ready," we said as one, out of four mouths.

He started a slight flow of energy toward us and Patty and I captured it easily into the mouth of the imaginary hose we had formed in our minds and sent it directly to the shield.

Expand the shield, I thought to The Smoke, so that it covers as much as you can with the energy coming to you.

He expanded the shield as Stan increased the energy until the shield covered all of the Las Vegas area. As more energy came in Patty and I let the natural flow expand the size of the hose protecting all of our minds. It worked easily for one god's worth of energy. Could we hold the containment for over six hundred gods' energy, all directed at the same spot?

If not, we would be four very dead superheroes.

SIX

STAN JUMPED the four of us back to the front of what looked like a large auditorium floating high over Las Vegas. We were suddenly standing on a stage facing six hundred very powerful gods who stared at us like we were a bad stage act that was bombing.

The colors and styles of clothing in the room seemed to not only cover every possible color in the rainbow, but almost every age of man. I didn't recognize more than one or two of them. I could see the Bookkeeper's bosses, the Gods of Mathematics, in their heavy sweaters and large glasses, but beyond that I had no idea who the rest of the gods were. I was pretty certain I didn't want to know.

Laverne, still dressed in her business suit and white blouse stepped up beside the four of us and started speaking to the crowd. "We have very little time if we are to avert a disaster of epic proportions. We have four superheroes here who need all of our help to solve this problem."

She introduced the four of us and which area of the deities we each worked, then said, "Poker Boy, please tell us how we can help your team solve this problem."

I took a deep breath, dug down deep into the calming poker face and manner that had gotten me through many a stressful tournament, and then with Patty's hand barely touching my arm for support, I explained what we needed and why.

Around the room I could see heads nodding, clearly thinking our plan would work. Others sat perfectly still, expressionless.

When I finished Laverne stepped forward. "I will help focus the power and contain it as it moves through the four of them so that they will not die from the extreme energy being poured through them."

I was very, very happy to hear Laverne say that.

She turned to me again. "Poker Boy, how long will we need to hold the shield?"

"Two seconds," I said, "but it will take a few seconds for us to power up the shield as well, so if the energy can be brought up over the first three seconds, then held for two seconds, it should solve the problem."

Lady Luck nodded, her expression deadly serious, then turned to the audience. "Thank you all for your help. Please be ready."

Burt appeared next to Laverne and said, "Twenty seconds."

"Screamer," I said and he nodded. He stepped between me and Patty and The Smoke moved in behind him. Then The Smoke put both hands on Screamer's shoulder while Patty and I took each of Screamer's hands.

Suddenly we were all together again.

Sure hope this works, the Screamer thought clearly.

Just hold us together no matter what happens, I thought back.

Burt and Laverne stepped in front of us and then turned sideways to the audience facing each other, leaving an opening between them from us to the audience.

"Ten seconds," Burt said.

Screamer's grip on my hand tightened.

Form the hose, I thought at Patty and we formed a very thick, very expandable imaginary hose.

"Five seconds," Burt said.

"Start easy for the first second, then increase the energy," Laverne said to the gods.

Not a sound could be heard in the huge room as every god sat forward, clearly focused on the task at hand.

Every ounce of energy we have to keep this hose together, I thought to Patty. Keep the shield on frequency, I thought at The Smoke.

"Two, one, Now!" Burt said.

The impact of the first energy staggered both Laverne and Burt, but they both adjusted and the energy hit us, caught by the now seemingly huge imaginary hose in our minds.

Even though Patty and I were focusing all our energy on the hose and holding it in place against the flood of energy, I could see the shield expanding as the energy increased and increased.

Time seemed to slow down as the energy increased. As far as I was concerned, it felt like the hose was the size of a ten-lane interstate and growing, all inside our group minds.

I could feel Patty starting to weaken, so I dug as deep as I could and held. Then I felt her also dig deep and strengthen as well. She was the strongest human I had ever met.

Somehow we held that imaginary hose in our minds together, even as it continued to grow. Just one leak from that stream of energy and we would all be dead. And I wasn't going to allow anything to happen to Patty.

I could sense a thought from The Smoke that the shield was full and holding.

I could feel energy coming from Screamer trying to help me and Patty as much as possible without losing the contact between us he was struggling to hold.

Time stretched and stretched and stretched.

I could feel myself and Patty starting to slip on our hold on the imaginary hose.

The strain was too much.

I couldn't hold this much longer.

It wasn't possible.

It's done! The faint thought came from The Smoke. The radiation is blocked.

"Stop," I said, hoping that was my out-loud voice.

The energy shut off instantly and all four of us slumped to the stage as one.

Screamer let our hands go and I had the sudden feeling of being alone.

Both Lady Luck and Burt staggered backward as well, then worked to catch their breath.

Slowly a sound filled the air and I looked at Patty, who was coming around and looking at me. It took me a moment to realize what the sound was, then I looked out at the mass of gods. They were all standing and applauding.

We were getting a standing ovation from a room full of gods! What a way to start a new year.

And then after a moment the sound stopped and they all vanished, leaving an empty room with only Stan, Laverne, Burt, and the four of us.

Stan helped me to my feet and I helped Patty. Screamer and The Smoke staggered up as well. My knees felt like they were held together by rubber bands, thin ones, but darned if I was going to fall down again in front of Lady Luck, so I braced my legs and Patty leaned against me and we held each other up somehow.

Laverne and Burt both looked tired as well, and there was actually a little sweat on her forehead that vanished after a moment.

Lady Luck actually could sweat. Who knew?

She thanked each of us for the great work, then looked directly at me. "Once again, Poker Boy, you and your team have saved us. All I can say is thank you yet again."

She and Burt vanished, leaving a tired-looking, but smiling Stan, the God of Poker. "How about we all go get something to eat? On me."

"I'm not sure if Madge can handle us three times in one day," I said. "Especially on the first day of the year."

"I was thinking more about the buffet at the MGM Grand. Don't you have some winnings to pick up?"

"I do," I said, smiling, remembering how my year had actually started with my tradition.

Everyone was nodding at the idea so I said, "Perfect. And besides, I wanted to talk to The Smoke here, see if he might be interested in joining us on a few cases down the road?"

The Smoke smiled, again without showing his teeth, then said, "I would be honored." Then he turned to Stan. "I hear the buffet at the MGM Grand has some great meat. Not cooked too much, I hope."

Stan laughed. "You know, you're as weird as the rest of this bunch. You fit perfectly."

"That he does," I said smiling at the werewolf named The Smoke, the newest member of the team.

A moment later the five of us were standing in line for the buffet. Even a god and four superheroes had to stand in line. Even after saving a lot of dogs.

The First Two Cold Poker Gang Novels
Available at your favorite booksellers.

Dean Wesley **Smith**

USA Today Bestselling Writer

Do you risk your life,
your safety,
and the women you love
for a dream?

The
Call *of the*
Track Ahead

Do you risk your life, your safety, and the women you love for a dream?

Sometimes just a single step from a moving train can provide the answer.

A heart-warming contemporary fantasy story.

THE CALL
OF THE TRACK AHEAD

ONE

TODAY HE WOULD JUMP.

The thought echoed around inside Mason Green's head and he sat upright in the coach seat, his two small blankets bunching across his lap and over his legs. Finally, after all the days, months, years of trying to decide, today he would jump.

He had decided.

The train rocked in its familiar motion of smooth track, a faint, consistent click-click as the wheels of the car ticked away the time. It was still pitch-black outside the cold, slightly fogged windows. The only light came from above the doors leading into the car forward and the car behind. The air held a chill, and around him everyone slept, the sounds of snoring mixed with deep breathing and the rhythmic clicking of the wheels on the tracks.

He knew those sounds well.

For as long as he could remember, he had called the front aisle seat of the fifth car back from the dining car his home. As of last evening, there were sixteen cars behind his. Sometimes there were more, sometimes less. Since the train never stopped, he had no idea how those cars were added or how the constant stream of new people came on board.

They just did.

He couldn't remember coming on board either. But he liked being here at first. He had always loved trains as a kid. Since his parents had both worked long hours at thankless jobs, and his room was in the basement of his house, they hadn't cared what he did down there as long as he didn't get in the way of the laundry room. So, in the unfinished large room next to his half-finished bedroom, he had built a very intricate model train layout, focusing at times on it instead of his studies or even girls. He built mountains, tunnels, rivers and lakes with train bridges over them. It became so real, that at times it helped him escape from the arguments going on upstairs between his parents.

As he had gotten older, he had dreamed of riding trains and seeing the country. He had a shelf full of books about trains in his room. He even thought of maybe going off and working for the railroad, but with all the pressures of college and starting his new corporate job, he had just never gotten around to it.

But more than anything, from his earliest memories, he had wanted to start and run his own toy store. He hadn't gotten around to that yet, either. In fact, he hadn't done anything at all with his life except school and work, right up to the point he found himself on the train.

He had been in his parents' old house, after his father's funeral, down in the basement, staring at the remains of his old train layout. His mother had just left it there for the decade since he had moved out. At times over the years, he had

packed up parts of it, hoping to rebuild it someday when he had his own house. He hadn't done that, so most of it still remained in his parents' basement, covered in dust just like his dreams.

He had been sitting there in the basement, staring at the old track and the mountains and lakes he had built when the next thing he realized, he was on the train.

No memory of how, no memory of what had happened between that moment in the basement and his first waking moment on the train.

For some reason, he sort of knew that no time had passed. And that no time was passing outside the train, either. But it felt like it passed in a normal manner on the train. He just didn't age.

Now he had been on the train for a very long time. Years and years. Over those long years, he had lived in every car, seen every type of human come through. Some people had become friends. Others enemies. He could barely remember most of their names. But almost without exception, they had all jumped. Taking the leap from a moving train car was the only way off, since the train never stopped, and everyone seemed to take it at one point or another.

Today he would, too.

Today he would jump.

Paula Simpson, his seatmate for the past four months, snored softly, her head on a pillow against the window. Even in sleep, she smelled of fresh peaches and the great outdoors.

That was one of the many things that had drawn him to her when they met over lunch one afternoon in the dining car. She had blue eyes, just like his, and she liked that. They both had blonde hair, and she liked that, too, even though his was thinning. Her nose was short and, as she called it, "perky." He had more of a Roman nose, which she said fit great with hers when they kissed.

Two days after they met, she moved her stuff up to the window seat beside him. She was special, the most special person he could remember meeting on the train.

Over the months, they talked a lot about their lives, about how they grew up, about their parents, about their dreams, and about jumping. Everyone on the train talked a lot about jumping.

Since she was new on the train, and he had been on board for so long, he had shown her all the normal places to jump. Passengers jumped at all places along the train's circular route through the mountains. Some jumped into the lakes or rivers as the train passed over the bridges. Mason was sure that none of them survived, but Paula wasn't. She said that if they hit the water just right it

would be fine. It depended on how well they planned it and how much control they had.

Some passengers went crazy and didn't pay any attention at all to where they jumped. They would step boldly into the night and let fate do with them as it would.

Mason doubted any of them made it and Paula agreed. She said planning was the important part of success, not jumping blindly.

Mason had always wondered why, when the train came around again in eighteen days, there was never a sign of any of the jumpers, and why no one ever came back on board. He took that to mean that he would only have one chance – and that thought had scared him even more, causing him to stay seated month after month, year after year, just thinking about what he should do with his only real chance.

Paula said the reason that there were no sign of the jumpers, or anyone else

Some Classic Dean Wesley Smith Stories
Available at your favorite booksellers.

along the tracks, was obvious. The world took care of the failures and the ones who made it moved on, away from the train, into their lives.

Actually it didn't matter to Mason. He firmly believed that most of the jumpers failed, and for some reason he couldn't shake that fear.

It was that belief that had kept him on the train for so long.

But he did have a plan in which he thought he could survive a jump. Carefully worked out and thought through, he had talked the plan over with Paula on the third afternoon after she moved to the seat beside him.

"There," he had said, pointing ahead into the wind as they stood arm in arm on the open deck at the back of the last car. The day had been crisp and cold and the wind cut at them. Mason had never had a coat, so he had a blanket draped over his shoulders. Paula had on the ski parka and gloves she had arrived with.

The train had slowed for slightly rough track right before the lake bridge. There was a steep slope of grass and dirt that fell away from the tracks and ended in brush at the bottom near the lake's edge.

"See," he had said, pointing down the slope as they went by. "If we timed it just right we would hit the slope and roll. We might get hurt a little, but at least we would be off the train."

Paula had nodded and watched the slope recede into the distance behind them, studying it the way he had hundreds of times. The train would be back at this exact point in eighteen days. They had time to think and talk about it.

On that first day, Mason had turned her out of the wind and looked her right in the eye to drive his point home. "We

would be alive again. Back in the real world. And we would be together."

Under his hands he had felt Paula shudder, either from the fear or the cold.

That had been four months ago. Every eighteen days they talked about jumping and decided against it. Paula just didn't feel ready yet. She needed more time to think about it, to plan. She just hadn't spent enough time on the train.

Every time around, Mason had decided to wait for her.

Mason glanced around the dark car, at all the sleeping people, and then at Paula, the faint light making her skin appear even more beautiful and soft than it really was. He stared at her for the longest time, just thinking.

He had to face facts. He was stuck on the train, just like so many others around him. He wasn't sure, but he would bet there were many who simply died of old age on the train, never finding the courage to jump, to get on with their lives. He didn't want to be one of those, but he was quickly headed that way.

His dad had been that way. He had never, ever, followed his dreams with anything. His fear and his wife, Mason's mother, had made sure that he stayed in a dead-end job, working in a miserable place he hated right up to the moment of his early death.

What a waste of a life.

Before the train, before his father's death, Mason had been doing the same thing. Getting by, existing, staying away from anything that might be risky, both in work and with women. True, he had been dreaming of bigger and better things, of his toy store, but it was the same dream he had had when he was a child.

When his father had died, Mason was thirty-two and had done nothing.

Where had all the years gone?

That day, before he had ended up on the train, he had sat in his old basement, staring at the remains of his train layout, feeling sorry for himself. He had nothing to show for the years, just as he had nothing to show now for the years on this train. Every eighteen days, he would start his path over again, following the same tracks, knowing every turn, every bump.

Around and around, waiting to gain a little courage and take some action.

Thousands and thousands of people had come on board since he had and then jumped off. He had had a number of lovers, some of whom jumped without him in the middle of the night, somehow knowing he wouldn't jump with them.

Through college and beyond, he had had the same experience with the women he met. They wanted more from him in the way of commitment than he was willing to give them. He had been afraid of that as well. They had eventually left him, too, sometimes in the middle of the night.

Sherry, his last seatmate before Paula, had jumped on his slope. He was supposed to have jumped with her.

He had been too afraid, and instead just stood on the train and watched as she tumbled and rolled down the slope and vanished into the bushes at the bottom.

There was no sign of her eighteen days later.

The slope was coming by again today. With or without Paula, he would jump.

It was time.

Actually, it was long past time. He might fail in the jump, but he couldn't die in this seat, without moving, without doing anything with his life.

He couldn't die the way his father had died.

He had to at least try.

TWO

HE COVERED PAULA with one of his blankets and she murmured a soft "thanks."

He stood and went through the double doors to the next car. It was dark, too. Running his hands along the overhead luggage rack to keep his balance in the moving car, he quickly made his way through the sleeping people and on forward until he reached the dining car.

It was still a good hour before breakfast, but the train's staff were cleaning and setting tables when he came in. After the coolness of the coach cars, the warmth and the smell of fresh coffee in the dining car was a welcome relief.

"You're up early," Hank said from the waiter's station in the middle of the car. "Coffee?" He held up a coffee pot in his giant hands.

"Thanks," Mason said and slid into a table that wasn't set yet. He'd been around the train long enough to know that the staff didn't want passengers in the dining car before meal times. But he had been on board for so long that Hank, the six-foot, five-inch tall waiter, had become his best friend.

Before he had started working for the train, Hank had done a little of everything, sort of a jack of all trades. He could talk about anything and Mason loved that trait. Hank said he loved working with people, and as long as he was working in someplace where he could talk to folks, he was happy.

A couple of times, Mason had asked Hank about the train and how Hank had gotten on board.

Hank's only answer had been that at one point or another, everyone was on the train for one reason or another. That was all he would say.

Their favorite conversation was about the toy and hobby store Mason wanted to start. As a kid, he had found safety and friendship in the local hobby store, saving his pennies and money from pop cans and later his paper route to buy a new piece for his train layout. His mother said that he sometimes spent more time in the toy store than he did at home.

Mason didn't tell her that she was right. He loved the store more than anything, with all the promises of all the fun each toy seemed to represent.

At home, it wasn't fun to listen to his parents argue so much. He couldn't understand how his two younger brothers stood it. They had rooms upstairs. He at least had the basement and his train layout.

Hank slid the coffee in front of Mason and then dropped into the seat across the booth, letting his long legs stretch out into the aisle.

Mason nodded thanks and sipped the wonderfully hot coffee.

"You're looking serious this morning."

Mason took another slow sip and then set the cup down. "I'm going to jump today. About ten, near the bridge."

Hank leaned forward slightly. "Going to miss you, but I think it's for the better. Paula going to go with you?"

"She might," Mason said.

"But she might not, huh?"

Mason took another sip from his coffee and didn't answer.

"How old are you?"

"Thirty-two when I got onto this thing," Mason said.

"And from what we talked about, you had been doing the same thing most of the years since college?"

Mason nodded. "Now, I've been on this train almost longer than I can remember. Seems like a lifetime, actually. Maybe ten years or so. I'm guessing, but I lost count a long time ago, as if time means anything here."

Hank whistled softly. "I knew it was a long time, but didn't have any idea it was that long. So what are you going to do with this jump?"

Mason laughed. "Take a wild guess."

Hank laughed. "Going to open that toy store finally, huh?"

"Yeah. The one I used to spend my afternoons in closed up when the owner died, about a month before my dad died. It was what I was thinking about in my parents' basement when I ended up here. If the store is still there when I get off, I'm going to make his son an offer. If not, then I'm going to just open my own."

"Hey, that's great," Hank said. "You got everything you need? Money and all that?"

Mason nodded. "I even know the suppliers and had set up business accounts with them before..." Mason indicated the train and just shrugged. "I'm hoping I end up back the same age, at the same moment after my dad died."

Hank just smiled and nodded his head as if that made sense.

Mason was glad Hank didn't ask the next question. Why had it taken him so long?

From down the car came the sound of rattling dishes and pans. Hank glanced over his shoulder and then back at Mason. "You better go wake Paula and tell her what you decided. You want to give her some time to make up her mind. She might be ready, too."

"Good idea," Mason said and downed the last of his coffee.

They both stood at once and Mason extended his hand. "Thanks for being a friend."

Hank shook his hand. "You're welcome. It's been my pleasure."

Mason let go of Hank's firm grip and turned to move back into the coach cars.

"Mason?" Hank said.

Mason stopped and turned back to his tall friend.

"You'll make it. Just believe that."

Mason smiled. "You know, for some reason, today, I actually do."

THREE

A FEW MINUTES LATER he softly woke up Paula and asked her to come with him downstairs so that they could talk.

They made their way down the familiar spiral staircase and locked themselves into the small woman's bathroom near the carry-on luggage compartment. The bathroom always smelled damp and unclean and this morning was no exception.

Paula dashed some water on her face, toweled it off, and then turned and faced him. "You're going to jump, aren't you?"

"At the slope," he said. "And I hope you'll come with me."

"The toy store?" she asked.

"The toy store," he said. "And my home town is a lovely place to live. And you told me you liked to ski and hike. There's a lot of that around there. There is no more beautiful place in the entire world."

She touched his face gently. "I know. You've told me a dozen times. It sounds wonderful."

"But," he said, "you're not coming."

Paula frowned. "I didn't say that."

"But I can tell."

Paula took his hand, her grip warm in his cold palm. "I've always wanted to play music. You know that. I've told you all my dreams. Your home town is a small town, with no real facilities for me to help my music. I need to go to a bigger city that has a good music community and maybe even a university with a good music program."

Mason took a deep breath and pulled her close to him. "I know that," he said, softly. "I just hoped you would come and visit me. I think you're ready to get your music career really going, start that group you've been talking about... and I want you to jump with me. That's all."

Paula pushed him back and looked into his eyes. Mason could see that she was fighting tears, but after a short moment she said, "You mean that, don't you?"

He nodded. "Of course. You need to get on with your music and I need to get on with my toy store. And you know, I've been trying to make up my mind on this for so long that I have finally realized that I have more than enough money put away. I might be able to help you a little along the way. As long as you come and see me in my store once in a while."

That did it. Tears ran down her face and she hugged him so hard he didn't know if his ribs were going to break or not.

Finally, she pushed him back against the sink and held him as best she could at arm's length. "Thank you," she said.

"For what?"

She smiled. "For believing in me. That was all it took. Just one person to believe in my dream. My family never did. My friends always laughed."

Mason smiled and kissed her, her lips wet from the tears. She kissed him back, hard. Then she held him and said, "You're going to make a great toy store owner, you know that?"

He stared at her. "Now I do."

A few minutes later they were back at their seats gathering their things. It was going to be a rough jump, but they'd both make it. Of that, he now had no doubt.

FOUR

THE BELL on the front door of Toys, Trains, and Gifts jangled lightly and Mason looked up from the main counter. The woman entering was dressed in a new ski parka, with matching ski pants and hat. She had long blonde hair drifting out of the back of the ski cap and the most striking blue eyes he had ever seen. Her skin looked soft, and she had the cutest perky nose. Instantly, he felt as if he knew her. But since quitting his corporate job and opening the toy store, he had felt that about a lot of people.

But this woman was someone really special. He could tell. And it was everything he could to not go rushing over to her and make a fool out of himself.

She saw him, glanced at him twice, as if recognizing him as well, then stopped beside a rack of Hot Wheels, actually studying them as if she knew what she was looking for.

After a moment, she turned and moved over to the working HO Scale train set running in a large layout under the main window and back into the corner of the shop. It was the same layout he had designed as a kid in his parents' basement. It took up a lot of floor space in his store, but for some reason, he had known from the beginning that it was worth it.

Now he never shut the train off, letting the cars run their course automatically with a new, state-of-the-art computer control panel. It was as if shutting it off might make him shut down his store. He had even rigged up battery backup systems to keep it going during power failures.

It turned out to be a real attraction. Late at night, when the nearby movie theater would let out, he would see people standing and just staring in his window, watching the train go through its eighteen-minute course. Sometimes they would be staring so intently, it was as if they weren't in their bodies anymore.

Customers did that at times during the day as well. Mason had learned to just let them stare. It didn't hurt business.

Mason watched as the beautiful woman studied the moving train for the longest time, just like he did every so often. The moment he had moved that layout from his basement to his new store and got it working again, it had seemed oddly familiar, not because he built it, but because of something else he couldn't quite remember.

Finally, she shook her head and turned away from the train as it went in behind a mountain. She came slowly toward the counter, winding her way in and around the miniature supplies and model kits, looking at everything as she came.

He never took his gaze off her.

To break the ice, when she got close enough, he stuck out his hand. "I'm Mason. I own this place."

He noticed again how really proud he was of those words. He was proud of his store. It wasn't the biggest by a long ways. But it was something he was very proud of. And it was all his.

The woman smiled a huge, beautiful smile and took his hand. "I'm Paula. I'm a musician, here on regional tour with my group." While still holding his hand, she waved her other arm around at the store. "You have a wonderful place here. It feels like I have been in here before, like I could stay forever."

"I'm glad you like it." For some reason he was even more pleased than usual. Her compliment felt very important to him for some reason.

She paused, seeming to not want to let go of Mason's hand. Mason hoped at that moment that she never would.

"Have we met before?" she asked hesitantly, looking him directly in the eyes."

"It seems to me we have," Mason said and her look of worry lightened.

He smiled at her and went on, "But it might take lunch for us to figure out from where."

Her smile and light laugh were so wonderful, Mason knew he would never forget them, and wanted to see and hear them a lot more.

She gave his hand one last soft squeeze and let go. "I'd love that."

Mason turned to Hank, his six-foot five-inch tall employee and close friend, who obviously must have overheard their conversation. He grinned at Mason. "I'll guard the store, boss. You two take your time."

"Thanks," Mason said to Hank and winked.

Then he turned and opened the front door for Paula. "There's this great lunch place just up the street called The Dining Car. Sound good to you?"

"Sounds wonderful," Paula said. She took his hand and pulled him through the door into the cold winter air.

The scale model train in his store window ran along a rough mountain slope, turned and disappeared into a tunnel.

Outside, in the distance, there was the faint sound of a train whistle, but neither of them noticed.

~

Some Classic Dean Wesley Smith Stories
Available at your favorite booksellers.

USA TODAY BESTSELLING AUTHOR

DEAN WESLEY SMITH

WRITING INTO THE DARK

HOW TO WRITE A NOVEL WITHOUT AN OUTLINE

A WMG WRITER'S GUIDE

With more than a hundred published novels and more than seventeen million copies of his books in print, USA Today *bestselling author Dean Wesley Smith knows how to outline. And he knows how to write a novel without an outline.*

In this WMG Writer's Guide, Dean takes you step-by-step through the process of writing without an outline and explains why not having an outline boosts your creative voice and keeps you more interested in your writing.

Want to enjoy your writing more and entertain yourself? Then toss away your outline and Write into the Dark.

WRITING INTO THE DARK
A WMG Writer's Guide

Part 2 of 2

CHAPTER SIX
SOME PROCESS HINTS

In this chapter, I'm going to talk about some process hints before we go any farther. Remember, trust the process.

That takes a belief system in your own work. Of course, believing in our own work is where the critical voice hits us all the hardest. And where our wall against the critical voice is the weakest.

But writing into the dark takes a belief system in story. It takes a trust that your creative voice knows what it is doing. And it takes a vast amount of mental fight to walk against all the myths and let the fine work your creative voice has done alone and not ruin it with rewriting.

Writing into the dark also takes a complete awareness that uncertainty is part of the process, a normal part, not something to be feared.

Remember, if you start focusing on the uncertainty too much, you allow the critical voice to come in and stop you cold.

So you have to know uncertainty is part of the process, but not focus on it or care about it.

So now to some hints about major areas we all run into while writing into the dark.

PLOT TIME JUMPS

First off, when dealing with time jumps in a plot you don't know, remember that it is fine to write extra words. You should have no fear of writing extra words. Writing extra words is often part of the process.

So in the book I talked about in the last chapter, I ended up having three major time jumps in it.

Of course, when writing the book I didn't know that. But as I was writing, working my two characters in alternating chapters through their journey, it became clear from what I had set up that there needed to be a section break and a time jump. The characters basically had nothing to do that was interesting for an entire year.

But where to jump to? When to jump to?

Without some sort of idea where the story was even heading, I had no idea.

So I kind of sat there and looked at what I had written and went, "It seems logical they would jump to this point in time."

So I jumped there, put them back into a rich, thick setting with depth, and started typing. About two thousand words in I discovered the point where I should have jumped the characters.

I shrugged, cut off the extra words I had written, and just kept on going.

I was not afraid to write extra and just explore.

Back to the exploring a cave analogy. When exploring into the dark, we are often faced with two possible paths: one cave goes to the right, one to the left. We have no idea what is ahead, so we pick one and explore.

If it's the wrong path, we back up and go the other way.

Part of the process.

Have a belief in the process, and jumping ahead in a story will never be a problem.

BOGGING DOWN

Every writer I know bogs down in a story at one point or another. For me, and for most writers, it means we have done one of two things.

First, we have written past an ending of a chapter or scene, and the creative voice is just going to make us stop typing.

Second, we are on a wrong path with the plot. (Wrong branch of the cave.)

The subconscious, when it realizes you have taken a bad path, will just bog you down and stop you from typing.

What I do when this happens is simple. I look back at what I have written in the last three or four pages.

Writing past an ending on a scene or chapter is usually very, very clear. The ending almost always just pops off the page.

So I cut off the extra typing, do the scene or chapter break, and head forward with the characters.

When I am on a wrong path, I go back searching for the branch in the cave, keeping that analogy going.

When I find the one spot where I could have gone another direction, I cut off the extra words and go off in the new direction. I'll know I'm going in the right direction because suddenly the story is flowing again faster than I can type.

So bogging down is part of the process as well.

Expect it and don't be afraid to write extra words or cut words to get back on track.

END OF BOOK

When you bog down near the end of a book or a story, it often means you have written past your ending.

I do that all the time on short stories. I'll be typing along with the sense that the ending should be coming up soon and then I'll just bog down. Usually I'll sit there trying to figure out the end before I have the realization to look back a little bit at what I have already typed.

Often, more times than not, the great ending is back a hundred words or so. I wrote it and then just kept typing.

THE ONE-THIRD POINT OF A NOVEL

On novels, almost every writer I know hits a stopping point about one third of the way into writing the book. It does not matter if you are writing into the dark or outlining—this one-third point is a deadly spot for all novelists.

And most beginning writers working at their first novel never make it past this spot. This one-third point stopped me on all my first attempts. On every novel, I still have troubles with it.

The reason I want to mention it in a book on writing into the dark is because this one-third point stop is often blamed on writing into the dark. Blamed on not having an outline.

It has nothing to do with it.

Nothing.

Here is basically what happens:

As writers, we are all excited as we get started into a novel. The characters are fun and new, the promise of the novel is like a shining star, the words are all golden, the story flowing like a perfect stream, everything is just powering along.

Then you hit that one-third spot.

Suddenly, your critical voice comes roaring in. And it's loud. Damn loud.

Everything you have written, all those golden words, suddenly look like crap. The middle boring part of the book is ahead, or if you are writing into the dark, the fear of not knowing what is next rears up and becomes a monster.

And then the critical voice hits you with the thought, "This book is so bad, so much work to finish, what's the point?"

That's the end of the book. It goes into the unfinished file with a promise to yourself you'll come back to it, but of course you never do.

Critical voice has killed the book dead.

Critical voice: 1. Writer: 0.

There have been some amazing articles written by professional writers about this spot in a novel. It really is a deadly spot.

So how do you get through it?

There is only one way.

Suck it up and write the next sentence. And then the next.

You must be aware that this stopping point in a book is part of the process and you can't let the critical voice in the door to kill it.

There are no easy solutions.

And sucking it up is not an easy solution.

Just keep writing, shove the critical voice down into the corner again, believe there will be value in your work, and stay inside the character's heads and keep writing.

Do not let yourself make any stupid promises to yourself. You are still writing the book, period.

Don't get sloppy because the writing suddenly got difficult.

Just stay with the characters and stay in their heads and write the next sentence.

Trust your process.

Eventually, the excitement will return and you'll find the end and be very glad you kept going.

CHAPTER SEVEN
UNSTUCK IN TIME

There is one critical element in learning how to be a creative writer and writing into the dark with larger projects. And this one element sounds simple, but is extremely difficult to take in and learn for almost all early writers.

That's right. You are going to think you know this, but you won't apply it.

You must learn how to be unstuck in time in your book.

Let me see if I can explain this critical element to learning how to write into the dark.

And in all creative fiction writing, for that matter.

And then in the next chapter, I'll use this very idea to show you how to drive your writing forward.

READERS READ FROM FRONT TO BACK

That's an obvious point, isn't it?

We readers all pick up a book, start on page one, and read to the end of the book and put the book down because the story is over.

There is a straight line through the book. Front to back.

Reading is a very lineal process.

And we are all readers.

So when we come to writing, we have the experience as readers. After all, we've read thousands and thousands of books, haven't we? We believe that from front to back must also be the experience of the writing process.

We believe, without ever questioning, that we must write the book just as the readers will read it.

So as beginning writers—and I was no exception to this rule early on—we try to write novels from the first word to the last word.

We believe, and are taught by people who don't know any better, that the writing process is a lineal process from word one to the last word.

This false thinking is what leads to the driving need for outlining.

This false thinking is what leads to the driving need for rewriting by beginning writers. Their critical voice cannot let them believe it is possible to write a book from word one to the end without mistakes.

Why is that belief there?

Because, as readers, when we picked up a book we loved, we read from word one, and we all thought the author was so smart as to put all that nifty stuff in, and clues, and foreshadowing, and no character got lost, and wow it all came together in this nifty climax at the end.

Wow, that writer was really smart.

So as early writers, we think, "I'm not that smart. I don't know story that well, or plot, or any of that other stuff English teachers teach, so I have to rewrite to put all that in."

Then, of course, to rewrite, we go back to the beginning and start through the book again like a reader.

Front to back.

The reading process is a lineal process.

The truth is that the creative process is far, far, far from lineal.

In fact, when looked at in a hard light, the creative process is a jumbled mess.

REMEMBER YOU ARE WRITING YOUR ONLY DRAFT OF THE BOOK

That is critical to remember and keep firmly in mind before I go any farther. More than likely you dismissed that in an early chapter, but right now is when this becomes a critical point.

You must fix everything as you go because there will be no second chance, no second draft, no rewrite.

So with that firmly in mind, you are typing along and you realize you forgot some important detail, or forgot to dress a character, or forgot to plant a gun.

If there will be no rewrite, what do you do?

You fix it right at the moment you think of it.

You go up out of the lineal line of your book, float over that lineal line like a creative ghost. And then go back in the lineal timeline of your book and fix the problem.

Then fix the problem all the way through to where you left off and go from there again.

All problems your creative voice thinks of MUST BE FIXED AT ONCE. You are writing in creative voice. Stay in creative voice and fix the issues the creative voice comes up with instantly.

If you write some dumb note to fix it later, or think it will be fixed in second draft, you undermine all the wonderful stuff your creative voice is doing.

Your creative voice, at that moment, thought of that need to fix a problem.

Fix it. Honor your creative voice.

If you don't you almost kill the creative voice right there and you let in the critical voice.

When the creative voice knows the critical voice will mess up something, it's like a little kid. It will just say "What's the point?"

And stop.

So get unstuck in the timeline of your book and be willing to jump around at will to do what the creative voice wants you to do.

WRITE AHEAD, WRITE IN PIECES, CONSTANTLY LOOP

There are so many ways that long-term professional writers do this unstuck-in-time creative process.

Some, such as my wife, often write a project in pieces. She's writing into the dark, no idea where she is going, and she listens to her creative voice.

If her creative voice wants her to write a scene, she writes it. And often she'll have parts of a book, all written out of order, and when her creative voice tells her, she prints them all out and puts it all together on the floor.

Some writers I know have a scene appear to them, they write it, then loop back and write toward the scene.

I constantly loop back every 500 words or so, and I'll talk more about that process, called *cycling*, next chapter.

Remember, the key is that you (as a writer) are unstuck in the timeline of your book.

That's right. Let me free you up right here.

There is no rule that says you must write your book like a reader is going to read it.

None.

Get unstuck in time.

BUT SOMETIMES STRAIGHT THROUGH IS THE BEST WAY

I tend to build most of my books from front to back. But if you diagramed out how my eye actually works, what I actually typed, as I write a book that feels like it is lineal, you will discover my writing is far, far from lineal.

I will write a few hundred words, loop back, fill in some other stuff, take out some other words, write forward from the place where I lifted out of the timeline, then loop around again and do it all again.

It feels to me at times like I am starting at the beginning and moving toward the end. But in all honesty, it's more like digging a tunnel through a mountain.

I dig for a little bit, go back, take out the dirt, shape the tunnel a little, dig a little farther, go back, take out the dirt, shape some more, dig some more, and so on.

Eventually I find the end of the tunnel and when I look back I have created a wonderful, smooth-sided tunnel. And that's what the readers think when they walk through the tunnel from one end to the other.

But sure not what the process was.

The belief that we MUST write a book straight through is what grinds writers down.

And what makes many writers believe in all the people who say we must outline.

Logical, actually.

If you believe, deep down, that the only real way to write a book is from word one to the end, then outlining is more than likely something you are going to have to do.

And plan for a short career.

For all of us, the reader must experience our book in a lineal fashion. And we are all readers. So this drive to write from front to back is strong.

But even if you start with word one on a novel and write lineal forward, kill your fear of jumping out of the book and be like a floating god over the characters and the path of the book and let your subconscious have that freedom.

When you can write in any fashion you want, you are not roped into traveling from word one to the last word in the writing process.

And that gives your creative voice the freedom to build that lineal process for the reader in any way it wants.

WRITE THE NEXT SENTENCE

That's advice I gave to help you through the rough points, the stuck points.

A key point to remember is that "next sentence" does not have to be the very next sentence the READER is going to read. It just needs to be the next sentence you are going to type.

The next sentence could be the start of the next chapter.

Or you could cycle back and write some extra description at the start of chapter two as the next sentence.

It all makes your book longer, it all pushes the book forward.

Sometimes the next sentence when you are stuck will be the next sentence the reader will read.

But often it won't be.

And it sure doesn't have to be to help you keep going.

UNSTUCK IN THE TIMELINE OF YOUR STORY

Again, this is the most critical point about writing into the dark, or even becoming a full-time professional storyteller.

You must realize you are the writer of your book, not the reader of your book.

You are unstuck in time in your own book.

In other words, you can jump around in your manuscript at will.

Creative minds do not tend to work in a straight line.

And as a writer, you don't need to.

All that matters is that the reader experiences your story in a straight line from word one to the end.

But no one cares if you write it that way.

And chances are, you won't.

Or shouldn't.

CHAPTER EIGHT
THE HINT OF CYCLING

Very little that is created is created lineally.

But in writing, our audience experiences a very clear order to a book. And if that order isn't clear, they leave the book.

So it is logical that new writers come at writing thinking they must create the book just as a reader experiences the work.

But thankfully, it doesn't work that way, as I talked about in the last chapter.

Or, at least, it doesn't have to.

MODERN COMPUTER AGE

The modern computer age has been both a blessing and a curse for writers. In the days of typewriters, or writing by hand, rewriting was a chore, to say the least, so professional writers quickly learned to not do much rewriting. Especially the top storytellers who were working for a certain amount per word.

They didn't get paid for rewriting. Only finished product.

The focus was to get it correct the first time through.

That should still be your focus, even though rewriting is easy in this new computer world, and myths of modern publishing expect it.

But back before the computers of the last 25-plus years, making a mistake and fixing it on a typed page was a pain. I know I personally went through bottles of Wite-Out because of my spelling and bad typing.

And the rule of thumb when submitting a manuscript to an editor was no more than ten corrections on a page. If you had more than ten, you had to retype it. And trust me, ten fixed mistakes on a manuscript page looked awful, so I retyped at five mistakes.

And I was a horrid typist. I hated typing, especially retyping.

So my two-finger hunt-and-peck method was slow. Very slow.

But now the fixes are easy.

And that causes the problem of too much rewriting.

But it also allows professional writers a wonderful tool that many, many of us have adopted. The tool is called cycling.

Now to understand this tool and use it correctly, you have to be completely unstuck in the timeline of your manuscript. Timeline of the manuscript is page one, followed by page two, and so on until the end of the book.

Those page numbers should mean nothing to you until the end of the book, and even the order of the chapters should mean little to you.

In creative mode, nothing is set in stone.

You are not locked into the moment you are typing. You can go anywhere in the story and type at any point in the manuscript.

CYCLING

I thought for the longest time that I was the only one who had picked this up. That's my ego for you. The more I talked

with other professional writers, the more I realized that in one form or another, all of us did this.

Let me explain what I do, so you get a clear picture of what I am calling *cycling* and find a form of it that will work for you.

I start into what I think is the opening of a story or novel. I climb inside a character's head and get the emotions of the character about the setting around the character, and I type for two or three pages.

500 to 700 words or so.

And I come to a halt.

Every time, without fail. This is now a dug-in habit.

I instantly jump out of the timeline of the story and cycle back to the first word and start through the story again.

Sometimes I add in stuff, sometimes I take out, sometimes I just reread, scanning forward, fixing any mistakes I see.

(Remember, this will be the only draft I will do.)

So when I get back to the white space, I have some speed up and I power onward, usually another 500 or so words until I stop.

Then I cycle back again to the beginning and do the same thing, run through it all until I get back to the white space with momentum and power forward again for another 500 or 700 words.

Then I cycle back about 700 to 1,000 words and do it again.

So if you were tracking how I write a story or novel, you would see me go 500 words forward, back, power to the white spot again, more forward, then back.

I am completely unstuck from the timeline of the novel.

Sometimes, when I get a nifty thought, I type it and then write forward until I get there.

But almost always I cycle back, all in creative voice, never once judging the work, just working to make it clearer, make the character better, the setting richer, and so on and so on.

I could never do this with a typewriter.

Only the last 25 years or so since I got my first computer have I been able to do this.

HOW CYCLING HELPS WRITING INTO THE DARK

When you have no idea where you are going with a story, momentum is often the key to it all.

I have great momentum for about 500 words, about two manuscript pages. Then I run into that "What happens next?" question.

So by cycling back, I am putting the character and the events solidly in my mind by going over them again. And when I hit the white space where I stopped, I have momentum to drive the story forward.

By going back and coming forward again, my creative voice knows what's going to happen next.

When I am really, really stuck, I often will cycle back a full chapter or so and take a run at the stuck spot, spending 15 minutes or so going over what I have done, touching it, getting my creative voice back into where it was going.

More often than not, that solves being very stuck.

Think of this as the white spaces being small hills and I need to get a run at each hill. And think of being very stuck as a larger hill, and I need to back up farther to get more speed at the larger hill.

FIXING MISTAKES

Cycling, knowing you will be done when you hit the end, makes you fix any problem or mistake instantly, the moment you see or discover the problem.

So say a character says something to another character and your creative voice goes, "Damn it, that wasn't set up."

You instantly pop out of the timeline and go back and set it up and then work toward the white space again.

You need to have a character wearing something different for a plot reason that came up in chapter four, you instantly go back and fix what the character is wearing, moving forward again through the manuscript until you get to the white space to make sure all the details match.

You need to look up a detail, you stop, look it up, put it in, cycle back and run at the white space again to make sure the detail is correct.

DOESN'T CYCLING TAKE MORE TIME?

Seriously, I get this question a lot and I imagine some of you reading this are thinking it.

But no, this takes far, far less time to get a story right the first time through than to try to fix it later. And that goes for putting silly brackets around something you have to research later.

Get it right and be done and move on to a new story.

By having that attitude, you power up your creative voice to get it right the first time.

You don't write sloppy.

You don't write for a second draft.

Now are some of my first runs through 500 words sloppy? I don't honestly know. I suppose so because I am not paying any attention, and I know I will cover those 500 words to clean them up at least twice more, if not more than twice, in very short order.

But to be honest, I don't notice or care. My subconscious knows this will be the only time through and I'm known for moderately clean manuscripts. Not perfect. No manuscript is perfect.

But I'm fairly clean.

So how much time does this take me?

I tend to think I write (that's finished, after cycling) about 1,000 or so words per hour, typing with three fingers and taking five and ten minute breaks every hour or so.

Sometimes I am faster. Not slower that often.

If I had to worry about going back for a second draft, I doubt I would be writing. I know the story, so it would be boring because I know the story.

I didn't rewrite when I wrote on a typewriter either.

I never reread my stories after I get to the end.

Why?

Because I have seen every word in the story two or three or four times in the cycling.

And I know I don't have to.

CHAPTER NINE
HELPFUL HINT #2

The first major hint on writing into the dark was being unstuck in time in your manuscript, learning to cycle.

So now, this second hint is to save you more time than you can imagine. It will help you be more productive and keep stress down.

And help you write better books.

Sounds magical, doesn't it?

Well, it sort of is.

OUTLINE AS YOU GO

I do not mean outline ahead in critical voice. Not in the slightest.

Remember, you are writing in the dark.

I mean that when you finish a chapter, write down quickly what you just wrote in a very clear form.

Let me explain what I do so you can find a way that works for you.

When I finish a chapter, I have a yellow legal pad sitting beside the computer.

(I would suggest you use something like a legal pad instead of doing this on a screen. Save the screen for creative writing.)

On that yellow legal pad I mark the chapter number, the viewpoint character, what happened in the chapter (one-line summary) and how the chapter ended.

That usually takes one or maybe two lines on the legal pad per chapter.

On that page, or another piece of paper, I also have what the character is wearing, and if they change clothes, I make a note on the chapter line that they changed clothes.

So by chapter six, I have six or so lines on a notepad beside my computer telling me exactly where I have gone and what I have written so far.

This takes me about one minute to do, if not less, at the end of every chapter.

But, wow, does it save me hours of time.

MULTIPLE VIEWPOINT NOVELS

Most of the books I write are multiple viewpoint novels. And I write one character per chapter. I tend to make each scene a chapter. So if you are writing scenes inside chapters, do a line on your reverse outline for each scene.

If I am writing a thriller, which is often five to eight viewpoints, this outline as I go becomes even more important for me to remember the last time I was in a viewpoint.

Instead of looking back through the book to see what the character was wearing and where did I leave them in their last scene, I just glance at my notebook and go, "Oh, yeah."

In essence, that yellow piece of paper is an external memory drive for me.

The more complex the book or the plot as it develops, the more detail I put into this outline as I go.

I had one very complex book where each chapter was actually three lines on the yellow legal pad. So my outline took three pages or so of paper when it was all done.

WHY TAKE THE TIME?

Because not a one of us can hold an entire novel in our minds. We just can't. Not how the human brain works.

And because of that, many people say that's another reason to let the critical voice outline ahead.

But instead of doing that, just outline as you go.

Write into the dark and outline what you have done.

That way, at a glance you can see the novel on a single piece of paper beside your computer.

You can see what characters were wearing. And where they ended up in their last scene.

One reason for this is to save you hunting back through the novel after being away from it for some life event.

Say you are gone for a week and come back and sit down with no memory of the book or even where you are at. Hunting back through a couple hundred pages of manuscript to figure out what a character was wearing or what they were doing takes a vast amount of time and is very annoying.

And does not help in a restart after a life event.

With an outline as you go, you never have to look back in the manuscript, or if you do, you know which chapters to look in.

This saves vast amounts of time.

And keeps you far, far more productive and moving into the dark because you can see the novel building.

Seeing the novel building right there on the paper is great feedback to the creative voice.

SENSE OF NOVEL STRUCTURE

Again, we can't hold a novel in our minds, so later in the book you are writing, when you start worrying about the novel structure, whether are things moving too fast or too slow—you know, standard worry questions—you can glance at the outline page and just see the structure.

It is amazing how clear a structure becomes when just spread out in notes beside the computer, in a quick summary of what you have written.

(Another reason to not let this summary get too complex. Keep it simple and easy to see.)

And if there is a problem in the structure of the book, you can see that quickly as well.

I was doing this once with a big thriller: I got to chapter thirty and noticed on my outline I had a viewpoint chapter from a character in chapter four that I had never returned to.

Uh-oh. I jumped back, reread that character's chapter, realized I didn't need it, and cut it. My creative voice had put it in back at the start, but then decided I didn't need it by the middle of the book. I never would have noticed without that outline of what I had written.

Some of you have watched me write books here on this blog and then say the book got shorter because I cut out stuff.

So, since I never reread what I write after I get to the end, how do I know to cut out something?

Simple. It shouts at me from the structure of the outline that I wrote as I was writing.

I can see that everything is on track up until, say, chapter nine, then the characters go off and do something in a loop and return to the regular through-line of the book in chapter thirteen.

And the end of chapter nine fits perfectly against the start of chapter thirteen. Nothing really important happened in those loop chapters, so I just cut them out.

Not much work at all because I can see the structure clearly from the notes I made after I wrote each chapter.

So again, the quick outline of what I have written saves me a vast amount of time and makes the novels stronger.

So a helpful hint to make writing into the dark so much easier: Outline in a very concise, simple, and fast method, on a piece of paper beside your computer, what you have just finished.

Chapter or scene.

Just write it down and then get back to writing.

Two Cold Poker Gang Novels
Available at your favorite booksellers.

About halfway through the book, when you need to find something to fix or to figure out a character, you will thank me.

ONE FINAL NOTE

The moment I see the ending of the book—which for me is usually about four or five chapters away—I stop doing this outline as I go.

I no longer need it, and I never think to do it in the typing rush to reach the end of the novel.

And I never save the outlines unless the book is part of a series. Then I toss the outline and character details I have sketched down in a file for the next book in the series.

That hasn't helped much yet, but I keep doing it anyway.

The outline is for only when you are writing into the dark. After you are done with the story, most of the time that outline is worthless. It did its job.

It saved you time and energy, and helped you write a better book.

CHAPTER TEN
HELPFUL HINT #3

One of the things I hear the most from writers working into the dark is trouble finding the ending of the book or story.

Or maybe better said, seeing the end of the book or story.

The ending is there. Recognizing it sometimes takes a special trick.

So let me try to ease some of the worry with this helpful hint.

JUST KEEP WRITING

I know that sounds silly, but it actually is the hint.

When you start feeling like your ending should be coming at any moment, but

Two Cold Poker Gang Novels
Available at your favorite booksellers.

you can't see it, just keep writing until you bog down.

Then, when you bog down, cycle back about a thousand words and chances are you'll spot your ending about a page or two back. Then just cut off the stuff you wrote extra after the perfect ending line.

If you don't spot it, write another three or four pages and do it again.

Now, if you know your ending, of course don't do this.

But if you are having trouble finding that perfect ending line, just write and then cycle back and you'll see it.

I know, sounds magical, but it tends to work most times. It's part of the process of writing into the dark and trusting your subconscious.

Also, back to what I talked about in the beginning of the book: For this to work, you need to have no fear of writing extra.

Writing extra is part of the process and it applies right at the ending. Just cut off the not-needed words and don't worry about it.

WRITING TO LENGTH

This is a modern world with a thousand ways to publish any book of any length, yet I often hear writers saying they want their next novel to be 60,000 words or some such silliness.

I shake my head and walk away.

When writing into the dark, just let the story be what the story wants to be.

Trying to write to some made-up word length is all critical voice, and that simple idea of wanting a book to be a certain length will pile in the critical voice and shut down the creative voice.

Let the story be what the story wants to be at the length it wants to be.

Trust your creative voice.

Write what you are passionate about or what you enjoy.

And to the length the story needs to be.

Some Classic Dean Wesley Smith Stories
Available at your favorite booksellers.

THE LAST KEY

To really be successful at writing into the dark, or with any creative fiction writing, you are always better entertaining yourself.

So let me give you a few hints to finish this book up. A few checkpoints to remember.

—Entertain Yourself

You are a reader, so write into the dark to entertain yourself. You are writing the story for yourself.

—Enjoy the Uncertainty

As a reader, you pick up the book and don't know the story or the ending. You are reading the book for the journey. There is uncertainty in that journey. When writing into the dark, there is uncertainty in the journey as well. Enjoy it. Welcome it.

—Write the Book You Want to Read

If you love a certain type of book or wonder why you haven't seen a certain type of book you used to love, write it. Back to the first point. Entertain yourself.

—Never Write for Anyone But Yourself

Basically, stop writing to market. If you entertain yourself, enjoy the uncertainty, and write the books you want to read, writing into the dark is a joy.

THANKS FOR READING

I sure hope this book helped some, and on your next book you'll write into the dark. You might be surprised at just how much fun it is.

And how much more productive you are.

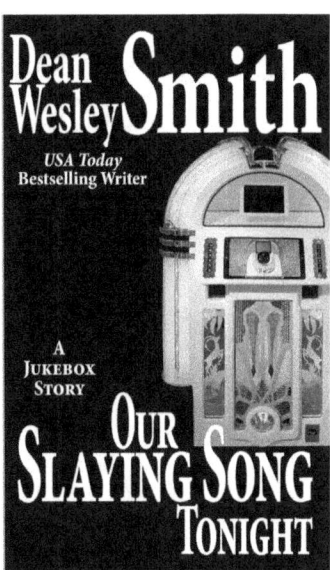

Some Classic Dean Wesley Smith Stories
Available at your favorite booksellers.

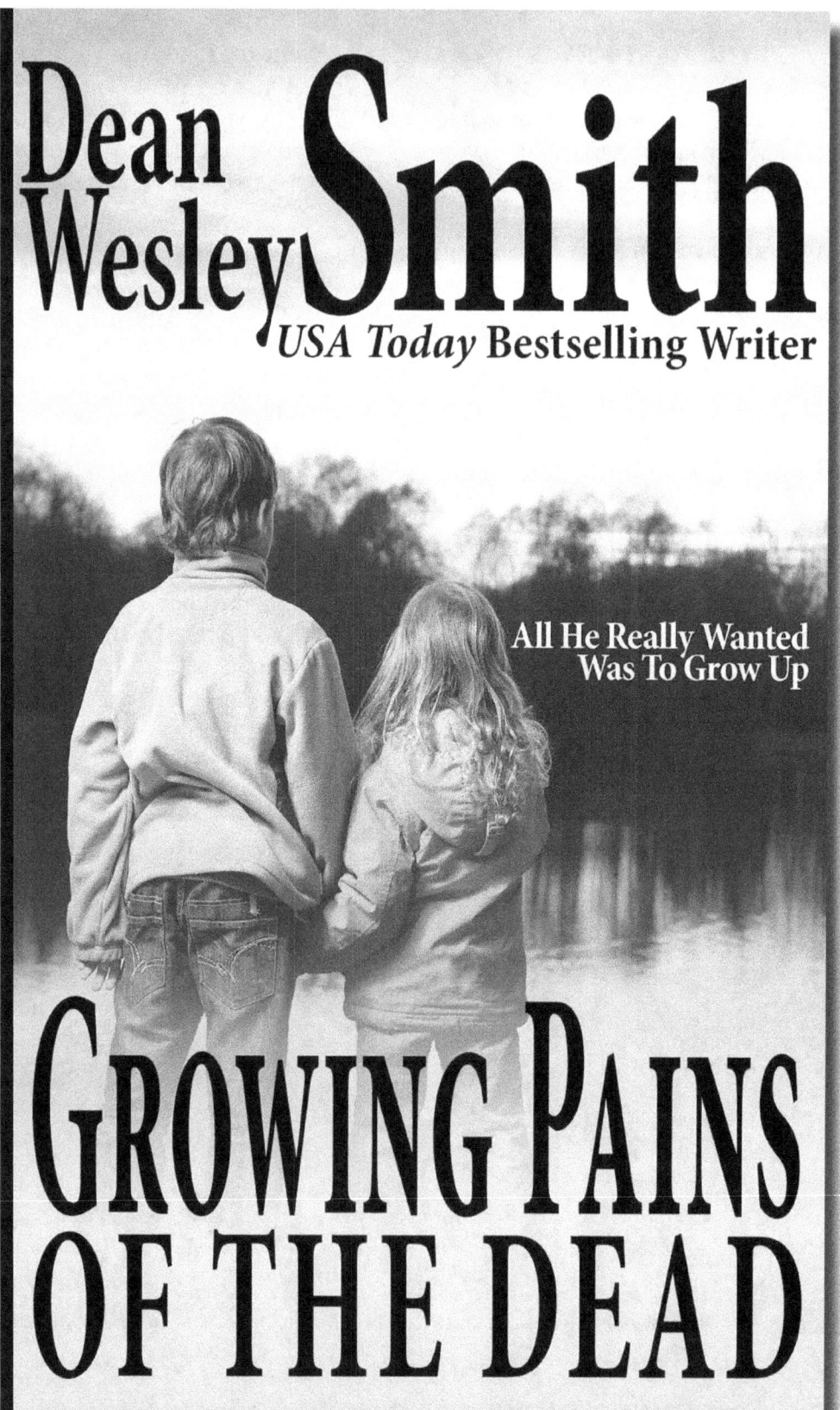

Dean Wesley **Smith**
USA Today Bestselling Writer

All He Really Wanted
Was To Grow Up

GROWING PAINS
OF THE DEAD

Mathew died at the age of fourteen, but that didn't stop him from wanting to grow up.

Set in the primitive area of Idaho, "Growing Pains of the Dead" tells a gentle ghost story of a young boy named Mathew who finally gets a chance to grow up one hundred years after he died.

GROWING PAINS OF THE DEAD

ONE

IN THE TOWERING mountains of central Idaho, storms sweep in almost without notice, sometimes dumping snow measured in feet in a matter of hours. In the summer, the heat can kill a human without water within days, and the steep slopes can trap even the most experienced hiker in a confusing mix of valleys filled with giant trees, thick brush, and fields of fallen rock. The area is now designated "primitive area" mostly because it is just too rugged to bother doing anything else with.

There are no towns.

There aren't even roads.

We live in a valley called Monumental Valley in this primitive area, off a creek called Mule Creek. From mid-September to late May, there is no way for humans in or out of the valley through the deep snow. Even in the summer, only a small trail leads over the summit and to the small human settlements in valleys beyond the steep ridges. I understand there are huge human cities beyond those valleys, but I cannot imagine them.

Going downstream in the Monumental Valley, the trail follows Mule Creek until it blends into a river called "The River of No Return." The trail ends there.

We have a very simple existence here, in our steep-walled valley. Once in a while a few humans visit, usually carrying too much weight in fancy-colored backpacks.

I like it when the humans come into the valley. They are always fun to watch, even though they never know I am there. A thousand years before my time, the first humans had come into the valley and stayed for a time. Then just over a hundred years ago my family settled here, to mine for gold, my father said.

A huge flood wiped out where we were living and the town we lived in, and the remaining humans just eventually all left the valley, leaving us to ourselves, wandering through the trees, waiting for something. Something none of us knew or talked about or even worried about. We do not worry about anything.

And we feel almost nothing as well.

I remember when my dad tried to show himself to a living human once, two men who had camped in a tent on the lakeshore above our old home. He tried to communicate, show them he was there, even tossed small rocks he could move into the water. It scared them and they stayed up most of the night acting real strange. In the morning they left at first light.

Dad just laughed, but I didn't think it was funny. I want to understand why we walk these woods, why I never grow older, why I don't leave the valley, even on the warm summer days when the trail is open and nothing blocks my way.

When I mention such things to my mother, who sits all day in the trees next to an old gravestone with the writing worn off by the weather, or my father, who wanders the main street of the old town under the water, they both just tell me that is the way of things.

When I asked them why we look like humans, but yet are not human, they told me we were human, once, but we died and can no longer be human. When I asked what death was, they simply told me it is the moment between being human and not being human.

I did not understand, and when I told them that, they smiled and said I was too young to understand. But on other times, they told me I will never grow older. Only humans grow older.

I want to grow older.

I want to understand.

There are fifty of us in this valley, from the summit to the raging waters of The River of No Return. We talk only rarely, and we do not often laugh. We simply sit or walk the deer trails.

The oldest of us is a mother with a baby, dressed in animal skins with colored beads made from clay. My father told me she has been in the valley for a thousand years, and she does not speak our language. I have never spoken to her, and in the one hundred years I have been in the valley, the baby has not grown, just as I have not grown. The mother has been carrying the baby on her back for over a thousand years. I cannot imagine that or understand it either, but there seemed no point in talking with my parents about it.

TWO

EVERYTHING CHANGED for me one warm spring day. I had decided to walk up the trail toward the summit, going to visit the three who lived in the ghostly image of an old hotel that used to stand at the crest of the trail. One girl there is my age, and I enjoy her company on warm days, even though she seldom talks. My parents told me I did not know her when I was a human. She died before we came to the valley.

I still like her, like her plain blue dress, her scuffed black shoes, her smile, when she does smile.

I am halfway up the trail, at a point where it crosses a rockslide, when a human hiker with a large blue backpack stops just ahead of me and stares.

On my left the slope goes almost straight down for a thousand feet into the trees around the stream below. On my left, the rock slope climbs very steeply, too steep to hike up, for almost two thousand feet. There is still snow on the top ridgeline, snow that feeds the streams below.

"You can't be here, too," she says.

I am used to humans talking even when no other human was around. This young human, a woman who was younger than my mother, is dressed in very short shorts and a soft shirt of some kind that was loose at her waist. My mother would have called her clothing indecent, but I have grown used to the way the few modern humans dressed who came to the valley in the summers.

My parents never understood why I even paid attention to the humans, but decided I was just being a normal, curious boy and after twenty or so years, they didn't bother to even comment on my habits.

I step up the slope, just off the narrow trail, and stop to wait for her to pass. I have never liked having a human walk through me, and decided that if I could help it, I would not let that happen. It felt like walking through a fire, from what I could remember of the heat of a fire.

We did not often feel much of anything. Feeling seemed to be a human experience that ended with death.

She does not continue forward, but instead stares at me, seeming to talk to me.

"Is there not any place on this planet you ghosts do not roam?"

My father had used the term 'ghosts' a few times to describe us, and every time my mother had hushed him, telling him we were not ghosts, we were simply waiting for the next stage of life.

"I do not know," I say to the young woman. "I live in this valley with my parents and others."

"I had so hoped," she says, pulling off her heavy pack, dropping it on the narrow trail, and sitting down on a large rock. Then she breaks into tears, something I have seldom seen humans do over the hundred years. I remember I used to cry when I was alive at times, but had never cried since I had left being a human.

"Hope what?" I ask, moving closer to her, but stopping within ten feet.

She looks up at me. "Hoped to find a place where there are no ghosts."

"Then you can see us?" I ask. It is an obvious question, but one that I needed to ask because in my experience humans could not see any of us.

She nods and the tears keep coming, even though now she seems to be looking out over the narrow but beautiful valley at the steep hillside beyond. "I started seeing you after an accident last spring. There are far more ghosts than there are humans in some places, did you know that? Even here."

"I can show you where there are none of my kind," I say, wanting to ask her more questions, but deciding not to at the moment.

53

She looks directly at me. "You can? Where?"

I point back toward where my parents are. "There is an old town named Roosevelt under a lake down the hill. A stream comes in near the lake. If you follow the stream up the hill, in about a half-day's hike, you will find an old gold mine. There are none of my people there and we have no reason to leave this valley and go there."

She jumps to her feet, clearly excited. "Will you show me the way?"

"I will," I say.

She bends over, grabs the strap of her clearly heavy backpack and swings it up on her shoulder. The weight makes her stagger, her foot slips on the loose rock of the trail, and she goes over the edge of the trail with a scream, pulled by the heavy weight of her pack.

I watch as she tumbles down the rock slope, gaining speed until a thousand feet below she crashes into the trees, followed by a small avalanche of stones following her. Her screams had stopped long before she reached the bottom.

THREE

I MOVE BACK DOWN the trail about a half-mile, then take a deer trail off toward the stream, moving up the valley through the brush. I find her sitting on a rock about ten feet from the remains of her twisted, bloody human body.

She sees me coming and smiles. "That wasn't very smart on my part, was it?"

"Did dying hurt?"

She frowns at her mangled human body. "No, actually. And I have a hunch I should be angry, but I don't feel much

of anything at the moment, to be honest. That's kind of nice."

"That's normal," I say. "I can still show you the way."

She points to a meadow through the trees, a small place where two deer are grazing in the sun. "I think I will stay here. It is so beautiful."

"May I come visit you?" I ask. "I would like to learn what the world outside this valley is like."

She glances back up the slope she had tumbled down when human. "Can you leave the valley?"

"Nothing seems to stop me," I say, feeling slightly worried about her question.

She nods. "Give me time to get used to this and I will tell you about the world beyond that ridge. What is your name?"

I am about to turn away, to give her time, but her question startles me and I stop. I think for a moment. "I was called Mathew when I was human."

I remembered my parents calling me that before, when I was human, and my mother continued using that name the first few years of us not being human. Now I was never called anything at all.

She smiles again. "Mathew, I am Connie. Thank you for offering to help me."

It is my turn to smile. "Connie, it is very nice meeting you. I am sorry you are no longer human."

She glances at her battered human body a short distance away. "I don't think I miss it."

With that, I turn and leave, going down the valley to where I can follow the deer trail up the path to the ridge, then on up to the old lodge on the ridge, continuing my original journey. I am now curious as to the young girl's name.

And how she became non-human.

I remember how I became non-human. I fell asleep one night, very sick, and at some point in the middle of the night, while the snow fell outside our small cabin, I was no longer human. They buried my human body in the small cemetery where my mother sits most of the time. My mother said I was only fourteen years old at the time, far too young to die.

My mother joined me as non-human one night that same winter when she sat beside my grave through a snow storm. My father was shot in a fight in a saloon in the now underwater town of Roosevelt while drunk a very short time later.

My friend in the scuffed black shoes who lives on the ridge tells me she is named Lareina, after her grandmother. She is surprised I ask her name and then she is surprised I tell her mine. It seems to please her, as it does me. She also died at age 14 she tells me, also from a sickness.

"Walk with me?" I ask her, and we start down the narrow mountain road that leads from the ridge toward the human settlements beyond. I am surprised there is no feeling that I should turn back, and she doesn't complain.

"A full day's walk down this road," Lareina tells me, "there is an old mining town called Stibnite. There are many of us living there."

"And beyond that?"

She shakes her head. "I have never gone beyond that, toward the next town where humans live."

"Why not?" I ask.

"I have never had a reason to do so," she says.

We walk in silence until I decide to tell her about the hiker who went from being human to one of us right before my eyes earlier.

"Can I meet her?" Lareina asks. "I also would like to learn about the world of humans."

"I do not think she will mind," I say. "We must just give her time to adjust to not being human."

Lareina smiles at me. "My mother says that time is something we have a great deal of."

I think I understand that.

We walk to the old town of Stibnite, walk around the town, then start back. It takes us two days. We walk both during the beautiful clear days and during the night under the stars.

There are more of us in Stibnite than in the valley I live in, but most seem to be miners who ignore us. There are only a few children our age and Lareina and I stop and talk with them, learning their names and telling them our names as well.

When we leave, they want us to come back.

For the first time, it seems important to me that someone knows my name.

Lareina and I stop to greet her mother, then Lareina decides to walk with me the length of the trail all the way to the waters of The River of No Return. It takes us four days. On the return we decide to stop and talk with Connie, the hiker.

Connie's human body has begun to decay and been torn apart by animals, but there is no sign of the non-human Connie.

I feel disappointment, and I tell Lareina. She says she feels it also. It is unusual for us to feel anything.

We start up the trail to the lodge. Connie is sitting on the same rock on the rockslide where she sat before she fell, staring down the slope where her human form died.

"It is very strange not being alive," she says as we sit down next to her.

"I do not remember very well being alive," I say.

"Neither do I," Lareina says.

"How long have you been dead?" Connie asks.

"I died of the flu in 1906," Lareina says.

I thought quickly, figuring I got sick in 1912 and I tell them that.

"Wow the year is 2012, a hundred years," Connie says. "Both of you, frozen in time. That is a very long time."

We sit on the trail in silence, then Connie asks, "So there is nothing after this for us ghosts, us non-humans as you call us?"

"I don't know," I say. "No one I've talked to seems to know. So we wait. But I would like to grow up."

Lareina agrees.

Connie stares at us, then back down at the valley below. We sit there like that for a long time, until finally Connie talks again.

"As much as it seems right for me to sit here and let time pass, waiting for the next life after this stage, I think I need to go back to the city, Back to New York, to where humans live, to where I lived before I attempted to escape from people like I am now."

"And what would you do there?" Lareina asks.

"Explore, learn, keep living, keep moving," Connie says. "Maybe find the answer to what comes next. Someone, somewhere should know."

"I would like to see the world beyond this valley," I say. "Can I walk with you?"

"I would like to see it as well," Lareina says.

For some reason, that pleases me.

"The more the merrier," Connie says, smiling and standing. "Shall we get going?"

I glance back down the valley in the direction of the lake and the cemetery and think about telling my parents. But I doubt that they would even notice I was not walking my trail as normal. Sometimes it had been a full year between times we spoke. There had just been no reason to speak after all the decades.

"I am ready," I say, standing.

"So am I," Lareina says.

I can feel faint excitement, faint fear, faint feelings of happiness. I like all three feelings and I smile. I remember feelings like that when I was alive.

"Is this an adventure?" I ask.

"I would say it is," Connie says. "Having adventures and experiences are part of growing up."

"I want to grow up," I say.

"So do I," Lareina says.

Connie reaches out and takes my hand, and for the first time in a long time, I can feel another person's hand in my own.

"Then let's go have some adventures," Connie says.

I take Lareina's hand in turn and she beams, staring at my hand in hers.

I like the feel of Lareina's hand, I like the idea of having an adventure in the human cities.

And most of all, I like the idea of finally growing up.

~

Now Available
from all your favorite booksellers
in trade paper and electronic editions.

USA *Today* Bestselling Writer

DEAN WESLEY SMITH

THE CASE OF THE DEAD LADY BLUES

A Pilgrim Hugh Incident

Private Detective Pilgrim Hugh loves solving strange cases. Very little stumps him for very long.

But a woman by the name of Deep Blue, dead in her empty apartment and dyed blue, seemed like an impossible case.

And more than Hugh knows depends on his quick solution.

Pilgrim Hugh once again rides to the rescue in his stretch limo driven by his brilliant assistant.

THE CASE OF THE DEAD LADY BLUES
A Pilgrim Hugh Incident

ONE

PILGRIM HUGH STARED at the body of the woman even though he had no desire to stare or look or even glance. Blue was just not an attractive color on a redhead, and this woman had clearly been very attractive in her pink-skinned time.

Dead was not attractive either. And she was most certainly dead, stretched out in the middle of the polished oak floor.

Her skin was deep blue, clashing with her long red hair. Her white slinky dress also seemed a pale blue from the shade of her skin showing through. The dress left little to the imagination, allowing Pilgrim to see clearly more than she likely wanted him to see in her own death.

Chances are she no longer cared, however.

The apartment where she lay had been scrubbed clean. The oak hardwood floors had been polished, the off-white walls all wiped down to a gloss, and not a stick of furniture or window blinds or anything else but a blue body remained.

And the temperature was set at a comfortable seventy degrees on the thermostat on the wall. Outside, the July day was a hot one for Portland, Oregon, one of those ninety-plus days the weather people liked to proclaim as dangerous. Just walking from his limo to the apartment building had forced him to break out into a sweat under his dress shirt, jeans, and tennis shoes.

The room around him had more of an antiseptic hospital smell than a crime scene, but Pilgrim was pretty convinced he was standing in a crime scene. He had seen his share over the years helping police with varied investigations.

This might be someone really sick who did this.

As a private detective who helped the police on cases, he was usually called to a crime scene long after a body was removed, however. This time he was the one calling the police to a body. Actually, his assistant Donna Marks was doing the calling just outside the door.

He had ended up a private eye through a series of strange events. First, three years of law school and a failed first marriage while working for a corporate law firm had convinced him he wasn't a normal lawyer.

Or a decent standard husband either.

Then his grandmother had died and left him more money than he could imagine, which sent him on a year of traveling and drinking, which also eventually got boring.

So he went back to school to become a private detective, but soon learned, after he hung out his shingle, that being a private eye wasn't what the books described. It was all computer work and long boring hours of nothingness trying to watch someone.

At that point, he had finally figured out that he bored easily and needed some excitement and challenges in his life. So with some of his grandmother's money, he set up Hugh and Associates, a combination law firm and private investigative firm. Then he had hired a couple great associates who took all the boring cases and made the firm lots of money and they hired even more associates that he had no desire to meet who also made him lots and lots of money.

And he bought apartments around the town that also made him money, so his grandmother's fortune had gotten bigger even with his best efforts to spend it all.

He had then offered his investigative state-of-the-art services for free to all the surrounding police forces. After a few years, he had solved a bunch of cases and was now called regularly. Interesting stuff.

Seldom boring.

For the first two years on being a private eye, his best friend from school, Carrie, had been his assistant, but she had fallen in love with the law side of the firm, gone back to law school, and now worked on the floor below his office doing law stuff that seemed boring to him, but that she seemed to thrive on.

Before she left, Carrie had trained Donna Marks to be his special assistant. At times he had to admit, Donna was better at her job being his assistant than Carrie had been.

At the moment, he could hear Donna's voice in the hallway outside the apartment. From the sounds of it, the Portland Police would be here shortly.

He looked at the apartment key in his hand. Nothing unusual about it at all. It had come to his office by Priority Mail with a simple typed note that read: Go

Now Available
from all your favorite booksellers in trade paper and electronic editions.

USA TODAY BESTSELLING AUTHOR

DEAN WESLEY SMITH

HEAVEN PAINTED
as a Christmas Gift

A GHOST OF A CHANCE NOVEL

here at noon for the most puzzling crime of your career.

Then the address of the apartment, no signature.

Had the person who murdered this woman sent the note?

Or had the woman even been murdered?

No clues in the note at all, just the reference to crime and all printed out on standard white paper. He had all of it in his limo to give the police.

This was puzzling. The note was right about that much.

He took a slow walk around the small studio apartment, looking for any clues or anything that seemed odd besides the fact that everything was scrubbed to an inch of its paint job. Even the small bathroom shone like a bad commercial.

Whoever had cleaned this place had done a great job of it.

He went back to the dead woman and just stared at her.

The blue woman in the white dress lay in the middle of the hardwood floor, her feet together and aimed toward the door into the hallway. Her hands were grasped over her stomach, as if resting. Her eyes were closed.

He moved closer and bent down carefully to not touch anything.

She had on makeup, but not too much. There was just enough to accent her face, even with the shade of blue of her skin. Her bright red hair was combed back and arranged around her face on the floor. She almost seemed to be smiling.

The blue skin color was clearly covering every inch of visible skin and from the blue tint coming through the sheer white dress, all of her body.

She had no obvious signs of trauma, but he sure wasn't going to move her to look for any. However, he did carefully, using one knuckle, touch her skin on the side of her arm.

Room temperature. And she had no smell at all.

None.

He had been in rooms after murder victims were taken away and the smell of death always remained.

No smell of life or death with this woman.

He stood and stepped back toward the apartment door as Donna came in. She was wearing white shorts that fit like a glove, a brown tank top, and tennis shoes. She had short brown hair and wide brown eyes and when smiling, she could light up a room.

She was divorced, thirty, and an expert on computers, high-speed driving, and weapons. So far he had only needed her for the computers, thankfully.

"You would think blue lady there would smell," Donna said. "And I don't see any blood anywhere."

"More than likely it would have been blue," Pilgrim said.

"Are we going down that blue road?" she asked.

"Not until the men in blue get here," he said.

She moaned and turned for the hallway. "I'm calling a blue moratorium on bad jokes until we get this solved."

"Deal," he said.

Over her shoulder she said, "I'm going back to the limo to do some research on how skin can become that shade and exactly who this woman used to be."

"The police will want the letter," he said.

"Already have it in a bag," she said without looking back.

He shook his head and went back to staring at the redhead with the blue skin resting peacefully on the floor.

The letter writer had been correct. It was a crime for someone so beautiful and young to be dead, no matter how it happened.

TWO

PILGRIM HUGH heard the police before he saw them as they thundered up the stairs and then along the hallway toward the apartment door. This apartment was on the second floor and since there was a park across the street, the only thing that could look in the windows were the birds in the far trees.

Since Donna had told the police there was a body, more than likely the first to arrive would be the closest patrol officers to secure the scene. The detectives would follow in their own sweet time.

"Sir," a policeman said, "please turn around."

Pilgrim did as he was told, arms away from his body. Then he smiled.

"Officer Daniels," he said. "Great seeing you again."

Daniels had been the officer on scene on a number of Pilgrim's strange cases over the years. He looked like the perfect image of a college quarterback, with strong shoulders, dark hair, a jutting chin, and a wide smile. He and Carrie had flirted a great deal at times, but as far as Pilgrim knew, nothing had come of it.

"Mr. Hugh," Daniels said, smiling and stepping forward and shaking Pilgrim's hand.

"Wow, a blue woman," the other officer said from beside Daniels.

"Yeah, real blue," Daniels said, looking past Pilgrim at the body. "And she was a looker before she got the dye job."

"Dye job?" Pilgrim asked. "Something I'm missing these days in the newest trend."

"Don't get me started," the other officer said, moving back into the hallway to stand beside the door.

"Some kids have moved past tattoos into full-body dye jobs," Daniels said, shaking his head. "The green ones are just flat disgusting and some of the dyes glow in the dark. Damn creepy if you ask me."

"You're kidding?" Pilgrim had no idea how he had missed this recent fad. He really needed to get out of that office at the top of the building a little more. It didn't help that his apartment was the penthouse above his office.

Daniels just shook his head. "Wish I was."

Pilgrim handed Daniels the key to the apartment. "This was sent to me with a note. Donna has the note and the envelope in the limo outside when the detectives want it. That's where I'll be waiting as well."

"Carrie not with you today?" Daniels asked.

"Working back at the firm," Hugh said. "But if you haven't met Donna yet, you'll love her."

"Looking forward to it," Daniels said, smiling.

Pilgrim took one last look at the blue woman and headed out.

Puzzling, yes.

Crime, maybe.

Solution, nothing yet.

THREE

"THE BLUE WOMAN used to be the renter of record on the apartment," Donna said as Pilgrim Hugh climbed into the limo.

This stretch limo was far more than just a nice ride around town. It had state of the art computer stations that folded down into hidden compartments and many other features.

The cool air in the limo felt good after the short walk from the front of the apartment building through the hot July afternoon. Donna handed him a bottle of cold water from the fridge near her station in the center of the limo compartment and then went back to her screens.

Pilgrim took a drink as he got into his seat and punched a button so that his computer station would come up and wrap around him.

"Incoming," Donna said.

She had sent him the image of the redheaded woman. The photo was a glamour shot with her standing with a white dress in a snowstorm of something white. Even with the images slightly blurred from the art work, it was clearly the blue woman.

"Her name is Deirdre Blue," Donna said. "But it seems she went by the first name of Deep and I am not kidding about the last name. Both parents dead, no siblings."

"Deep Blue?" he asked, staring at his screen.

"Deep Blue," Donna said. "And I'm sticking to the moratorium on the jokes."

"Think that name might be a reason she ended up the way she did?" he asked.

Donna laughed. "Wouldn't bet against it."

Pilgrim had his computer screens up and Donna was giving him all the data she had found about Deep Blue. She had worked at a downtown clothing store until a month ago, and also as a professional clothing model. She had been twenty-six and single, and had a degree in design and business. Not a dumb woman by any means and clearly successful in a hard field.

"So what happened a month ago at her job?" he asked.

Donna shook her head. "I hacked into the store employment records to save time and it only shows that she quit with standard notice. No reason given."

Pilgrim ignored the hacked part and nodded. Clearly Deep had no criminal record, had worked as a model at times and at the clothing store and had lived in a small studio apartment. It all seemed so standard.

He dug deeper into the records for the apartment and found that she had given notice at the first of the month and moved out, paying for a professional cleaning service to clean everything and give all her furnishings to charities. The apartment was still paid for until the end of the month.

"What the hell was this woman planning?" Donna asked, staring at her screen. "Quit her job, gave up her apartment, and then dyed herself blue to match her name."

"I'm not sure she did that to herself," Pilgrim said. "And I want to figure out who would kill her and then take her back to her own apartment, one that she had already moved out of. And then why write us to find her?"

Donna looked over at him. "It's the writing us that is the key to all this."

"You're right," he said. "Who and why?" That was the part that made no sense to him at all.

"The package came priority mail," Donna said. "At least a full day, maybe two. She would have had a pretty ripe odor after two days on that floor."

Pilgrim knew exactly what Donna was thinking.

"Any cameras around this building on the street or the alley behind the building near the garbage bins?"

Donna's fingers were flying over the keys of her computer. After a moment images of traffic cams started appearing on his screen.

"I figured the person who staged her would make sure we got the mail first," Donna said, "then stage her right ahead of us getting there, so I'm checking traffic cams from an hour or so ago going backward in time."

"Doing that would show a respect for Deep," he said. "Not that she was killed."

Donna glanced at him and nodded, then turned back to her screens.

"I got another idea as well," he said. "How much you want to bet this person is still watching in some fashion."

"No bet in a blue moon," Donna said.

He shook his head.

"Sorry," she said. "Slipped out."

"Can you scan that building around the apartment for any stray signals. I didn't see any hidden cams in that apartment, but doesn't mean they aren't there."

As Donna's fingers sort of danced a happy dance on her computer keyboard, he started through the videos. It didn't take him long since Donna had narrowed the choices down so much. A mortuary van had turned onto the street where the three-story apartment building was situated just thirty minutes before they got here.

Stanton Mortuary.

Deep Blue had been embalmed and the marks covered. No wonder her skin felt room temperature.

He suddenly knew that even though the body didn't smell, he was getting a distinct odor of fish in all this.

He quickly hacked into the Stanton Mortuary files to find the records of a Deep Blue who died five days ago from a massive brain tumor. She had spent most of the last month in hospice care. Her service had been yesterday.

As he looked quickly through the photos of family and friends, he ran across one photo of five girls in college. And with one look at the photo, he knew exactly what had happened.

"Got it," Donna said. "Camera signal from the apartment to a nearby source."

He pointed to the hidden computer area that Carrie used when with them. "Check her computer and I think you'll find the signal."

Donna looked really puzzled, but did as he suggested and ten seconds later Donna nodded. "The signal is being transferred from here. But how, these systems are guarded better than any system I have ever seen. I know, I set up most of the walls."

"Break into the signal and tell Carrie we solved it."

"Of course," Donna said, smiling.

He glanced at the clock on his computer screen. "Tell her it only took twenty-one minutes. Tell her to send in the mortuary van again to pick up Deep. And ask her how her dates with Officer Daniels have gone."

Donna just frowned at the date part, but did as she was told.

Pilgrim clicked off his computer and let it retract back into its hiding spot, then sat back with his cold bottle of water and waited.

It took exactly fifty seconds for a knock to come to the side door of the limo.

"Get the chief a cold bottle of water," he said to Donna, who opened the door for the chief to climb in and then handed him a bottle of water from the fridge.

"Man, that was fast," Chief Craig said as he sat across from Pilgrim with a sigh. The chief was a thin man, who seemed to dominate every room he was in with his combination stern look and smile. He had worked up through the ranks and was a popular chief, both with his officers and with the city government, a hard trick to pull off.

"How did Carrie get you to allow this stunt?" Pilgrim asked as Donna let her computer screens vanish back into their home so she could turn and join the conversation.

"It wasn't Carrie," the chief said. "Carrie just helped. I was friends of the family with the Blues and before they died, I promised them I would watch over Deep."

"But then she got the inoperable brain tumor," Pilgrim said.

The chief nodded, clearly sad. "She had heard so much about you from Carrie at their girls' nights out, that she wanted to use her death to test you, for the fun of it. Sort of a last request."

"You tried to talk her out of it, I presume," Donna said.

"We all did," the chief said, laughing. "Deep was really strong-willed when she wanted to be, even right down to the end."

"And beyond, it seems," Pilgrim said. "But I have a hunch there was more to this than just a last wish."

The chief laughed and then nodded. "Deep had a lot of money from insurance after her parents died. She wanted it to go to good causes, but couldn't decide which cause to give it to or how to divide it up."

"You're kidding me," Donna said. "Us solving this will result in some charities getting money and others not so much."

The chief nodded. "All the charities get some," the chief said, "including a few police funds, but with you solving it in twenty-one minutes, the large share goes to a fund to help the fisheries on the Columbia."

Pilgrim was just shaking his head. Only his best friend Carrie could have come up with such a strange test. But he had to admit, it had kept him entertained for a bit.

"We were going to pull the plug at one hour," the chief said.

"Did Carrie say it would never take us that long," Donna asked.

"Actually," the chief said, "she wasn't sure."

"How much money is the top charity getting?" Pilgrim asked.

"Quarter of a million."

"And how many charities were standing to gain from this?"

"Five total."

Pilgrim smiled. "I'll toss in enough so that all the charities get the same quarter million, as long as it all comes in under Deep Blue's name."

"I'm sure Carrie can make that happen," Chief Craig said. "And thanks."

"Thank you for honoring the tragic death of a young woman by following her wishes," Pilgrim said, "even as strange as they were."

The chief nodded. "I just wish you two had taken another ten minutes."

Pilgrim laughed.

"Why?" Donna asked.

"I had thirty-one minutes in the office pool."

"Who had twenty-one minutes?" Donna asked.

"Let me guess," Pilgrim said. "Daniels."

"Got it in one," the chief said, laughing. He handed Donna back his empty water bottle.

"Thanks again for the donations. Very kind of you. Now I got to go make sure Deep gets back to where she needs to go to be cremated."

The chief started to climb out into the warm air. Then he turned back and said, "Thanks also for keeping the blue jokes under control. The Blue family were really nice people and Deep was a wonderful woman. All gone far too soon."

He left and closed the door.

Donna took a long drink of cold water, then asked, "Back to the office, Boss?"

"Let's go get some lunch first and let Carrie wonder for a while how we reacted to all this," Pilgrim said, smiling. "Your choice."

She nodded and climbed out to move up to the driver's seat. He had a hunch he knew exactly where they would be eating. The Blue Diamond Grill. It was close and had great sandwiches.

He was right about that, but surprised when Donna ordered the Blue Plate Special and they actually had one. Who knew?

~

DEAN WESLEY SMITH

SMITH

USA Today Bestselling Author

the **First Tee Panic**

AND OTHER VERY REAL GOLF STORIES

Former PGA Golf Professional and USA Today *bestselling writer Dean Wesley Smith walks you step-by-step, club-by-club from your car to the first tee and beyond in a laugh-out-loud style that not only teaches, but entertains.*

A perfect gift for the golfer in your family.

Now Available
from all your favorite booksellers
in trade paper
and electronic editions.

DEAN WESLEY SMITH

SMITH

USA Today BESTSELLING AUTHOR

GRAPEVINE

SPRINGS

A THUNDER MOUNTAIN NOVEL

Could the entire history of an Old West mining town be false?
Did Grapevine Springs ever really exist?
Duster Kendal wants to know the answer to that question. But to get the answer, he must turn for help from two top researchers who must risk everything, including their lives, to find the answer.
A gripping new adventure in the Thunder Mountain series.

GRAPEVINE SPRINGS
A Thunder Mountain Novel

For Kris

Authors's Note
Parts of this novel was published originally in a much altered form
as a short story in the collection *Stories from July.*

PART ONE
A Missing Town

ONE

June 27th, 1909
Grapevine Creek Valley, Idaho

DUSTER KENDAL SAT high in his saddle, turning slowly in all directions, staring at the surrounding small valley in the warm afternoon sun. The hills were pine covered, the valley floor itself fairly wide for a mountain valley, with a gentle fall from north to south that allowed Grapevine Creek to meander back and forth from one side of the valley to the other, forming great stream banks under grass and weeds for trout to hide.

He wore his long oilcloth brown duster over a thin long-sleeved shirt and jeans. His face and head were sheltered from the high-mountain sun by a brown cowboy hat.

At six feet tall and with the long, flowing coat, he made an imposing figure in the saddle.

The air around him had a hot-pine smell and only a very faint breeze even rustled the brush under the trees.

Beautiful valley.

Very peaceful.

A place he might want to spend some time in.

But it shouldn't be.

This was the location, he was sure of it.

He just shook his head and rode slowly over to a stand of tall pine jutting off a ridgeline and into the valley floor, working his way through the grass. The trees would give him shade, a place to camp, and time to figure out what was happening.

He dismounted, allowing his horse, Sandy, to graze close by while he took his canteen and a map from his saddlebag.

He had printed the map before he left 2020 to come back to 1901. It looked like an old map of 1900, only with far more detail than most maps of this time could manage.

He studied the map, then the valley around him.

This was the right place.

But he should be far from alone standing here.

It had taken him eight years to finally get to this remote valley north of the Salmon River in Idaho, even though it had been the stated reason for his trip back into time.

He had spent the first years helping once again to build the big log Monumental Lodge on the ridge above the mining town of Roosevelt, Idaho. He loved the two years building that lodge every timeline he helped build it. And he loved more having it always there to stay at.

Then, after building the lodge, he had gone to Denver to play some poker for a couple years. That had been fun. The poker games in Denver just after the turn of the century were the best anywhere in the country.

But now he was back in Idaho, on a mission that had puzzled him and others for years, both here in the past, and in the future.

His mission: To find Grapevine Springs, the mining town.

He again studied the steep-walled valley as he took a drink from his canteen, letting the cool water wash down some dust.

For the next thirty minutes he checked and double-checked every detail. He was in the right spot.

But there was nothing here but a remote valley.

Nothing.

At this point in history, Grapevine Springs should be winding its mining days down, but at least five saloons and two thousand people should still be in this area right now.

But clearly that had never happened. There were no trails into this valley, let alone a wagon road. As far as he could tell, the entire area hadn't even had anyone go through it besides Native Americans, let alone been settled by miners.

But it was supposed to have been.

Grapevine Springs was a very real town in 2018. A former mining town turned tourist and ski town. The tall hill across from him was covered with snowboarders and skiers in the winter, with runs cut through the stands of pine.

In January of 2018 he had stood on this very spot, actually, on the deck of a condo he owned, watching the skiers on the hill across the valley.

The history of this town was well documented in a museum in the town's center, plus in the Idaho Historical Society.

Supposedly, a married couple named Watts, prospecting out of the Missoula region, had stumbled upon color in pans in Grapevine Creek around 1901. Good color, from all reports.

They and a dozen silent partners out of Boise had managed to get claims in on most of the ground in this valley and had built the town of Grapevine Springs, selling off parcels of land to stores and saloons and other businesses.

At one point, Grapevine Springs had bragged that it had over ten thousand people in it working dozens of mines up and down the valley. That had been before the gold died down and the town receded back to almost a ghost town with only a few winter residents and a couple hundred landowners coming in during the summer.

In 2002, a group of investors, looking to build a major ski area destination resort like Sun Valley, visited the ghost town of Grapevine Springs and liked the beauty and the fantastic mountain and the winter snow, acclaimed to be some of the best and lightest in the west.

Three years later the resort opened, and it grew every year since into a major tourist attraction for the State of Idaho.

But in all of Duster's years living in the past, beyond ten thousand years now from what his wife Bonnie told him, almost all of it in parts of Idaho, he had never heard of Grapevine Springs as a mining town.

In fact, at one point or another, he had been the town sheriff or marshal for most major towns in the west.

So it would be impossible to not know about a major mining town here, especially that late into the gold-town period.

So Grapevine Springs flat didn't exist in this timeline. Or any of the other thousand timelines he had visited.

Someone, for some reason, had planted the history of Grapevine Springs in historical records.

So it actually was a real ghost town, because in the past it had never existed.

At least not in this past.

TWO

August 3rd, 2018
Boise, Idaho

PROFESSOR Sophie Silverman sat on the grass in the shade of a small poplar tree watching the people in inner tubes and on small rafts and air-mattresses float by in front of her on the Boise River.

The river was about as wide as Broadway in New York City and the water was clear and blue and reflected the bright sun. The air near the river smelled of dampness and had a slight fish odor that was actually pleasant, reminding her of days at the beach in New Jersey.

The ages of the people going by were from elderly to very young children and everyone seemed to be smiling and having a good time. Clearly all were very relaxed, seemingly without a care in the world. All of the younger children had on bright orange life jackets and a few of the elderly did as well.

From large yellow numbers on the sides of the inner tubes and small rafts, it appeared most of the flotation devices were rented.

Many of the small tubes and mattresses were tied together like a floating party and numbers of dogs sat on their own small platforms, drifting past with their people.

She loved dogs; just hadn't had time or felt settled enough over the last ten years to get a dog again.

The warm afternoon sun had baked many of the rafters by the time they got to her location, and she had no doubt a few of them would be wishing they had used more suntan lotion tomorrow.

But from where she sat up on the grassy bank, it sure seemed like fun. From what she understood, the rafters took busses from the Julia Davis Park area just down the river from her and rode up to Barber Park about six miles up the river. From there, they could rent rafts or inner tubes and drift downriver to Julia Davis Park, going over a few rapids along the way, but nothing really dangerous.

Mostly the float was just a wonderful time to relax and get away from the world on the calm, cold water as it wandered through tree-lined banks.

From an article she had read in the Boise Statesman newspaper, sometimes thousands of people on a nice summer weekend were floating the river at any given time. She could see why. What a wonderful way to spend a lazy summer afternoon.

Sophie adjusted her wide-brimmed floppy hat to make sure it covered her fair skin. She had short, pitch-black hair and skin so white she swore she glowed at night. And not a blemish on her skin either, which meant she didn't just tan, she went from white to bright red and painful if she wasn't careful.

That was one of the reasons she hadn't tried the river float yet this summer. And on top of that, she wasn't much of a swimmer, so she wanted to be with other people, but in her six months in this wonderful city, she had been so busy with her research, she just hadn't made many friends.

She had come to love Boise, with its warm, dry days and chilly nights. Everything about the city seemed to be beautiful, from the rafters in front of her to the mountains beyond the city in the distance.

The city was full of trees and seemed to be more like an oasis tucked down in a valley between tall mountains on one side and barren desert on the other.

It was a far, far cry from her home in New Jersey.

She had been born and raised in the small town of Phillipsburg in western New Jersey. In a few places, Boise reminded her of her hometown, mostly in the historic downtown area, but compared to Boise, Phillipsburg barely filled one neighborhood.

Both cities had rivers as well. But the Delaware River was nothing at all like the wonderful clear blue waters of the Boise River in front of her.

And the air in Boise was dry. Scary dry, actually.

Here on the edge of the desert, she had gone through tubes of Chapstick in just the first week, and moisturizing lotion sometimes seemed to just soak into her skin faster than she could apply it.

Humidity was called high here when it reached thirty percent. In her home town, that would have been the driest day on record.

But now, after four months, she had to admit, she liked the dry better. And she loved how it cooled down at night and when a storm came in, it actually cooled things off instead of making the air more sticky and hot.

"Professor Silverman?" a deep voice said from the sidewalk on the top of the grassy slope behind her.

She turned around and then scrambled to her feet.

"Director Parks," she said, moving up and standing on the edge of the wide sidewalk beside him.

"Hope I didn't startle you," he said, smiling.

Parks was the director of the Institute for Historical Research, the reason she was here in Boise. He had broad shoulders and seemed to be about thirty, with short-cut hair and a smile that seemed to always reach his eyes. He towered over her five-five height. She liked him and his wife Kerri a great deal.

Both Sophie and Parks had on what seemed to be the standard uniform of the summer in Boise. Jeans, tennis shoes, and light shirts. She also had on over a light blouse a light jacket in case she ended up sitting in air-conditioning at one point or another. Plus it kept the sun from burning her through her blouse.

He wasn't wearing a hat, but he often wore a cowboy hat that made him look more like he should be riding a horse instead of directing the most prestigious research facility in the world.

"Didn't startle me at all," she said, indicating the constant flow of rafters going past. "Just enjoying the show for a short time."

Parks smiled. "It's great fun and very relaxing. Have you tried it yet?"

"I want to," she said. "Just haven't taken the six hours needed to put on enough suntan lotion on this white skin."

Three Seeders Universe Novels
Available at your favorite booksellers.

He laughed. "Yeah, good point. The sun on that river can really burn a person faster than normal. But still worth it."

"I hear a voice of experience in that warning," she said.

"Hard earned," he said, laughing.

Then his face got serious. "I need your help on something if you wouldn't mind."

"Anything," she said.

That had stunned her. Why Director Parks would need her help was beyond her. She had felt that over the last four months she had barely been noticed by anyone else at the institute. She had just spent days and nights buried in her research and often barely managed to stagger back to her condo to fall into bed with exhaustion.

"Good," he said. "Thanks. We have a new researcher applying for a position this afternoon. His area of expertise and study is similar to yours and we were hoping after we accepted him, you could show him the ropes and help him get settled."

She wasn't sure if having another researcher close to her area of study was good or bad, so she flat decided to ask.

She stammered out her question and Parks laughed. "Actually, not in the slightest. That's why we figured you could help him get up to speed not only with Boise and the library and the living situation, but with some of his work. We like having more than one person working in similar areas and that's one of the reasons we are going to accept him, not counting the fact that he is a brilliant researcher."

"What exactly is his focus on his research?" she asked.

"His name is Doctor Olsen Wade," Parks said. "He's got an MD, but also degrees in history and teaches history at UCLA. His passion is the research of the medical condition of men in the Old West."

Sophie laughed. Her area was family life and women of the Old West, so the Director was right, her area and Doctor Wade's focus were similar. And matched in many ways.

"I'll be glad to help him get up to speed here," Sophie said.

"Wonderful," Parks said, indicating they should head toward the institute about a half-mile up the river from where they stood.

The walk was wonderful, the conversation with the director light and about the rafters floating past.

In all her years of college and then teaching for three years at the University of Massachusetts, she had never expected to be this happy with life in general.

There was just something about being free to do her research as she wanted.

And about Boise and the warm, dry summer days.

THREE

August 3rd, 2018
Boise, Idaho

DOCTOR OLSEN WADE stood near the door of the front reception area of the Institute of Historical Research. He had had no idea what to expect when he came to Boise for this interview, but finding the institute headquartered in a beautiful Victorian-style mansion perched on a ridgeline overlooking a river was not it.

The building had been designed to impress from the moment it had been built in the late 1880s, and it impressed him completely.

Warm Springs Avenue in front of the institute was lined with similar style mansions and clearly, back at the beginning of the last century, this neighborhood had been for the wealthy.

The very wealthy.

This front room just inside the massive wooden front door had towering ceilings, all with fine detail woodworking that would be far, far too expensive to do today. Windows filled two sides of the room. They had to be almost fifteen feet tall, framed in beautiful mahogany and old-fashioned heavy drapes pulled open to let in the light.

A wide stone fireplace filled the corner between the windows. It was made of smooth river rock laid in a clean pattern and it extended all the way through the ceiling.

From what he could tell, the fireplace was still used in the winter and wood was stacked neatly beside it.

Period furniture sat in front of the fireplace on a large ornate area rug over the dark floors. A couch and two overstuffed chairs were arranged in such a way as to take advantage of the fireplace in the winter. A mahogany coffee table with claw feet sat in front of the couch with old lace coasters.

He moved over and sat in one chair, letting his six-foot frame ease down into the soft cushions. Even ancient, the chair was comfortable and he could imagine himself spending an evening in the chair reading in front of the fire.

He stood and made sure his dress shirt was still tucked into his jeans. He ran a hand through his longish brown hair, wishing for the tenth time in the last few hours that he had gotten a haircut. His hair never seemed to stay in place.

At least he had managed to shave in the airport restroom on the way.

Across the room from the fireplace was a beautiful ornate grand staircase with polished mahogany rails and dark-stained pine stairs covered with a carpet runner up the middle. He moved over to it and ran his hand along the railing, feeling the polished smoothness of the wood.

The archway into what must have been a formal dining room in the past was partially blocked by a large wooden desk from the same period. Even the chair behind the desk fit the time period of the room. There was nothing at all on the desk.

He couldn't see a detail out of place. What an amazing front office for a historical institute.

He stood there by the staircase, not really knowing what to do with himself at this point. He had left his travel bag near the front door and it looked tempting to just pick up and head back to Southern California.

But he knew if he did that, he would always regret not seeing this through.

He forced himself to take some deep breaths to try to calm down some. He had no idea why he was so nervous. He had more than enough money to do his own research on his own pace, so the institute financial help didn't matter. But there was just something about the institute and its reputation for only accepting the best that challenged him.

At twenty-nine, he had grown tired of teaching and wanted a break. Actually, he needed a break. He had liked Southern California. Clearly different from his hometown of Boulder, Colorado. And he had liked the sun and the excitement of living there, even though he seldom got out or down to the beach or anywhere else for that matter.

And his former fiancée, Jean, had finally gotten tired of waiting for him and his strange ways of staying up all night lost in medical records in old books from western towns. She had met another humanities professor from Berkeley and had moved there in May to be with her new love.

Wade had no doubt he would be hearing that they were married at some point this winter. Jean hated waiting for him and really, really had a desire to be married. Pathological desire, at times, as far as he was concerned.

He had loved the fact that they fit together, loved that they both loved to surf, loved her passion for politics and her passion in bed. But as time went on, he had realized he didn't really love her as a person.

After a few months now since she had left him all alone in their condo, he realized that his hesitation on getting married to her had been his subconscious telling him it wouldn't be right.

At that moment a man about Wade's height and age entered the room from the back, followed by a short, black-haired woman wearing a wide floppy blue hat. Both of them wore jeans and light shirts and the woman had on a light blue thin jacket as well that covered her arms and neck.

"Dr. Wade?" the man said as he came forward, extending his hand. "I'm Director Parks."

Wade shook the director's strong hand, smiling. "Great meeting you and thanks for allowing me to interview."

Parks laughed. "Our pleasure, I assure you."

Parks turned and said, "Dr. Wade, this is Professor Silverman."

At that moment Professor Silverman looked up and into Wade's eyes and Wade damn near froze as he extended his hand.

She was the most beautiful woman he had ever seen.

And when they touched, he never wanted to let go.

And clearly as they held each other's gaze, she was surprised at meeting him as well.

"Nice meeting you," he finally managed to say.

He didn't want to let go of her wonderful hand, but he did.

She nodded and just kept staring at him.

Director Parks didn't seem to notice their interaction, thankfully, as he said, "Let's sit and talk for a moment. And I hope we didn't keep you waiting too long."

"Not at all," Wade said, desperately trying to gather his wits about him like they were lost marbles scattering across the hardwood floor. This was an important interview. He really, really needed to get it together.

And fast.

Real fast.

FOUR

August 3rd, 2018
Boise, Idaho

SOPHIE SOMEHOW managed to take a breath as Dr. Wade turned to follow the director to the couch and chairs. She wanted to just sit down at the desk on the chair there because her legs were feeling strange, like she had had too much sun.

But she knew she hadn't. She knew the reaction was to meeting Dr. Wade.

And watching him walk toward the couch and chairs didn't help. He was built like an athlete, with narrow hips and wide shoulders.

The man was the most attractive man she had ever seen. He was as tall as Director Parks and had the most wonderful green eyes and tanned skin. His brown hair looked like it needed to be cut and combed, but she had a hunch it always looked like that, giving him a boyish charm that she would never suggest he change.

And his touch had been heavenly. She had wanted to just hold onto his hand for a lot, lot longer, but she had a hunch Director Parks would have frowned on that with a new recruit to the institute. The director had asked her to help, not tackle Dr. Wade.

She had had her share of boyfriends along the way. A couple had pretended to get serious, but both of them had moved on to others, calling her remote and unavailable. She had only shrugged at that. It was saying something when she liked her research work more than the man she was dating.

It had been seven months since her last fling, and after a few lackluster attempts in bed, she had moved on from that guy, not even giving him the chance to do so first.

So Dr. Wade's touch had certainly set off something inside of her she had kept sort of under control over the summer since arriving here. She wasn't sure if that was a good thing or a bad thing. But she sure wanted to find out.

Dr. Wade sat on the couch and Director Parks took the chair closest to the fireplace and turned it toward the couch. Sophie took the other chair, also turning it toward the couch.

Dr. Wade looked at her and smiled as she sat down.

Her breath caught with that. His smile was as good as the rest of him.

Thankfully, he turned his attention to the director and gave her another chance to gather herself. She could never remember having a reaction like this to any man before. And now certainly wasn't the best time to start.

"Thanks for applying to the institute, Dr. Wade," Director Parks said, getting this all started.

"Thanks for taking my application," Dr. Wade said. "And please just call me Wade. Everyone does."

The Director nodded and Wade turned to Sophie and she nodded.

"I just go by Sophie."

Wade again nodded and smiled at her and then turned back to the director.

And once again she was glad he gave her the time to catch her breath again. She really, really needed to pull herself together very quickly.

"The board here at the institute has looked over your credentials," Park said.

"Anything I can fill in?" Wade asked.

The director shook his head. "No, I think we're satisfied and would like to offer you a research position here starting today."

Sophie watched as Wade opened his mouth, then closed it. Clearly he was shocked, as shocked as she had been thinking she was coming for an interview and being offered a position instead. It seemed the institute and directors did a very complete job of researching perspective candidates.

"A research position comes with a nice condo down along the river," the director said. "All food and supplies are furnished, plus you have use of a car any time you need one."

"Wow," Wade managed to say.

Sophie smiled at that. She hadn't even gotten that much out for the first two minutes.

"The institute will also cover any travel you need to do," Parks said, "and a five-thousand-dollar-a-month stipend you can do anything you would like with."

Wade only nodded to that, but Sophie bet he was barely holding it together.

"We ask for no credit at all in your research or any papers you write while here. However, we do ask that you sign a nondisclosure agreement as to anything you see here or the terms of our agreement."

Wade again nodded.

The director went on. "You can stay as long as you need for your research. No limits and no hurry and we do not ask to check your work in any fashion."

Sophie nodded to that. In the last few months, she had met a few researchers who basically were just living here and publishing books and had been for years. She certainly was in no hurry to leave, and her $5,000 per month was already building up into a pretty good reserve fund for when she did move on.

"Are you interested in our offer?" Director Parks asked.

Wade nodded for a moment before he managed to say, "Yes, I am honored."

"Actually," Director Parks said, "We are honored to have you here."

With that, the director stood and shook Wade's hand as Wade stood.

"Welcome aboard," Director Parks said. "I'll have the paperwork drawn up over the next few hours. Sophie has generously offered to show you around in the meantime. Her area of research is similar to yours, so I'm sure you'll have a lot to talk about."

Sophie stood and smiled at Wade, who looked completely shocked.

Director Parks went to the clean wooden desk and punched a hidden button on the side. A computer screen lifted up and Parks quickly typed in a code, then turned to a hidden printer in a cabinet behind the desk.

A moment later he turned back and handed Wade a couple of plastic cards. "These are your pass keys into the buildings, library, and your condo. Sophie will show you how they work."

"Which condo is Wade in?" Sophie asked.

Parks glanced at the screen, then said, "10-19."

"Great," Sophie said, smiling at Wade. "I'm in 9-12 in the complex next to yours. It's beautiful there. You will be amazed."

"Any furniture or supplies you need," the director said, "feel free to just buy them using that card."

Wade looked at the cards in his hand with a puzzled look. They looked like simple hotel keys with nothing at all written on them. But Sophie knew around Boise those white cards were better than the top charge cards in existence.

"I'll explain it all," she said, letting Wade and Director Parks off the hook.

Wade nodded and then smiled. "Thanks."

Sophie smiled back at him. She understood exactly what he was thinking and the confusion he was feeling.

She just wished she understood what she was thinking, and why she couldn't get the idea of getting him naked out of her mind.

FIVE

August 3rd, 2018
Boise, Idaho

THE FIRST HOUR with Sophie was like a dream.

A wonderful dream.

She had to be the most beautiful and alluring woman he had ever met. And when she had taken off that large, floppy-brimmed sunhat when she sat down in the meeting, he had almost melted. He had been attracted to his share of women over the years, and had been in lust with a lot more.

But never had he felt such sudden attraction and lust at the same time with another person, let alone another historian and professor. Before today he would have bet that wasn't even possible.

As Director Parks had gone up the stairs, she had asked him if he minded a half-mile walk along the river in the warm afternoon sun.

"Might clear my head some," he said, laughing.

She had indicated that he grab his shoulder bag and follow her.

She led him out the back of the old Victorian Mansion and down past three other buildings. The entire complex was shaded by massive old oak and cottonwood trees, giving it all a sense of privacy and protection.

"Those used to be the stables," she said as they went by the first two, "but now they house cars we can use if we want. I've never really checked one out, since I like walking everywhere. But I'll show you how later."

He nodded. After living in LA for so long, he found it hard to imagine living without a car. And in Boulder you pretty much needed one all the time as well.

In LA he had parked at the airport his BMW convertible. He was going to need to head back down there and either park it somewhere or bring it up here. He would decide that later.

The warmth of the sunny afternoon felt good, slightly cooler than what he was used to. Sophie had put her hat back on the moment they stepped outside, laughing at how her fair skin didn't do well without lotion in the sun.

He didn't say anything, but he found her skin frighteningly alluring, so much so that it was everything he could do to just not touch her hand at times as they walked.

The path beside the river wound along in the shade through tall poplar and oak and cottonwood trees.

About two blocks down from the institute, the river path ran into a street and they crossed over the bridge and took the tunnel on the other side under the road to continue to follow along the river.

"What is all that?" he asked, trying to make sense out of the hordes of people floating past, many of them sitting in inner tubes. He didn't even know inner tubes were still made.

"That," Sophie said, "is one of the many wonderful charms about this city. Seems like a summer pastime for vast numbers of people here is to float the Boise River from about six miles upstream to a park just down from us."

The more he stared at the people going past, the more he liked the idea, especially if the river was as clean and cool as it looked.

"You ever done it?" he asked.

She shook her head. "Only been here since May and haven't had a chance to yet. But it sure looks like fun, doesn't it? I like to sit here on the grass and just watch them float by. Gives me time to think."

"It does look like fun," he said.

At that moment, he came out of his shock from the meeting and realized how little he knew about this person walking beside him. In fact, he knew nothing about her at all besides her name.

Nothing.

They walked for a moment in silence before he asked, "Were you on the committee that approved my application?"

She laughed, the sound high and soft, like it belonged in the grass and trees around them.

"I was the last person accepted here before you," she said. "They surprised me in the same way and it was Director Parks' secretary that showed me around. I'm guessing the director thought that since I was new at this as well, it would help you figure out stuff quicker."

"So you know as little about me as I do about you?"

"Yup," she said. Then she shrugged. "And not much more about the institute, actually. Got a hunch both of us are going to be asking questions when I realize how much I really don't know yet about this place."

He laughed. "So how about we start with the important stuff in the getting to know each other area. What are you researching?"

She laughed as well. "Family, mostly women's lives in the Old West, specifically the women living in the old mining towns. How about you?"

He was shocked at that. The director had been right. Their areas of research were very close.

"I'm trying to research and dig up what medical records that exist about the health of the people living and working in the old mining towns."

She looked up at him from under her floppy hat. He could tell she was surprised as well.

And he decided right there he hoped to spend hours staring into those dark eyes to find out what was behind them.

"I ran across some old medical diaries from a mining town called Stibnite last week," she said. "Glad to show you how to get to them."

"Fantastic," he said. "Thanks. Director Parks was right about our areas of research. They really are close."

She laughed. "Some day I just hope to meet Dawn Edwards, since both of us are clearly jumping off the fantastic work she has done."

Just the sound of that name made Wade jerk a little. Dawn Edwards had done some of the most definitive books on the people and lives of the people in old mining towns that had ever been written.

"Is she around here?" Wade asked.

"I think she is at times," Sophie said. "But again, haven't had enough time to dig into that. Just hoping is all. I wouldn't actually recognize her if she walked past us right now."

"With that I agree," Wade said. "But it would be an honor to shake her hand and tell her how much I loved her books at some point."

"It would at that," Sophie said.

SIX

August 3rd, 2018
Boise, Idaho

SOPHIE DIRECTED Wade along a sidewalk away from the river and toward some two-story condos scattered in the trees. Each complex had eight or ten condos and they were staggered in such a fashion that each one had a private backyard and a view of the river.

Sophie couldn't even image how much these had cost to build, but no one lived in them but the researchers at the institute. And even then most were empty as far as she could tell. There were never any cars in the small parking lots, that's for certain.

"I live in that complex," she said as they came to a branch in the sidewalk. "Complex number nine. From what I understand, all the condos look the same, but I have never been in more than mine."

"These are all for the researchers?" Wade asked, looking at the complex of buildings.

"From what I understand," Sophie said.

"Wow," Wade said.

Now that she really looked around, that was amazing.

"Any idea where the institute gets its money?"

"Not a clue," she said. "One of the many things I've been meaning to ask but just never have."

"They clearly have a lot of it," Wade said. "And they don't check anything you are doing?"

"Nothing," Sophie said. "I asked for help a few times finding stuff in the institute library, and they were glad to help."

"The library in that mansion?" Wade asked.

She laughed as they continued to walk along the path toward his condo. "No, the library is the size of a major warehouse building and is about four floors, at least. I haven't managed to get to it all yet. You

will have an office in there if you want. I would suggest it."

"They give us offices?"

"They give us everything we want," she said.

Now that she said that, she wondered why she hadn't questioned that before now. Strange place, this institute.

At that point they reached his door. It had the label 10-19 beside it.

"Take either one of your white cards out and just hold it in front of the door handle," she said.

He quickly dug into his back pocket and pulled out the two white cards. He moved one toward the door and the latch clicked and the door opened slightly.

He shook his head and pushed open the door.

"Welcome, Dr. Wade," a female voice said. "And Professor Silverman."

"Thank you, Goldie," Sophie said, smiling at Wade's shocked expression.

"The condo complex is called the Gold Rush Village, so everyone just calls the computer that takes care of everything in our places Goldie."

"Monitored?"

Sophie remembered being worried about that as well. "No, just security at the doors and windows and audio response inside when asked. Some tech guys from the institute showed me how it worked. You might want to have them show you as well."

"Well, nice meeting you, Goldie," Wade said as Sophie closed the door and Wade dropped his bag nearby.

"It is good to have you here, Dr. Wade," Goldie said. "If you have any questions, feel free to just ask by using my name."

"Thank you," Wade said, shaking his head.

Sophie laughed. It had taken her a month or so to get used to Goldie as well, but now she wasn't sure how she would survive without her at times. She had far too many traits similar to an absent-minded professor than she wanted to admit and Goldie tended to keep track of things for her, including what time of the day or night it was.

She led him to the huge living room and told him to go explore as she sat down on one of the large chairs.

The ceiling in here was high, with wide windows looking out over the river beyond. And the temperature in here was set perfectly.

There were three large overstuffed chairs, a love-seat, and a couch in the living room, with a river-stone fireplace dominating one side of the room. Everything, including the soft carpet and drapes were done in various brown tones that seemed to complement the wood trim and the dark wood deck beyond the window.

She loved how comfortable the place felt. It really did feel like a home to her.

After a few minutes, Wade joined her, coming back down the open wood staircase and going through the living room and to the state-of-the-art kitchen on the other side of the living room.

She didn't say a word.

Sophie doubted there was much she could say.

The kitchen had a counter with bar stools. The counter was open and looked out over the living room. A polished wood dining table with four chairs was tucked to one side of the kitchen in an alcove with windows that also looked out at the river.

The granite counters seemed to match the stone of the fireplace and the cabinets were also a light brown.

This place was almost identical to her place, just flipped so that her kitchen was on the other side.

Finally Wade came down the two steps into the sunken living room and dropped into a chair beside her facing the river. She just stared at his handsome face and messed-up hair and trim body as he looked out over the river.

Damn he was handsome. She just wanted to go over there and kiss him, but she kept her spot, watching him instead.

She let the silence just last, since more than likely he needed time to gather his thoughts.

Finally, he looked away from the view and turned in his chair to face her directly. "You are saying this place is mine to use while I am doing my research?"

"It is," she said, doing her best to not get lost in his wonderful green eyes. "I've added some personal details to my place and some pictures of old mining towns and friends from college, but otherwise this is exactly the same as my place."

"Rent free?" he asked.

"Rent free," she said, laughing. "Thankfully. I couldn't afford a nice place like this."

In fact, her condo was the nicest place she had ever lived in her life, but she didn't say that. There would be time for the two of them to get to know each other.

Or at least she hoped there would be time.

SEVEN

August 3rd, 2018
Boise, Idaho

AFTER HE TOOK his bag up to his room and checked with Goldie about sheets and blankets and towels and soap and other things. All provided and Goldie told him where it was all stored. He could see why Sophie liked Goldie, but he would have a tech person from the institute at some point explain the limitations of Goldie just to be sure.

Then he and Sophie headed off to find some lunch.

He hadn't realized just how hungry he was until she said something. He had only had a snack at the airport while waiting for his bags and nothing since. Breakfast in his condo in LA was a very long time ago.

In fact, his condo now seemed like years ago, even though he had slept there last night.

They ended up two blocks from the condos in what looked to be a sports bar near a football stadium. The place had dozens of large-screen televisions, all turned to different events.

They found a spot in a back corner booth that was quiet enough that they could talk.

It seemed that from what Sophie understood, college football here in Boise was like a religion in the fall. She warned Wade to stay either in the institute or in his condo or on foot on Saturday nights of home games. It seemed that Boise State University was a pretty good party school when it came to football and something called Smurf Turf.

They both had the bar's equivalent of a French Dip sandwich and iced tea and large glasses of water. Sophie downed half her water when it arrived and laughed when she saw him watching her.

"East Coast humidity girl doesn't do well with western dryness."

That he understood. He didn't do well in the thick, humid air of the East Coast either.

Over lunch they talked about their backgrounds. He was surprised that she had been teaching at U-Mass and she seemed just as surprised about his teaching at UCLA.

She planned on taking a year's leave this coming year, and he did as well if he got the research position. Telling the school was going to be something he needed to do fairly soon. He might ask for help from Director Parks with a letter to make sure he didn't jeopardize his position at the school.

Neither of them had family they were close to and both of them considered themselves loners. Both had no interest in organized religion at all and both enjoyed exercise when they could. She said she really enjoyed walking and hoped to build up to running since the path along the river was such a good runners' path.

What had really surprised him was when Sophie mentioned snow skiing. But she had actually no idea about it other than she understood it was very popular here and many of the staff and researchers at the institute skied and were looking forward to the winter already.

So when a guy about twenty with sandy hair and a neck that looked like he had played football returned carrying their meals, Wade asked him.

"I'm new in town and I hear there is good skiing nearby in the winter."

The guy laughed and pointed in a direction over Wade's shoulder. "Nineteen miles beyond the city limits, a resort called Bogus Basin. Four mountains, two mountains for night skiing. Some of the best skiing in the country."

"Thanks," Wade said, shaking his head.

"You a skier?" Sophie asked as the guy left.

"Born and raised in Boulder, Colorado," he said, laughing. "I think I was skiing before I could walk. How about you?"

"Born and raised in a very small town in the rolling hills along the upper Delaware River in eastern New Jersey," she said, smiling. "Snow was something you put up with."

"Ever wanted to learn how to ski?" he asked.

She looked puzzled, then said, "Honestly, until you asked, I had never given it a thought."

He laughed at that and the rest of the lunch was fun as they slowly got to know each other better.

And the more he learned about her, the more time he wanted to spend with her. She just kept stunning him with her sharp mind and piercing dark eyes and bright smile.

He had been really happy to hear she had no boyfriend and she seemed very pleased when he told her in return that he was very single. Clearly she was attracted to him as much as he was to her.

And he had no idea if there were any rules about two researchers having a relationship or not. More than likely he would learn that this afternoon. But Sophie sure didn't seem to be concerned about the attraction, so until he learned otherwise, he wouldn't be concerned either.

So after lunch they headed back to the river trail and up the river toward the institute. The rafters were still going by in a steady stream.

The weather was warm, but not too warm.

And Sophie was the best company he could ever imagine having on a beautiful summer walk. He had only known her for a few hours and it felt as if she had always been a part of his life.

He just hoped she was feeling the same way. Otherwise, he was going to be in for a really hard fall.

But she was worth the risk, of that he had no doubt.

EIGHT

August 3rd, 2018
Boise, Idaho

SOPHIE KNEW THAT the paperwork Wade had to do was pretty minor. The institute wanted nothing in return for their financial support but nondisclosure. So all the paperwork was basically making sure all of Wade's rights and work remained completely with him.

All the paperwork was done at the front desk in the large room and Director Parks was the only one there to do it. He had been the only one with her as well, so it seemed the director took clear personal interest in each new researcher.

When Wade had said something about the fact that the agreements protected only him and not the institute, Director Parks had laughed and said that was the only reason for the paperwork. The institute needed and wanted nothing in return but the knowledge they were helping in the research.

The nondisclosure to the institute was the only important document.

Wade had had the courage to ask about where all the money came from and again Director Parks had laughed. "We have a board of obscenely rich people who believe in the institute. All this may look like a lot of money from the outside, but to our board, it is just pocket change."

Sophie had nodded to that. She had heard of people that rich. Never met one, but they were not uncommon back east.

Wade had asked one more question that Sophie had not thought to ask. "So I am free to come and go as I want?"

Parks nodded. "Once accepted you are in. If you feel like you need to teach for a semester or a year, your place here will be waiting for you when you come back. And if you need to travel for your research, the institute hopes you will ask for funds to help with the travel. Again, money is no object when it comes to helping you with your work."

Sophie just shook her head at that one. So far she had had no desire to go anywhere but here, but it was great to know that was an option.

So when all the paperwork was done, Sophie and Wade wandered down the river path once again to the institute library to get Wade an office there. Then to a nearby grocery store to order supplies for Wade and have them delivered.

The manager of the grocery store had told Wade they would be waiting on his counter and in his fridge when he got back to his condo.

Sophie had had to explain to him how the grocery delivery was part of the service and Goldie only let authorized delivery people into the condo and tracked them.

By the time that was all done, it had been four hours since lunch.

"I'm betting you are getting tired," Sophie said to Wade as they left the grocery store and stood in the shade on a large tree. The river was a few blocks away and beside them traffic moved past in an orderly fashion. It wasn't yet five o'clock. "I sort of remember my first day here and how crazy it all seemed."

"I think I'm more numb than tired," Wade said. "This is a lot to take in."

"An understatement," she said. "How about an early dinner and then you can head back to your condo to get settled in."

He nodded to that.

"If you don't mind a little walk," she said, "I know a wonderful place."

"A walk would feel good," he said. "Might clear my mind."

"You like Italian food," she asked, hoping he said yes, because what she had in mind was her favorite restaurant.

"Love everything about it," he said, smiling at her.

Damn, she could look at that smile for a very, very long time.

She pointed down the sidewalk and together they turned and started off.

Twenty minutes later he sat across a wooden table from her in the moderately crowded Brooks Garden Restaurant. Most of the crowd was in the bar for happy hour, which gave them a lot of open seating in the restaurant.

Around them plants and wooden barriers gave each table a sense of privacy even when the place was full of people. At lunch this place was full of people taking breaks from all the tall office buildings in this downtown area.

The restaurant's high ceilings and the wooden planter barriers and enough plants and small trees to start a greenhouse kept the noise down. Without a lot of people, it felt to Sophie as if just she and Wade were the only two people in the world.

She had instantly loved the place the first time she wandered in here. The smell of garlic and fresh baking bread seemed to just drift between the trees and plants and always made her mouth water.

"I really am hungry," Wade said, "More than I had thought."

"It's the smell of garlic bread that can do that to you," Sophie said, smiling.

"This place seems great," Wade said, looking around. "I like all the old western pictures on the walls and the private booths."

"One of my favorites," Sophie said. "Glad you like it. The food is as good as the smell, I promise."

"Then I'm in heaven," he said, smiling at her.

Once again she just let herself stare into those wonderful green eyes and his handsome face.

And he didn't drop his gaze either.

Finally a waiter with a red apron and a deep voice broke their moment by dropping a basket of hot-buttered breadsticks on the table. They both ordered iced teas and also placed their food order, since they were both suddenly hungry. He went with a deep-dish pasta with thick red sauce and she went with lasagna, her favorite.

Finally, as both of them were chewing on the soft and warm garlic bread stick, he asked, "So ever heard of a mining town by the name of Grapevine Springs?"

She actually laughed. "North-central Idaho," she said. "Above the River of No Return."

"Now a major ski resort," he said nodding.

"Why?" she asked. "I've been gathering some data on it at times."

He shrugged. "I was thinking that town was isolated enough that the medical records, whatever I could find of them, would be a good study for part of my research."

She nodded, thinking back to what she knew about that old mining town. "It really would be, actually. One of the most isolated mining towns in the west with its location."

"Interested in sharing information we find about the place, Professor Silverman?" he asked, smiling at her.

"I would be honored, Dr. Wade," she said, returning his smile.

And once again their connection was broken with the waiter appearing between the plants with their drinks.

She liked Wade's offer more than she wanted to admit, actually. Anything that would give her a reason to be near Wade was a good thing in her mind.

Two hours later she said goodnight to a very tired Dr. Olsen Wade on the path where it split to her condo and his.

"Mind showing me around for another day or so?" he asked.

"I would love to," she said. "Can you find your way back to the same restaurant we just left?"

"That wonderful smell will lead me there I'm sure," he said.

"We'll meet for late breakfast there at 10:30. How does that sound? They do fantastic omelets and coffee."

"That sounds perfect," he said.

She wanted to just move forward and pull his head down to her height and kiss him, but instead just said, "It's wonderful having you at the institute."

"I think I'm going to enjoy it," he said, smiling a very tired smile at her.

"Get some sleep and see you in the morning," she said.

With that, she turned and started away.

"Professor," Wade said behind her.

She stopped and looked back.

"Thank you."

"Trust me," she said. "It was my pleasure."

He chuckled at that and they both turned away, even though she didn't want to.

And she had a hunch he didn't want to either.

PART TWO
The Mystery Deepens

NINE

July 2nd, 1909
Grapevine Creek Valley, Idaho

DUSTER KENDAL spent a week exploring the wonderful, hidden valley. He caught large rainbow trout from the stream and ate trout for both lunch and dinner. He never got tired of fresh rainbow trout cooked in butter so that the meat fell off the bones.

This valley was so peaceful, he might have to come back here more often, at least in the summer. He knew for a fact that the winters in this area were brutal and the snow deep.

In the future, he had watched skiers on the mountain right above him.

Then on the third day, he had decided to do a little gold panning himself.

It had turned out amazingly simple to pull color on a pan.

He hit ten different areas of the stream for a mile upstream and a couple miles downstream from his campsite, finding gold every time.

A lot of it.

There was no doubt there were some rich veins in this valley somewhere.

This area really should have been found, and how it hadn't been, he had no idea. More than likely the area was just far too remote.

For him to get here, he had had to go up to Edwardsburg and then over to the main Salmon River on the south side. He followed the trail down the river to Campbell's Ferry and crossed there, then went up the drainage of a side creek, going North, working his way without much more than game trails until he found the valley.

So after a week of camping in the Grapevine Valley, it was clear something was very wrong.

Very wrong.

No town by the name of Grapevine Springs ever had existed here.

Now he needed to get back to 2018 and find out why this fake had been played.

It took him a good two weeks to make his way to the Monumental Lodge, and he stayed there until just before the first snowfall in late September before heading back to Boise and the Historical Institute.

The institute had been started by him and Bonnie and twelve others who knew about timeline jumping to help historians in their research. Most of the historians working there at the institute knew nothing about being able to actually jump into the past of an almost identical timeline to do hands-on research.

And since each jump into another timeline only lasted two minutes and fifteen seconds, a person could stay in that other timeline, live a full life, even die, and find themselves having only a few minutes pass in their real life.

That was how he and Bonnie had lived so long.

Twenty-two others now knew about the massive hidden caverns under the main institute building and had jumped back into the past of another timeline at different points. He and Bonnie and the other twelve founders of the institute were very selective in who they chose.

When he finally reached Boise in late September, the year was 1910. He and others from 2018 had gone back into the past to 1880 and built this institute so that through all periods of time, they would have a place as a base.

He got his horse settled in the stable behind the main mansion, patted her a goodbye, and went in through a hidden door in the stable that took him directly to the caverns under the mansion.

He quickly dropped off the gold he had panned in the regular safe, left his saddlebags in the preparation cavern, and, with only the map from the future in his hand, jumped back to 2018 by unplugging a wire from a machine he and Bonnie had invented.

The machine was simple. It was hooked to a crystal that looked like a glowing quartz crystal. The machine allowed a person touching it to step into the past of the timeline held in that crystal.

Every time a decision was made, a new timeline was formed.

An infinite number of timelines for almost all major decisions.

By Duster simply being in the past of that timeline, he had caused millions of new timelines to be formed in the Nexus, the place where all energy, matter, and time combine into gigantic caverns full of crystals, each crystal holding a unique timeline.

A person could go back and alter a past, just not their own past. Only the past in another timeline.

The thousands of crystals brought to the institute in Boise from the Nexus were all timelines virtually identical to their own. And every year or so 2018 time, all the crystals that had been used were returned to the Nexus and new ones brought out to replace them.

Now, by removing that simple wire, he had returned to 2018. August 4th, actually.

TEN

August 4th, 2018
Boise, Idaho

SOPHIE SAT in Brooks Garden Restaurant, in the same wooden booth she and Wade had sat in last night. She figured Wade would find her easier there than anywhere in this plant-filled place.

She had on jeans, a light blouse, and a thin dress jacket to keep the sun off her arms. She had picked a different wide-brimmed hat today, one that had a style more like the type women wore in the Old West and matched the blue in her blouse. She had found the hat in a vintage clothing store and just loved it because of its distinctive weave pattern around the top.

She was sipping on her coffee and studying some information about the old mining town of Grapevine Springs on her tablet. She had spent a few hours earlier this morning in her office in the institute library digging up information about the town that Wade had mentioned.

And the more she dug into it, the more she liked the idea of studying it and the families and people who had lived there. It was a perfect sample of the Old West mining towns. A contained sample because of the remote nature of the valley.

The town had had a newspaper for ten years called the Grapevine Gazette, and also much of its news was also printed in the Grangeville paper, a larger farming town to the north.

The society page in the town's paper was larger than most mining town papers, which allowed her some basic start on the residents. Amazing what she could find by combining census data with the social pages and obituaries.

She had no doubt she was going to also need to go into the valley in person and check out the old cemetery and the historical museum that existed there now.

The town even had an unusual share of photos from a couple of the most famous western photographers of the time, Jackson and Watkins. Plus numbers of other uncredited photographs.

Perfect for her research.

The entire idea had her excited.

"Morning," Wade said as he slid into the booth across from her.

She looked up into his wonderful green eyes and smiling face and that just made her stomach flutter like a high school girl on a first date.

He looked to be a little flushed from his walk.

"Getting warm out there?"

"It's starting to," he said, taking a drink from a glass of water on the table.

"You look refreshed this morning," she said, smiling back and him. "Get some sleep?"

"Solid for almost eight hours," he said, shaking his head. "I never sleep that long normally. And I already have a list of things I need for my place and a list of things I want to bring up here with me from my place in LA."

"Wow, you got some stuff done already," she said, laughing. "I'm impressed."

"Feels like I have only scratched the surface."

"I still feel that way and I've been here since May."

At that moment the waitress in jeans, a white blouse, a red apron and bright red hair brought them both menus and asked if Wade would like coffee by holding up the coffee pot in her hand after she refreshed Sophie's cup.

"Please," Wade said.

He took a sip almost immediately, looking almost relieved.

For some reason the fact that Wade drank coffee black the way that she did pleased her far more than it should. She pushed the thought away of breakfasts regularly with him.

At least for now.

"So what are you working on?" Wade asked, indicating her tablet, "If you don't mind telling me."

She laughed. "No trade secrets around here that I know of. I got interested in learning more about Grapevine Springs after you mentioned it last night."

"What do you think?"

"I actually think it's perfect for both of our areas of research," she said. "I downloaded a bunch of pictures from it as well."

She slid her tablet toward him and he took it, looking at the images while she enjoyed watching his face and his wonderful hands as he slid one picture after another aside.

Then suddenly he stopped and stared at a picture, frowning.

He was even handsome frowning. How was that possible?

"What did you find?" she asked.

"You got family from the Old West?" he asked, glancing up at her and then back at the picture on her tablet.

She actually laughed at that. "Silverman. New Jersey." She said the state name with her deepest New Jersey accent, something she had trained out years before.

"You sure?" he asked, still frowning and staring at a picture on her tablet.

"My family is all from Europe, both sides, moved over in the thirties ahead of the Second World War. Not the type to go beyond sight of the Atlantic Ocean. I think it was pathological."

"Wow," he said, shaking his head and sliding her tablet back to her. "You had a twin back in Grapevine Springs."

She looked at the picture. It was of the wooden sidewalk in front of three buildings. One was a general store, another a lawyer's office and barbershop with the candy-cane pole and the third building was a saloon with its doors propped open.

Five people stood on the boardwalk in a group, clearly not realizing they were having their picture taken. One was a short woman in riding clothes of the time. She was facing the camera and her face was clear under the hat.

It did look exactly like her.

And then Sophie noticed the hat the woman was wearing and got chills down her spine.

Then she looked at the other four people in the group. One of the men in a long oilcloth-style coat she recognized from dozens of photos around the west. His name was Duster Kendal and he was often a town's marshal.

And the man standing beside him, wearing a dress shirt, dress coat, and jeans, with his back to the camera looked exactly like Wade.

She took a deep breath and laughed.

"That's very strange," she said. "Take a look at this?"

She slid the tablet back to Wade and then reached down on the booth beside her and pulled up the hat and put it on.

He looked at her, then down at the picture, then back at her. "Now that's creepy. Same hat as well."

"Take a look at the guy beside the woman with his back to the camera," she said.

"Yeah," he said.

"That looks exactly like you from the back," she said.

"It does?" he asked, staring at the picture more.

"Your hair is just like that from the back," she said. "And besides, after watching you yesterday, I would recognize that nice butt of yours anywhere."

He laughed and looked up, blushing.

And she had no doubt she was blushing as well.

He pointed to the picture. "I have a hunch this guy's butt is pretty bony by now."

"Then I guess I'll just have to stare at yours some more."

With that they both laughed and she blushed even more. She had never been that forward before. No idea what had gotten into her this morning.

Thankfully the waitress saved them from even more embarrassment by coming to take their order.

ELEVEN

August 4th, 2018
Boise, Idaho

AFTER BREAKFAST, Wade and Sophie walked back along the river to the institute library. Sophie wore her hat, the same one that was in the picture, and when he mentioned that as being weird, she suddenly stopped, letting him go a few steps ahead.

"Yup, same butt as in the picture," she said, smiling at him. "But nothing at all weird about that."

He laughed and just shook his head. He was really, really falling for this wonderful, smart woman. More than he wanted to even admit to himself.

Around them the city seemed to be alive and there were already people floating by on the river. He was really starting to like this city and he didn't even know that much about it. Most of that liking, he had a hunch, was because of Sophie.

They spent two hours in the library with Sophie showing him all the details of the massive place and introducing him to some of the staff who were there to help the researchers. They all already seemed to know who he was and seemed genuinely glad to meet him.

Feeling welcome didn't even begin to describe all of this.

From there they headed to the main institute building to check out a car. He had thought it would be a good idea to get a sense of Boise and Sophie had agreed on the condition that he drive. She didn't much like driving and that was one of the reasons she hadn't gone much past the area she could walk around the city.

He had a hunch that driving in Boise would be a cakewalk compared to driving in LA.

The car they checked out was identical to twenty other cars in the large garage that had been clearly converted from a barn. It was a white Cadillac SUV.

"And they are all new this year," Wade had said as they walked into the garage. "Does this place ever do anything cheaply?"

"Sure doesn't look like it, does it?" Sophie said, clearly as surprised as he was at seeing twenty brand new Cadillac SUVs just waiting to be used.

The one they decided to take because it would be the easiest to back out had seven hundred total miles on it.

"Never had a new car," Sophie said, inhaling the new car smell and the smell of new leather like it was life-saving oxygen as she got in and buckled her belt.

"Grew up poor, huh?" he asked. Then felt instantly bad about asking it in such a crass fashion.

"Not poor," she said. "Just working class. I got a scholarship to Harvard and got my doctorate at University of Massachusetts and liked it so much just stayed to teach and do research. Never needed a car there. How about you?"

He seldom told anyone the truth about his background, but he felt he needed to tell Sophie and not dodge the question as he always did.

"Parents were fairly well off from family money before them," he said, not even glancing at her as he worked to get the car out of the large garage. "They managed to make the family money even bigger. They are divorced and when I finished my MD, they both wanted to help me, so they tossed a lot of money and property and investments my way. It seems a few of the properties I ended up with became very expensive and I made some nice money selling them last year. So I'm doing fine."

Sophie looked at him as they stopped in the driveway of the institute to turn onto Warm Springs Avenue. "Doing fine is what rich people say."

"Guilty I'm afraid," he said, smiling at her. "Does that change the look of my butt?"

She laughed. "Not in the slightest."

"Oh, good," he said. "I was worried."

He felt amazingly lighter telling her about his money. Not sure why that was, but it felt great.

For the next hour they explored the area around the downtown part of Boise, then stopped and got a quick lunch before heading to the west down a beautiful, tree-lined boulevard with old homes on both sides. The boulevard ended as the foothills started and the road went up toward the ski resort.

He really wanted to see some of the resort in the summer and figured that up on the hill there might be a place to look at the entire valley. Turns out, there was.

They had wound up the twisting road for fifteen minutes before he pulled over on a wide gravel area and stopped, facing out over the valley below them, leaving the car running to keep the air-conditioning on.

"Wow," Sophie said, "This place is beautiful."

He couldn't agree more. Spread out below them was a lush, green valley full of trees and houses and businesses. In one area, the taller buildings of the downtown stuck up through the trees, but most of the buildings and roads were hidden by the lushness.

They could see three major parks along the river and then the more suburban areas beyond the river and up on slight hills that stretched out toward the brown desert beyond. A freeway cut through that area and the airport was out there along the desert as well.

The valley ended on their left not that far above where he figured the institute was, but it spread as far as they could see to the right.

"They call this the Treasure Valley, I think," Sophie said.

"I can see why," he said.

They sat and stared for a while at the valley, trying to pick out some landmarks and get the feel of their new home. He had a good sense about this place. The air was clear, the water clean, the mountains and valleys beautiful.

This made where he had come from in the heart of LA look very sad. It was really a hidden secret.

After a time, they decided that their next stop would be on the other side of the city at the large old cemetery, just to get a sense of the history of the town. Cemeteries were a wonderful place for that.

But just before he was about to put the car in reverse and get turned around on the two-lane road, Sophie said, "Hold on."

She unbuckled her seat belt, climbed up on her knees on the seat and reached over and kissed him.

He was so surprised it took him a moment, but then he kissed her back.

After a wonderful minute or so, she broke the kiss, sat back down and put her seatbelt back on.

He was sure his face was flushed and he was breathing harder than normal.

That kiss had been something special. Very special and he wanted to repeat it very soon.

"There," she said, looking forward out the window, her white skin slightly red as if she had a slight tan, "now I can say we parked and made out on our first date."

"This is a date?" he asked, laughing.

"It is now that you took me up in the hills to go parking," she said.

Then she turned to him, smiled, and then laughed.

All he could do was laugh along with her.

And try to catch his breath from the kiss.

Now Available
from all your favorite booksellers
in trade paper and electronic editions.

DEAN WESLEY
SMITH
USA Today BESTSELLING AUTHOR

MONUMENTAL
SUMMIT

A SCIENCE FICTION NOVEL OF THE OLD WEST AND TRUE LOVE

TWELVE

August 4th, 2018
Boise, Idaho

SOPHIE JUST COULDN'T believe that she had just kissed Wade like that. She had never really been that forward before, but there was something about him that she just wanted to be closer to.

She felt at certain points that she had known him for a very long time, and then at other points realized she really didn't know anything about him yet, other than his passion for history.

They spent a wonderful hour walking around the historical section of the Morris Hill Cemetery, hand-in-hand, talking about names and historical references from some of the major names they ran across.

The giant oak trees and freshly-mowed grass kept the temperature almost comfortable, but she kept her hat on just in case. Burning her head and face was never a fun thing to have happen.

She loved the feeling of his hand in hers, but she loved even more his sharp mind and passion for all things historical.

At one point they stopped near some family graves and he talked about how the family buried there had been behind the construction of a number of mining towns in Nevada and Northern California. He was actually surprised they had ended up in Boise and made notes to himself to look up how they ended up here.

From there, they headed to the State Historical Society down off of Capital Boulevard just to walk among the exhibits. The institute had a far larger reference library, but they both wanted to just see the exhibits of mining equipment and a mock-up of how a pioneer lived in a log cabin in the 1870s.

She hadn't taken the time to go there, even though a few at the institute had suggested that she should. She was pleasantly surprised, actually at the detail and the research done for each exhibit.

To Sophie, seeing it displayed made it all real. And made the fact that her research was about real people and real lives and real emotions. That's what they both wanted to write about. That way she could imagine better the reality of the people living in those mining towns.

The fact that he wanted to see and experience the same thing for the same reason was another detail she really liked about Wade.

On one exhibit of a mining town, a number of the pictures showed one of the same people in the picture they were looking at from earlier.

"I see that guy all over old west photos," Wade said, pointing to a man in a long oilcloth duster and matching cowboy hat. "You know who he was?"

"Marshal Duster Kendal," Sophie said. "I got a hunch someone could do a book about him, but no one has. Mostly when he is mentioned, it is either in a photo or as a marshal of a mining town. He seemed to do that a lot over a forty-year period."

Sophie also had noticed Marshal Kendal in a lot of pictures. Just never thought to investigate farther.

As they were finishing up their walk-through of the exhibits, Wade asked, "Do you like to cook?"

She laughed. "I guess I need to remind you one more time about my last name."

He just laughed at that.

"I know, I know," she said, "a horrid stereotype, but in my family we followed every one of those stereotypes to a letter like they were gospel. So yes, I love to cook. But most of the dishes my mother taught me to cook are not healthy, so I have managed to learn in college a bunch of new ones. How about you?"

"Typical southern California," he said. "We barbeque everything if we can. I was thinking I would get us a couple of steaks, some corn-on-the-cob and some salad-fixings and cook us a dinner."

"Wow, that sounds great," she said. "A real summer-type meal."

She hadn't had a good barbequed steak in a long time. Just the idea of it made her mouth water.

"Of course," Wade said, "I'll have to buy a grill, but I have a hunch we can find a few in this town this time of the year."

"You think?" she said, laughing. "But I hate to tell you I already have one on the deck of my condo."

"You're kidding?" he asked, clearly surprised. "They furnish that as well."

"Actually, they did," Sophie said, laughing. "But I have never used it. So let's get the steaks and corn and salad and cook at my place. What do you say?"

"I'd love that," he said.

She had no doubt she would love it as well.

PART THREE
Closer and Closer

THIRTEEN

August 4th, 2018
Boise, Idaho

DUSTER KENDAL dropped the map off on a table in the massive preparation cavern under the Warm Springs institute buildings and went out into what they all called the Living Room.

Don't Miss an Issue!

Subscribe
Electronic Subscription:
6 Issues... $29.99
12 Issues... $49.99
Paper Subscription:
6 Issues... $59.99
12 Issues... $99.99

For Full Subscription Information
Go To:

www.SmithsMonthly.com

He knew that his wife Bonnie and Dawn Edwards would be there, since from this time he had only been gone the ten minutes it took him to prepare, the slightly over two minutes to live the nine years in the past, and the few minutes to walk back to the Living Room area of the cavern under the mansion.

Bonnie and Dawn were both sitting at a long kitchen counter, talking. A fire was burning lightly in the huge stone fireplace that dominated the far wall, and no one was using the dozen couches and chair arrangements that filled the area between the fireplace and the kitchen with its long, granite-topped counter.

The Living Room area just seemed to be the center hub of everything under the institute and for the going and coming of travelers to other dimensions. They had built it for that purpose, actually, back in 1880. Duster liked the area, felt comfortable here.

Bonnie and Dawn both glanced up at him and Bonnie smiled.

Bonnie was as stunning as ever, in her light summer blue blouse, long brown hair that was pulled back and tied, and jeans. She was about two inchers shorter than his six-foot height and she carried herself with a force. She had been his partner for more centuries than he wanted to imagine and he loved everything about her. Even with all the time they had lived in other timelines, both of them were in their mid-thirties in this time.

"Any luck?" Dawn asked.

She was shorter than Bonnie, but also had long brown hair like Bonnie. Dawn and her husband Madison had been the first two Bonnie and Duster had taken back into the past with them. The two of them were major historians and had written many books from their research trips into the past.

Dawn and Madison loved the Monumental Lodge and always stayed and ran the lodge every time they went to a different timeline and built it in 1902. In fact, he had just said goodbye to Dawn and Madison when he left the lodge in the past.

They usually had a number of children and raised them in the lodge, not vanishing from that timeline until the kids were up and out, and leaving their share of the lodge to their kids.

But saying goodbye to Dawn in the other timeline and seeing her sitting here now sometimes felt odd. Jumping through time into varied timelines got complicated like that.

Damn, he had missed Bonnie, her wonderful smile, her beautiful brown hair, and those eyes that kept him intrigued all the time. Even after thousands of years together, he couldn't believe he was still madly in love with her.

He knew that to her, he had only been gone twenty minutes or so. To him, he hadn't seen her in years.

He walked over and kissed her, then pointed to the showers. "It was a long ride from the lodge. I'll take a shower and tell you all about what I found."

"Good plan," Bonnie said, smiling and pretending to wave her hand at his smell.

He laughed and turned away.

"How many years?" she asked.

"Nine," he said without turning around.

Again he heard her wonderful laugh.

"Denver poker games that good?" she asked.

"Wonderful," he said, as he walked to the showers. "Just wonderful."

After his shower, Duster told them about his trip, mostly focusing on the Grapevine Valley and how absolutely nothing was there.

Nothing.

As he expected it would, that got both Dawn and Bonnie even more interested, especially since Bonnie had gone with him to the condo at the Grapevine Springs Resort and they had really enjoyed it.

And they had enjoyed learning about the history of the old town in the museum there, even though they had never visited it in the past.

"I have some contacts at the Idaho Historical Society," Dawn said after they had talked for a while. "I'll get them and two of our researchers upstairs working on this and bring what I find to our meeting in a month or so at the lodge. We should be able to find out exactly where and when the information was planted. And maybe who did it."

Duster could only nod to that. He hated when someone made up history. Real history was wonderful enough on its own without people fabricating it just to make money off a ski resort.

FOURTEEN

August 4th, 2018
Boise, Idaho

WADE MANAGED to not burn the steaks or overcook the corn while Sophie put together the salad. They both went with large glasses of iced water to drink.

They decided to eat on her patio staring out over the lawn and the river and trees beyond.

It was still slightly warm, but it was clear to Wade that the night was cooling off quickly. The shadows were growing longer, but there were still people floating past on the river, often laughing and talking which made everything in the air seem filled with a joy. He couldn't remember feeling anything like that before in any of the places he had lived, let alone in LA.

Nothing like a perfect summer night with a beautiful and very smart woman to make Wade's evening as well.

Over dinner they talked about their family history and their studies. And a couple times even waved at floaters as they went past. He'd only been in this city for two days now and was coming to like it more and more. He could see why Sophie said she flat loved it here.

And it had a ski resort only nineteen miles away. He couldn't even imagine that, even though they had gone most of the way up to the resort today. Skiing to him had always been a weekend-long adventure, sometimes including flying.

Going from his condo and being on the slopes in less than forty minutes seemed impossible. He hoped to find out this winter just how impossible that was.

Actually, everything about the institute and Boise seemed too good to be true, so part of him was waiting for the other shoe to drop. But until it did, he was going to enjoy everything.

They took the plates and silverware and glasses back to the kitchen that looked exactly like the one in his condo, only Sophie had a lot more various appliances tucked around along the back of the counter. Some of them he wasn't even sure what they were, but it was clear they were used.

She put her dishes in the sink, took his plate and silverware and did the same thing, ran some water over them and then turned to him.

"Thank you for the wonderful dinner," she said.

She moved to him, pulled his head down to her level and kissed him again, hard and passionate. She felt wonderful against him, her skin smooth and soft, yet her body firm and clearly in shape.

After a moment she broke the kiss, smiling up at him.

"Wow, that settles it," he said as he managed to catch his breath. "I'm cooking all the time."

She laughed and kissed him again.

Then still holding him while they stood in the kitchen, she looked into his eyes. "I am not normally this forward, Dr. Wade."

"Professor Silverman," he said, smiling. "Do you hear me complaining in the slightest?"

"Oh, good," she said, smiling.

She took him by the hand and led him from the kitchen. "Then I think I'll just continue my new-found courage."

"Please," he said.

A moment later they were up the stairs and into her bedroom. She had a couple of large quilts on the bed that looked like they were family made and she quickly swept them off and onto the floor.

Then she told him to sit on the bed.

He did as she took off her clothes, not even pretending to do any sort of tease, just taking her clothes off as if she were getting ready to get into a shower.

It was the most alluring thing he had ever watched.

Ever.

Her white skin was perfect, her body proportioned for her size so that nude and without comparison, there was no way of telling she was so short. She actually looked tall and thin.

Her black pubic hair matched the black hair on her head and her breasts were perfect, with dark nipples.

He wanted to watch her undress like that every night.

After she was standing in front of him, totally nude, she smiled at him and said simply, "Your turn."

She sat on the edge of the bed as he stood.

"Has anyone ever told you that you have an amazing body?" he said.

"Actually, no," she said, a slight red blush on her neck.

"Well, you do," he said. "Stunningly amazing and alluring."

The flush on her neck deepened a little and she motioned that he get started.

"One of us here is way overdressed and it sure isn't me."

He laughed and did exactly what she had done, simply undressed as if climbing into bed at night.

She just stared at him, her dark eyes studying every movement he made until finally he was done and facing her, clearly aroused by what was happening.

At that moment she came off the bed and into his arms, kissing him and pressing her wonderful naked body against him.

He kissed her just as passionately and even though they were only a step from the bed, they barely made it back onto the bed.

Barely.

FIFTEEN

August 5th, 2018
Boise, Idaho

THE NEXT MORNING they had a wonderful breakfast and then headed for the institute hand-in-hand like two high school kids. Sophie loved it, every minute of it.

It was just before ten and the air still had a slight bite to it from the night, but it was clear it was going to be warm fairly shortly.

Last night they had made love three different times since dinner, including one while they were getting a late-night snack in the kitchen around one and another time before breakfast. She should be feeling it, but all she really felt was a sense of completeness and lightness.

She was a distance from being a virgin, but nothing before had been like last night. Not even close.

The rest of the night between talking, they just slept and held each other. She could never remember feeling so right sleeping with another person. And Wade had said he felt the same thing.

And both of them had promised they wouldn't get afraid and slow this relationship down in any fashion for any stupid reason without fully talking with the other. She had no desire or intent of slowing down anything about this relationship with Wade.

It was just after ten when they reached their offices in the institute library and a message was waiting for them, both of them, from Director Parks. He wanted a meeting with them at eleven if they could make it in the front room of the institute.

So Sophie managed to get a little done and find a book she had been looking for before Wade knocked on her door and said it was time to go.

His smiling face in her office door was something she wanted to see all the time and she got up from her desk and went over and kissed him. Then they headed, again hand-in-hand, for the main institute building the five blocks down the river path.

No rafters or tubers were on the river yet this morning, but Sophie had a hunch they were putting in up river by this point. The sun had warmed things up enough that she was glad she had her floppy hat on and a bottle of water in her hand.

They got into the institute main room just as Director Parks was coming down the ornate staircase from his office with a woman following him.

The director was smiling and so was the woman behind him. She was a number of inches taller than Sophie and had dark brown hair she had pulled back. She wore jeans, a white blouse, and a light dress jacket over the blouse.

Sophie thought she looked familiar, but couldn't place her instantly.

The director shook both of their hands, asking how Wade was getting settled in.

"Loving the city and everything here," he said. "I can't thank you enough."

"We are honored to have you here," Director Parks said.

Then he turned and introduced the woman with him.

"Professor Silverman, Dr. Wade, I would like you to meet Professor Dawn Edwards."

Sophie had her hand out and her mouth open before the name registered.

This was the Dawn Edwards, the best historical writer Sophie had ever read and one of the main reasons Sophie had decided to go into this area of study.

And from a conversation yesterday, she knew Wade felt the same exact way.

"Wonderful meeting you both," Professor Edwards said. "Just call me Dawn."

"Sophie," Sophie managed to say.

"Wade," Wade said to Dawn. "I just go by Wade."

Sophie was impressed that Wade had managed a full sentence. She was just proud of herself for getting out her own name.

As she and Wade took seats side-by-side on the couch and Director Parks took one large chair and Dawn took the other, Sophie managed to calm her heart a little and take a few deep breaths. Dawn seemed to have this easy-going way about her and didn't look much older than Sophie was. But Dawn felt much, much older.

"Thanks for meeting with us," Dawn said.

"I have been a fan of your books since your first Roosevelt book," Sophie said.

"As have I," Wade said. "So this is an honor."

Dawn laughed and waved her hand to dismiss that. "We are all just historians here. And that's why I need both of your help on a project if I might? But I don't want to interfere with your own research too much."

Sophie damn near lost her breath on that one again. Dawn Edwards was asking for her help.

"Anything I can do," Wade said.

"Same here," Sophie said. "Just name it."

"It actually is along the lines of both of your areas of research," Dawn said. "That's why when I heard Wade was

coming here and I knew you were already here, Sophie, I figured this would be perfect."

"You knew I was here?" Sophie asked, completely startled.

Dawn laughed. "I'm on the institute board of directors and help vet researchers we want to invite to join us."

"Oh," Wade said, sitting back slightly.

Sophie nodded. "Now I am doubly honored to be asked to help."

"So what we need to learn," Dawn said, "is as much as you can find about an old mining town in north-central Idaho by the name of Grapevine Springs."

Wade actually jerked and Sophie laughed.

Dawn looked suddenly puzzled and looked at Director Parks, who only shrugged.

"We were talking about that mining town yesterday," Sophie said.

"I thought it would be a great study in both of our areas of focus," Wade said. "So we had planned on sharing the research on it."

Dawn laughed and shook her head. "Great minds clearly think alike."

"Were you thinking of writing a book about it?" Sophie asked, now suddenly worried. No way in the world did she want to even slightly intrude on the work of Dawn Edwards. She wanted to expand off of Dawn's work instead.

"Nope," Dawn said, shaking her head. "I'm going to leave that up to you two."

"So why did you want us to focus on that old mining town?" Wade asked.

Dawn glanced at Director Parks and he nodded, so Dawn turned to them. "We think the history of the old mining town might have been planted."

Of all the things Dawn Edwards could have said, that was the most surprising.

History of the Old West faked? Why?

"Ski resort money?" Wade asked, clearly jumping to the why as well.

"We honestly don't know," Dawn said. "And we might be wrong in our suspicions, but if someone did fake it, they did an amazing job of planting the information and we figured two professional historians would uncover anything that might be fake or not."

"So sounds like this favor is actually right into the middle of what you both were already going to work on," Director Parks said.

"Smack in the middle," Wade said.

Sophie nodded. This was now even more exciting.

And a very solid reason to work even closer with Wade. And maybe get to know Professor Edwards, her idol.

She couldn't see one thing wrong with any of this.

Not a thing.

And in the back of her mind, that bothered her.

PART FOUR
Surprises

SIXTEEN

October 16th, 2018
Boise, Idaho

JUST OVER two months after Dawn's conversation with Sophie and Wade, Bonnie and Duster Kendal had flown into the Monumental Lodge by helicopter from Boise. The flight had been stunning since the day was crisp and calm and the sky a bright blue over the rugged snow-covered mountains.

Row after row of rugged ridgelines went past under them and even though he hated to wear them, Duster had on sunglasses under his cowboy hat from the glare of the fresh snow.

Duster wasn't so much excited about the meeting they planned on having at the lodge, but at this point he was more interested in what Dawn and the two researchers had found out about the fake history of Grapevine Springs.

For two months that had bothered him and nothing he could find on his own made any sense.

In this timeline, that mining town had never existed, yet it had because of history from the ski resort.

So even if Grapevine Springs mining town had existed in another timeline, how did the owners of the ski resort in this timeline know about it?

Every few months, all of the fourteen founders got together at the institute to talk about who to accept into the research area of the institute and who might be ready to be told about the timeline travel part in the caverns under the institute.

But before that larger meeting, Bonnie and Duster and Dawn and Madison had a private meeting about the candidates with the head of the institute and another founder, Jesse Parks, now the director.

It wasn't a secret meeting, just what Duster called a "make sure" meeting. Make sure that all five of them were on the same page going into the larger meeting.

Duster loved the feeling of the lodge. He and Bonnie, along with Dawn and

Madison, owned the massive log structure that sat high in a saddle overlooking the Monumental Creek drainage. One mountain to the south of the lodge was called Thunder Mountain, the mountain that gave the entire region its name.

The entire second floor was only for founders, and Bonnie and Duster had their own room that no one but them had slept in for over a hundred years.

Dawn and Madison also had a suite in the back where in various timelines they had raised children. Duster didn't want to know how many children they had raised here in different timelines. He was actually afraid to ask.

The massive polished logs and the 1900s furniture had been kept exactly as it had been when built all those years ago. That locked-in-time charm was one of the reasons that made getting a room in the Monumental Lodge one of the most sought-after reservations on the planet.

The fact that only ten rooms were ever rented and the food was top-flight didn't hurt the demand either.

As Bonnie and Duster arrived, snow covered everything but a dug out path from the helicopter pad to the lodge and the deck that looked out at the view over most of the central wilderness area of Idaho.

To say that view was spectacular would be a giant understatement. When you can see a hundred miles over some of the most rugged mountains in the world, on a crisp fall day like today, it was just hard to breathe when looking at the beauty of it all.

The first time he had stood on this saddle between the two tall peaks and looked out at the view, he knew it had to have a lodge here. And he had been right. They had built it in a hundred different timelines so far. And he never tired of building it again.

And always the exact same way with the exact same floor plan and the exact same furniture. There were some things in history that just shouldn't be messed with in any timeline and the Monumental Lodge was one of those things.

Bonnie and Duster put their overnight bags into their room, then headed down to the main dining room.

The fire was crackling in the stone fireplace that dominated one side of the room and the entire space felt comfortable. Massive logs supported the strong roof overhead and every log was polished and protected.

Parks and Dawn were already there, talking at a wooden table in the middle of the room. The table was covered by a cloth that looked like it was straight out of 1900 and most likely was. Both had hot teas in front of them from a pot on a sideboard.

The table had been set for five, with water and silverware and cloth napkins. Duster could not even begin to count the thousands of wonderful breakfasts he had eaten in this room over the centuries.

Duster poured himself and Bonnie cups of tea and sat down next to Dawn.

Before Parks had ended up meeting his wife Kerri, a historian and writer, and learning about traveling into timeline pasts, Bonnie and Duster had often hired him and his private investigative firm to find out about candidates. Parks still did that for the institute, as well as run everything.

He and his firm dug into a person's history while his wife Kerri dug into the candidate's research and work ethic. Between the two of them and how strict they were, it was amazing any candidate got through to even be considered for a research grant at the institute.

But Duster liked that.

"Any luck on the Grapevine Springs strangeness?" Duster asked Dawn as he and Bonnie got settled at the table.

"None," Dawn said. "Whoever made up that history and planted it, did a perfect job of it. None of us can find a seam anywhere to pick at. At let me tell you, between me and Sophie and Wade, we have picked."

"Damn that's weird," Duster said. "But someone had to have made it all up, since I camped for a week in that valley in the year the town should have been going strong and there was nothing at all there. Nothing."

"In that timeline," Bonnie said.

Duster shook his head. "There's got to be a way to figure this out. How did the different timelines I go to not have the town and yet in this one it supposedly existed?"

"I'll tell you, it's driving me crazy as well," Dawn said.

They all laughed and the conversation continued until Madison joined them and the five of them had a wonderful meal of trout, pan-fried better than Duster could have done over a campfire.

Finally, after a wonderful sorbet for dessert, the dishes were cleared, coffee served, and the five of them got down to the meeting.

"We had thirty-five applications for funding this summer," Parks said. "Ten of the straight funding for projects Kerri and I just approved."

He handed each of them a sheet with a two-line description of the funded projects and the amounts.

Duster only glanced at it. The institute had more money than any one place should ever have, and was constantly generating more from all the investments around the world. They could have given a thousand times more away than those

---

Don't Miss an Issue!
Subscribe

Electronic Subscription:
6 Issues... $29.99
12 Issues... $49.99

Paper Subscription:
6 Issues... $59.99
12 Issues... $99.99

For Full Subscription Information Go To:
www.SmithsMonthly.com

requests and not even have it be noticed in the petty cash fund.

But Duster knew that to remain an institute that seemed aboveboard and well-funded, Parks and his people had to do all this stuff and keep the levels within reason. Duster was just glad they had someone in that position he trusted to do it.

"We turned down another twenty projects," Parks said, "from people who just wanted the money and had no capability of even following through on the research."

"So that leaves five," Bonnie said, nodding.

Parks nodded. "All research requests for the person to come to the institute and research specific historical projects for varying amounts of time."

Duster nodded. They had almost sixty researchers at any point working in the various libraries and buildings in Boise that the institute owned. And if a person was accepted to the institute, all expenses were paid, including food, plus a large salary, and no claim was made against the researchers' final product.

That kind of package was why so many quality researchers applied to the institute. And it also allowed Parks and everyone to observe them over months or a year to see if they might be candidates for learning about the timeline jumping that went on under the institute.

Historical research always tended to be so much better when a person could go back into another timeline and actually see the place they were researching.

"Any good ones?" Bonnie asked.

"Actually," Parks said, "I think all five are good. One wants to do a definitive book on those who fought at the Alamo, not only who they were, but their families and their histories that took them to that place."

"Nifty," Dawn said. "A lot more than one book."

"A lifetime project, clearly," Bonnie said.

Parks nodded and handed a folder full of information about that person to Bonnie. She glanced at it and handed it to Duster.

Duster also just glanced at it and handed it to Dawn. He knew later tonight that he and Bonnie would go over each candidate's application. All of them would, and if there were any questions, they would talk it out at breakfast before flying back to Boise for the larger meeting.

"Two of the candidates are a couple working together on a project," Parks said. "They want to take an old mining town population and backtrack each inhabitant's history as much as possible. And do various books on the reasons why certain people and families ended up in these old boom towns. They are focusing on Northern California mining the most."

"That's kind of taking my research and expanding it," Dawn said, nodding. "I like that."

"They quoted your books a great deal in their presentation," Parks said, nodding. "They don't know you are involved with the institute, but are clearly major fans of your books."

"As Sophie and Wade were," Madison said, smiling at his wife.

"I'm looking forward to meeting the two new ones," Dawn said.

Actually, Duster had a hunch that Dawn would stay away from them until they proved their stuff. Dawn didn't much like to be worshipped.

Parks handed the folder to Bonnie, who glanced at it and then handed it to

Duster who passed it along with only a glance.

"So anyone ready for the caverns?" Madison asked.

"I have two," Dawn said. "I think that if Sophie and Wade are ever going to get to the bottom of this Grapevine Springs problem, they need to go back and understand why we are having a problem with the research."

Duster nodded. He had been following them both and liked them, even though he had never had a chance to meet either of them yet. And he knew Bonnie liked them as well. And both Sophie and Wade were about as smart as they came.

"Anyone have any objections?" Parks asked.

"I think they would be a great addition," Bonnie said.

"They are amazing," Dawn said. "It has been a real joy to work with both of them over the last few months."

"So we present it to the full meeting of the founders tomorrow," Duster said.

"I'll present it," Dawn said.

Duster laughed. He knew, without a doubt that would guarantee that everyone would agree. It was hard to argue with Dawn.

SEVENTEEN

October 18th, 2018
Boise, Idaho

"WE NEED to show Dawn the pictures," Wade said, handing the photos back across Sophie's desk to her. They were in her office in the institute library and Wade was perched on the corner of her big desk as he often liked to do.

Sophie took the photos back and just nodded, her stomach twisting like she had eaten something horrible the night before. But Wade was right. No matter the outcome, they needed to show Dawn.

Over the last two months, she and Wade had worked closely together on the Grapevine Springs project, while at the same time adding in research details for their own projects.

He was constantly finding wonderful things that she could use and she had found him numbers of medical references in journals as well. Every time she did, he got like a kid at Christmas opening up a present. She loved the look of joy on his handsome face when he got that way.

And she loved how focused he was on his research.

As a couple, things had just gotten better and better by the day. They hadn't slept alone one night since that first night in her condo. It had just never felt right on the two times they had tried.

Once they had both made it to their own places and just turned around and met back out on the sidewalk in the rain, laughing.

But they still maintained their own places and their own identities in their living spaces, made easier by the fact that their two condos were a hundred steps apart. So one night they were at her place, the next at his.

And they shared cooking dinners as well and had spent many a wonderful evening exploring the cities restaurants. She had really been amazed by the Basque food. She never had known food like that existed.

She couldn't imagine, after two short months, not spending her days with him close by.

And her nights.

She was, without a doubt, head-over-ass in love with Wade.

Thankfully, he seemed to feel the same way.

But now, what she held seemed to threaten both of their research projects. But at the same time might help win them favor with Dawn.

In the two months they had found numbers of pictures of the old mining town of Grapevine Springs, including the one that seemed to have a relative of Sophie's in it. All seemed to be perfectly legit.

But Sophie, by tracking down the living family members of someone who had lived in Grapevine Springs, had unearthed about forty old photos from a family album.

It seemed the family member, a man by the name of Bryce, loved to take photos and had set up a shop in the town along with his legal practice. And he had kept records with each photo, including the names of those he photographed.

Two of the photos showed Sophie and Wade, standing side-by-side in front of a general store, their backs to the camera, but their heads turned so it was clear it was them. The names on the back were Sophie and Wade Olsen. It said they owned the general store and had founded the town.

And they were talking with Dawn and Marshal Duster Kendal. Both were also named. And another unnamed woman and unnamed man.

"The photos prove Dawn's theory that the town was a fake," Wade said.

"But how did these photos get planted in that old family album?"

"Money?" Wade said, smiling at her. "Enough money will buy anything."

"But why have us in the photos?" Sophie asked, shaking her head. None of it made sense.

"Maybe the people behind the fake know we are investigating it and are just poking fun at us," Wade said. "Amazing how much arrogance a lot of money can buy."

Sophie sighed and stood. On that, she would have to trust Wade since she had never been around people with a lot of money before now. They needed to go to the institute and try to find where Dawn might be.

They were just outside her office when Dawn appeared, smiling.

"Wow, you two look worried," she said.

"We have something to show you about Grapevine Springs," Wade said.

Sophie indicated that they should go back into her office and then Wade closed the door behind them.

"That serious, huh?" Dawn asked.

"We think the people who faked the town know we are investigating them and are poking fun at all of us," Wade said.

"Seriously?" Dawn asked, looking surprised.

Sophie opened up the envelope with the pictures and handed the one with them in it to Dawn.

Sophie hadn't felt this nervous about anything for a very, very long time.

"These were in a family album," Sophie said, "handed down from a man by the name of Bryce who lived in Grapevine Springs and liked to take photos. Our names are on the back."

Dawn looked at the photo, then at the back, then laughed and handed the photo back to Sophie.

Sophie had not expected Dawn to laugh.

"Actually," Dawn said, smiling first at Wade, then at Sophie, "that photo is on the topic of why I came to see you today."

"How?" Sophie said. "I just got the photos in this morning's mail."

"The reason is very long and difficult to explain," Dawn said, laughing. "But actually that photo proves a lot. Just not what we were expecting."

"I'm not following," Wade said.

"Director Parks and a few others want to explain to you better than I can," Dawn said. "Come on, I got a car waiting out front to take us back to the institute."

Dawn laughed and then asked, "Do you two trust me?"

Sophie nodded and saw that Wade nodded as well.

"Then come with me," Dawn said, taking the picture and opening the office door and heading out. "I'm going to change your lives and in doing so explain this picture."

EIGHTEEN

October 18th, 2018
Boise, Idaho

WADE FOLLOWED Dawn out of the front door of the institute library to a white Cadillac SUV parked at the curb. A man was sitting behind the wheel and Dawn indicated that he and Sophie get in the back seat while she climbed into the front seat.

"My husband, Madison," Dawn said, introducing Madison Rogers, another famous historian as if he was just her cab driver. Madison had on jeans and a tan shirt that looked like it was comfortable and well worn.

Wade managed to not choke and beside him Sophie coughed.

Madison Rogers was one of the top experts on the mining wars that had gone on in the west and his books were the bibles in anything to do in that area. Wade had read them all a number of times and used one in his classroom in LA.

"Nice finally meeting you both," Madison said. "Heard a great deal about both of you."

Wade just choked again.

"Wonderful meeting you as well," Sophie said.

"Look what they found just today," Dawn said, handing Madison the picture.

He looked at it and then laughed, handing the picture back to Dawn. "Wow, great timing. You two are as good as your reputations led us all to believe."

Dawn laughed as well, but Wade wasn't sure what was so funny. Or even what Madison had meant.

"Hang on and we'll start explaining everything in a few minutes," Dawn said, turning to buckle her seat belt.

Sophie reached over and took Wade's hand and he felt better just knowing they were going into this together.

Whatever it was.

It took only a minute for Madison to pull the Cadillac into the driveway of the institute main building.

The main garage doors opened as he went past the big house and toward the garage and he pulled into a spot.

The garage doors closed behind him.

"Is it clear, Goldie?" Madison asked into the air as they all got out."

"Yes," Goldie said.

Both Sophie and Wade glanced around.

Dawn smiled at them. "All the interactive computers in the institute are called Goldie, even here in the big garage."

"Makes sense," Sophie said.

"First off," Dawn said as they all stopped near the back of the Cadillac, "I need to remind you about your Do Not Disclose agreement. Do you both stand by that still?"

"Completely," Sophie said.

"Completely as well," Wade said.

He felt odd that she had asked them that here in a garage, but clearly he and Sophie were about to be shown a secret of the institute that Dawn and the others didn't want out.

Sophie took his hand and they both moved to follow Dawn and Madison.

Madison headed toward a wall that held a workbench covered with some gardening tools hanging on pegs. As he approached, a hidden door opened.

Sophie squeezed Wade's hand in sudden worry.

"If you love secret rooms and passageways," Dawn said, "you're going to love what we are about to show you."

Wade wasn't sure how he felt about secret passages, but he didn't say anything as they went into what appeared to be a fairly modern tunnel that was well lit and allowed he and Sophie to walk side-by side.

"We are going in under the main institute building," Madison said as he and Dawn walked ahead.

After about a hundred paces the tunnel opened up into a small room and Madison opened a door and indicated they go on ahead, following Dawn.

On the other side of the door was a staircase leading both up and down.

"Up goes into a hidden room in the main building above," Dawn said as she headed down. "This goes down into the main cavern below the institute."

"Cavern?" Wade asked.

"All safe and very large," Madison said from behind them. "The large mansions on either side of the institute building are also part of this property and the caverns down here are three levels deep and run under all three properties."

Wade couldn't even begin to imagine that size and Sophie said nothing, just held onto his hand tightly.

After what felt like two flights of stairs, Dawn opened a door and led them out into what clearly was a large cavern carved right out of the dark lava rock.

Wade just felt stunned. The room was huge and with very high ceilings carved out of stone. What looked like a dozen couch and chair groupings filled the main part of the area, many of them turned to face a large stone fireplace.

Along the far wall was a long kitchen counter with a modern kitchen behind it. Two other people were there, one sitting with his back to them, the other was a woman standing behind the counter.

"Welcome," the woman said.

At that point the man turned around and smiled at them.

Wade wasn't sure his legs would move. The man was wearing a cowboy hat and had on a long oilcloth duster.

The man was Marshal Duster Kendal, the same man who had been in a bunch of photos they had found.

NINETEEN

October 18th, 2018
Boise, Idaho

IF NOT FOR holding Wade's hand, Sophie wasn't sure if she would have been able to go with Dawn and Madison down into the big cavern. Her mind was just not processing what was going on and what she was seeing.

In the middle of Boise there was a huge cavern carved out of the rock? How was that even possible?

None of this made any sense at all.

And then the man at the long kitchen counter had turned around and it was the man from the pictures out of the past. The very same man, yet that wasn't possible either.

Why would this guy pretend to be a historical figure?

Sophie and Wade stopped, hand-in-hand, facing the two new people and Madison stopped beside them. Dawn went around the end of the counter to stand beside the woman.

"Professor Silverman, Dr. Wade," Madison said, "I would like you to meet Bonnie and Duster Kendal, two of the greatest mathematical minds of all time."

Wade actually moved first and shook Bonnie's hand, then Duster's hand.

Sophie did the same, just staring at Duster.

Mathematicians? What were they doing here and why was one pretending to be a person from the past? Dressed the same and all.

Dawn handed the picture Sophie and Wade had found to Bonnie who glanced at it and laughed and slid it to Duster, who also laughed.

"Seems you might know who I am," Duster said.

"You got photographed enough," Bonnie said, shaking her head like a wife would shake her head at her husband. "Anyone looking at any picture from the west would know you."

"How?" Wade asked.

Dawn held up her hand. "We have a story to tell you and we need to tell it in some sort of order, but first let's all get something to drink and move over to more comfortable chairs."

Both Sophie and Wade just wanted water.

Sophie wasn't sure with all this if her stomach could handle any more than water, actually. She had no idea what was going on, but two of the greatest historians of all time were going to try to explain it all to her.

Thank heavens Wade was beside her, going through the same thing.

The seating area they went to was close to the long kitchen bar and consisted of two couches and two large chairs, all done in brown cloth. An area rug was under the grouping that was of a light-tan pattern color and a large wooden coffee table sat in the middle.

Bonnie and Duster sat on one couch and Duster put his cowboy hat beside him on the edge of the couch. Dawn took one end-chair and Madison another and Sophie and Wade took the other couch facing Bonnie and Duster over the coffee table.

Dawn then handed them each tablets she had brought from the kitchen counter area. "Before we go any farther, we need you to look up Bonnie and Duster Kendal."

Sophie did just that as beside her Wade did the same thing.

Thousands of articles came up about the two people sitting silently across from her in this impossible cavern.

It didn't take long for her to discover that they really were major mathematicians. And from a quick glance, they also had funded hundreds of scholarships in history and mathematics, and buildings on many major campuses were named after them.

She came across picture after picture of them. Clearly the two people sitting across from her were who they had been introduced to be.

So now she found herself sitting in an impossible cavern with two top mathematicians and two of the most acclaimed historians of all time. This was just flat strange.

And getting stranger by the moment.

There was the sound of a door closing and Director Parks came walking in, smiling.

"Got you a bottle of water," Bonnie said, pointing to a bottle on the coffee table in the middle of the chairs and couches.

"Thanks," Parks said. He pulled over another chair to sit beside Dawn and then took his water.

"This place is really something, isn't it?" Parks asked Sophie and Wade as they put the tablets on the coffee table.

"It is," Wade said. "But what is it?"

"And that's the story we're about to tell you," Dawn said.

"Oh, good, I got here in time for the fun," Parks said, settling back in his chair and smiling.

Sophie looked at him and grew even more tense. What in the hell was going on?

She reached over and took Wade's hand in hers. Thank heavens Wade was with her.

TWENTY

October 18th, 2018
Boise, Idaho

WADE FELT calmer suddenly when Sophie took his hand. The two of them

really were stronger together than apart, and even after just two months of being together, that didn't worry him at all. He just wanted to do everything in his power to make it last.

"Feel free to ask questions," Dawn said. "But I must warn you, what we are about to tell you will sound totally crazy."

"This isn't crazy enough?" Wade asked, indicating the cavern around them."

The rest laughed.

"No," Dawn said, "this will be the tame part when this story is done."

"But what we ask," Duster said, "is that you keep an open mind and then allow us to prove to you what we are saying. Can you do that?"

"And after we have shown you our case," Bonnie said, "you are both free to just be part of this, stay and research, or leave if you want. We just ask that you honor the do-not-disclose contract you signed."

Wade nodded and beside him Sophie did as well.

"All right then," Dawn said. "Here we go. First off, I have to tell you that only twenty-two people in the world know about this place and what we are about to tell you. With you two, the number is now twenty-four."

Wade was shocked at that low number. But he said nothing.

Dawn pointed to Duster.

"In the 1870s," Duster said, "a distant relative of mine opened a gold mine that quickly worked out. But in the process over the years of looking for another vein of gold by digging deeper into a hill, he broke into a fantastic cavern of what looked like glowing rose-quartz crystals."

Duster took a sip of water, then went on.

"My ancestor closed up the mine and passed it down through the family,"

Duster said. "A year after Bonnie and I were married and were both working on our first doctorates in mathematics, my father took us to the mine and showed us the vast crystal room."

"We had a hunch what it was," Bonnie said, "but it took us three more years and two more doctorate degrees in theoretical physics and mathematics to figure it out for sure."

Wade nodded. He had seen in his quick search that both of them had many higher degrees, none honorary.

"In physics," Duster said, "the accepted knowledge now is that energy and matter and time are all linked together in some fashion."

"And also a major theory is that with every decision," Bonnie said, "or every turning point, no matter how large or small, two different timelines split off."

Wade was following fine so far. And from what he could tell, Sophie was as well.

"What my ancestors found," Duster said, "was what we call the nexus, where energy and time and matter take a physical form in their connection."

"Each crystal in those massive caverns is a timeline," Bonnie said.

"That would be impossible to contain in one cavern," Sophie said. "The numbers of timelines would be infinite."

Wade was impressed. He had been sort of thinking the same thing, but wasn't anywhere near with the idea of such a place as Sophie clearly was.

"That's correct," Sophie," Duster said, smiling and nodding. "The caverns are infinite and go off into other dimensions. What my ancestors broke into was simply a small area of timelines very close to this timeline."

"What happened next is that Duster and I invented a very simple device that allows us to step into the past of another timeline," Bonnie said.

"We are limited to the time of the mine opening," Duster said. "And we can't be in another timeline when we are alive in that timeline, so we are limited to not being too close to the present by our age."

Wade just stared at them. "You were right. This now has gotten completely crazy."

"Are you saying you can travel back in time?" Sophie asked.

"Not really, no," Duster said, shaking his head. "But we can travel back in time in another timeline. But we can't go back in this timeline to change this past."

"But the other timelines are basically identical to this one," Madison said.

"Research," Sophie said and Wade instantly understood where she was going.

Dawn nodded. "It's how we can get such incredible and accurate detail in our books."

"It's why we founded this institute in the first place," Director Parks said.

Wade was just shaking his head. This was the wildest fairytale he could have ever imagined being told by seemingly smart people. The problem he had was that it all sounded logical and this cavern was most certainly real.

So why the tall tale?

For what purpose?

Duster laughed and glanced at Bonnie and then Dawn. "Seems like it's time for the show part."

"We asked you to trust us and that you would not believe us, but give us a chance to show you," Bonnie said, her voice and look very serious. "Are you willing to do that?"

Wade glanced at the worried look in Sophie's dark eyes, then he turned back to Bonnie and Duster and nodded. "I'll give you the rope because I want to know why you would tell us this story."

"I have a hunch you aren't making up a thing," Sophie said. "And that flat scares me even more. But I'm willing if Wade is."

"Great," Duster said. "Let's go."

"Madison and I will wait right here," Dawn said. "We'll get sandwiches and hot soup going."

Duster laughed. "Good idea."

Wade had no idea why that was a good idea, but with Sophie's hand in his, they followed Bonnie and Duster and Director Parks toward a door beyond the kitchen area.

He was sure he would never be doing this without Sophie at his side.

He wasn't sure if they should be doing it now.

TWENTY-ONE

October 18th, 2018
Boise, Idaho

THE DOOR opened into a stairwell that led downward. Sophie wasn't sure she wanted to go deeper underground, but she followed Duster and Bonnie, holding onto Wade's hand.

Thank heavens he was with her.

Finally, about two more floors down, another door opened into yet another huge cavern. As they went in, the lights came up and Sophie saw table after table full of historical supplies.

There were racks and racks of clothing from different periods of history.

And historical equipment like saddles and guns and saddlebags.

Everything, just everything.

Sophie had never seen or even imagined anything like this huge room. And right at that moment she knew, without a doubt, that what they had been told was accurate.

And that scared her more than she ever wanted to admit.

"Wow," Wade said. "What a costume shop."

"Not costumes," Duster said. "All authentic. Has to be."

Director Parks moved over and took a suit jacket from a rack and had Wade slip it on while Bonnie had Sophie put on a dress over her clothing and not button it.

Sophie could tell the dress was from around 1890s or so. It was blue with a dark ribbon around the middle and a few sizes too big for her so that it fit over her clothing.

"Just in case you are seen," Parks said as they turned toward the other side of the cavern.

"Seen when?" Sophie asked.

No one answered her. She dropped the question because she had a hunch she would know in a moment.

On the other side of the storage cavern was a wall of about thirty doors spaced evenly along the carved-stone wall like hotel room doors. Duster went through the door closest to the right wall of the supply area and into a long room.

The room wasn't more than a normal living room wide, but it must have been the length of a football field long, if not longer, carved out of the solid rock.

It had to be the strangest cave Sophie had ever seen.

Wooden tables stretched along the length of the center of the room with a simple wooden box on each table.

A wire fence that went from floor to ceiling ran along both walls on both sides of the room, making the room look like it had a fenced-in hallway down the middle.

And through the fence Sophie could see thousands and thousands of slots carved into the rock.

Each slot held a glowing pink crystal.

"This isn't the cave your ancestors discovered, is it?" Wade asked.

"Oh, no," Duster said. "That's a long ways from here in the mountains."

"Each crystal here has been brought to the institute from the original cavern and basically represents a timeline," Bonnie said.

Wade squeezed Sophie's hand and she just held on. Her mind was numb. It was becoming clearer by the moment that Bonnie and Duster were telling the truth.

Wires ran from each box on each table and through the fence. All the wires were on the ground.

Each crystal was clearly marked on the wall under its slot with a lined sheet of paper on a board. Some sheets had notations on them, others were blank.

"Oh, shit," Wade said softly as he studied everything.

Sophie couldn't even manage to say that much.

"We want to show you what exactly we are talking about," Bonnie said to Sophie, "as we promised."

Sophie watched as Duster moved over and opened up a gate in the fence near the closest machine, then Duster put on thick leather gloves and hooked up two wires to one of the crystals.

"Never touch a crystal with your bare hands," Duster said to Wade and Sophie as he came back out of the fence-protected area and shut the gate. "Extreme energy. Far, far more than we've been able

to calculate so far at least. We don't even know what kind of energy it is."

Sophie just stared at the crystal with the wires hooked to it with a soft band. Could that actually be an entire timeline there? How was that possible?

Duster turned to Director Parks. "You mind staying behind for the two minutes as an example?"

"Glad to," Director Parks said, smiling.

With the leather gloves still on, Duster adjusted a fairly plain-looking dial on one side of the wooden box, then hooked up both wires and took off the gloves.

"Move in close to the wooden box," Duster said.

"Trust me," Dawn said to Sophie and Wade, "this will not hurt and if you want to really understand what is happening here, this is the easiest way."

Wade squeezed Sophie's hand and together they stepped closer to the wooden box on the table.

The two of them were now between Bonnie and Duster.

"On the count of three, just touch the wooden box at the same time," Bonnie said.

Director Parks moved around so that he was standing just across the table from Sophie and Wade, smiling at them.

"One, two, three," Bonnie said.

Sophie touched the wooden box at the same time as Wade and Bonnie and Duster.

Nothing happened at all, or at least that was what it felt like.

Nothing.

She didn't know what she had expected, but not simply nothing.

Except that Director Parks just vanished without a trace.

Or a sound.

"Where did Director Parks go?" Wade asked, his voice sounding almost panicked as all four of them stepped back from the box.

Sophie didn't even trust herself to speak. When she felt like this her voice just squeaked and very few words could be understood.

"He didn't go anywhere," Bonnie said. "We did. We are now in the timeline that is represented by that crystal there on the wall. In December of 1885."

She pointed to the crystal.

All Sophie could do was stare at the crystal. Could they really be inside that crystal?

Duster turned to Bonnie. "You want to wait here and pull the plug in twenty minutes, save us the walk back down here?"

"Glad to," Bonnie said, smiling.

"Let me show you the reality of what is really going on here," Duster said, turning and heading for the door.

Sophie took a deep breath and, with her hand firmly in Wade's hand, they followed a famous man from the past who was also a famous mathematician in the present.

Their old present, if what Duster was saying had actually happened.

TWENTY-TWO

December 17th, 1885
Boise, Idaho

WADE STAYED beside Sophie as they followed Duster out of the fenced crystal room and through the warehouse of old clothes and supplies. The room did not look as full as when they had gone through a few minutes ago.

That fact alone bothered Wade far, far more than he wanted to think about. And Director Parks just vanishing right in front of his eyes seemed flat impossible.

But if the story they had told was right, both things would be logical. Director Parks was still back in the present of their own timeline and since they were so far back into the past, no need for as many supplies in the warehouse cavern.

Part of him just wanted to stop and shake for a moment because he knew, just knew, they had been telling them the truth. But he still didn't want to admit it even to himself.

Sophie seemed to be handling this a slight bit better than he was. But at the same time she wasn't saying anything at all. And she kept squeezing his hand.

The three of them got into an elevator that looked like an antique.

"This isn't as old as it looks," Duster said, indicating the elevator. "We just had to camouflage it in case someone who wasn't supposed to be in here got in. We update it every decade or so along the way."

Wade was very glad to hear that because this looked exactly like the elevator that had been in early hotels around the 1890s or so. And those had not been safe by any stretch of any imagination. A person could do an entire book on the deaths and accidents in early elevators.

The ride up three floors was quick and the elevator emptied them into a wide room with no furnishings at all. Just polished pine floors, painted walls, and two doors.

"We in the main building?" Sophie asked.

"We are," Duster said. He pointed to his right. "That goes into the back part of the institute main building." He moved to the second door. "This one goes into the main room."

"I don't remember a door into that main room," Sophie said. "Besides the front door. Only archways."

"Lots of secrets around here," Duster said, laughing.

Duster looked through what seemed to be some sort of viewfinder, then turned to them and pointed to the viewfinder. "This will tell you if anyone who doesn't belong is in the main room. As expected, no one at all is there."

He pushed the door open slowly and led the way into the main room of the institute, the one where Wade had met Sophie months before.

The big desk was there and a fire was crackling softly in the fireplace. The same furniture sat in front of the fireplace. Even the drapes on the windows were the same and were pulled closed.

For some reason that made Wade feel better. They really hadn't traveled in time. But then he noticed that the room had a slight chill to it. It had been a warm day outside, so some sort of hidden air-conditioning must be on, set too low.

Sophie and Wade both looked around as they stepped into the big room and the door slid closed with a click behind them.

Wade was impressed. The door now looked exactly like a wall with a large framed picture on it.

"Now that's something from a novel," Sophie said. "You would never know there was a door there."

"Good," Duster said. "Latch to open it is built into the trim on the column there beside the door."

He pointed to it and Wade and Sophie both nodded.

"Now let's take a look outside," Duster said, turning toward the front door.

Duster opened the big front door and stepped outside into the gray light beyond the door.

Wade felt the incredible cold hit him almost instantly as he and Sophie moved toward the front door.

Duster moved out onto the front porch and Sophie and Wade followed. Duster pulled the big front door closed behind them.

Wade was having a very hard time grasping what he was seeing and feeling.

Impossible.

It was all impossible.

A light snow was blowing through the trees in front of the mansion. The leaves were long gone from the big trees, and it had to be ten degrees, if that.

The cold cut through his thin suit jacket and shirt like it wasn't there.

"Wow, this is cold," Sophie said beside him.

Through the snow he could see the stone wall along the front of the mansion, but it had no hedge growing on it as it had when he went through the main gate months before.

And the Warm Springs Avenue that he could see beyond the wall wasn't anything more than a wagon trail.

"Welcome to December 17th, 1885," Duster said. "It's about two in the afternoon."

"Amazing" Sophie said, moving toward the front of the porch.

"How is this possible?" Wade asked. His mind still wasn't letting him accept what he was seeing and feeling.

"We stepped into another timeline," Duster said. "One that is for every intent and purpose identical to our timeline."

"So you were telling us the truth?" Sophie asked, looking back at Duster.

Wade could see her eyes wide and round and intense.

"We were," Duster said, nodding. "Every word. And we have a lot more to explain, but you would not have stood for it without seeing and experiencing this first."

"Mind if we walk out to the road?" Sophie asked, turning back to stare out into the snow.

Wade just shook his head, but he wasn't going anywhere without Sophie and if she needed to see more, then so be it.

Duster laughed. "Be my guest. I'll be inside."

Together, hand-in-hand, they went carefully down the front steps and along the front stone walk quickly getting covered with snow.

Wade was so cold, he could barely feel his arms and feet, but that didn't matter at the moment. He needed to prove to himself as well that this was actually happening.

They walked through the blowing snow without saying a word until they reached the front gate.

Wade managed to get the wrought-iron gate open and they walked into the middle of the wagon road that went past the mansion.

This was a major five-lane road.

Or it will become one in the future.

Clearly they were in the past.

And at a different time of the year as well.

The two mansions on either side of the main institute building were all that was here. No sign at all of anything else being built along this wagon road.

"They were telling us the truth," Sophie said simply after looking first one way, then the other along the wagon track. "We are standing in 1885."

"They are offering us this so we can research our books better," Wade said, finally realizing what this was all about. "No wonder Dawn and Madison's books have such crisp details."

"I know, I just realized that as well," Sophie said. "And if I wasn't so cold, I'd be jumping up and down with excitement."

"Yea, me too," Wade said. "The impossible really is possible. We can go meet and actually talk with the people we want to write about."

"That's just amazing," Sophie said.

Wade looked both directions down the wagon road, then back at the institute buildings over the wall. Then he let go of her hand and put his arm around her shoulder. "I've seen enough. How about you?"

She nodded.

"Let's head back," he said.

They had made it back through the gate and were about halfway to the front porch, both of them staggering from the intense cold, when suddenly they found themselves touching the wooden box in the long crystal room three levels underground.

Bonnie had a wire in a gloved hand and was smiling at them. Director Parks was basically standing in the same place he had been.

Bonnie and Duster were also touching the box.

Wade could feel Sophie's legs start to get weak and he caught her and held her up. She was shivering and wet and he was colder than he had ever remembered being before.

Bonnie got on one side of Sophie and together they all headed out of the long room with Duster leading.

Wade couldn't feel his feet, but somehow he just kept walking, helping Sophie along.

"Let's get you both to a hot shower, dry clothes, and some hot chocolate," Bonnie said as they headed for the door of the crystal room. "Then over some early dinner we can explain all this in more detail."

All Wade could do was nod, but he had to admit, that sounded wonderful.

"Perfect," Sophie said. "Especially the hot shower part."

TWENTY-THREE

October 18th, 2018
Boise, Idaho

AFTER THE HOT shower and some chicken soup that tasted wonderful, she finally got around to asking a few questions. She and Wade had both had to change clothes, but luckily Bonnie and Dawn had predicted the outcome and got them some exercise clothes to change into that would get them back to their condos just fine.

While they were in the showers, Director Parks had gone back to work and Madison had headed to his office to do some research, leaving just Bonnie and Duster and Dawn to explain things.

Wade sat beside Sophie at the big kitchen counter in the cavern. Duster, Bonnie, and Dawn all leaned against the back counter in front of Sophie and Wade like three bartenders waiting to serve two customers.

All three had bottles of water in their hands and all three gave off an air of complete control. Nothing seemed to worry these three much. And Sophie was starting to understand why.

"So tell me how this traveling into the past of another timeline works, exactly," Sophie said, finishing up the last of her soup. The chill wasn't completely gone, but she felt a lot better and actually refreshed. That had been extreme cold. Not at all something Sophie was used to without preparing ahead of time.

And going from a warm fall day to the dead of winter in a few minutes was not preparation in her mind.

Duster nodded as Bonnie pointed to him to start.

Duster had taken off his oilcloth duster and cowboy hat and had tossed both over one of the stools down the counter. He didn't look at all fazed by the few minutes he had been in the cold.

"We spent just over twenty minutes in that timeline," Duster said. "We have recorded on the ledger under the crystal who went back and to what date and the duration of the stay in the past."

"So others can use that same timeline?" Wade asked.

"Exactly," Duster said. "And if we had stayed long enough to start to alter the timeline, new crystals would have formed in the original nexus caverns."

"Wondering how the unlimited timelines didn't instantly fill those tunnel rooms here," Wade said.

"We would not have been able to do that if new timelines didn't just form in the nexus instead of here," Bonnie said, nodding.

"So we were there for just over twenty minutes," Sophie said. "But I remember you asked Director Parks to just stay for the two minutes we would be gone."

"The time elapsed here is just two minutes and fifteen seconds," Bonnie said. "No matter how long you stay in the past of another timeline."

Sophie sort of stared at Bonnie with that answer. Her mind just wouldn't wrap itself around what she had just heard.

"So we could have spent ten years in that timeline and only two minutes and fifteen seconds would have happened here?" Wade asked.

All three nodded.

Silence.

Sophie still couldn't grasp what that meant entirely.

"You can live full lives in other timelines," Dawn said, "and even die in other timelines and only just over two minutes will pass here."

Now Sophie really had a problem. "Die? What happens when you die in another timeline?"

"In that timeline, you actually die," Duster said. "But when the wire is pulled from the machine or the crystal here, you end up back in your original timeline, alive and with just over two minutes and fifteen seconds older."

"Madison and I have raised families at the Monumental Lodge now in sixty-three different timelines," Dawn said. "We always stay until our kids have grandkids every time before we come back."

"And those kids and grandkids still existed when you left?" Wade asked.

"Yes," Dawn nodded. "They all think we are lost at sea or some other way that our bodies will never be recovered."

"You actually live in the other timeline," Duster said. "So anything you do creates still more timelines."

"Infinite number of timelines," Sophie said, more to herself.

"Exactly," Bonnie said. "But all the timelines we can reach in our area of the nexus are so close to this timeline as to be indistinguishable."

"So you three have all actually lived for a very long time, even though you don't look much over thirty now," Sophie said.

"A very long time," Dawn nodded. "Thousands and thousands of years, actually."

Silence once again.

Sophie was trying to understand what it would be like to live for entire lifetimes and then get a chance to simply restart. How was that possible?

"So the historical research you do is accurate?" Wade asked Dawn.

Sophie could feel a slight bit of excitement returning as Wade brought back in their research.

"It is," Dawn said. "I lived many lifetimes in Roosevelt and again many lifetimes in the lodge we build up the valley from Roosevelt."

"So why did you want us to research Grapevine Springs?" Wade asked. "You could just go back and visit it."

"It's not there," Duster said. "I did go back."

Silence once again in the big cavern.

Suddenly, everything they had been saying snapped into place and it all made sense to Sophie.

Complete sense.

"When did you go back to look for the town?" Sophie asked, smiling and laughing a little. "When in this timeline?"

"Right before we accepted you to the institute," Duster said, frowning. "It's why we had you both research the old town."

"And in all the other timelines that are similar to this one," Sophie said, "you would have accepted us at the same time? Correct?"

All three nodded.

"And this timeline is your base timeline, correct?" Sophie asked.

"The one we leave from is the base timeline," Bonnie said.

Sophie turned slightly and smiled at Wade. She stuck out her hand to him like she was offering to shake his hand.

He looked puzzled, but took her hand. "Nice meeting you, Mr. Olsen. I'm Mrs. Olsen."

For a moment she saw the puzzled look in Wade's eyes and she just kept smiling because she knew in just an instant he would understand. They had shared all the research on Grapevine Springs. Every detail that they could find.

Then, after just a second or so, she saw the understanding come over his face. He laughed and shook her head back, "Wonderful to meet you, Mrs. Olsen."

She laughed and kissed him. Then they both turned to face the puzzled looks from Duster and Bonnie and Dawn.

"You want me to tell them, Mrs. Olsen?" Wade asked, smiling again at Sophie. "Or would you like to?"

"Oh, we can share," Sophie said, laughing. "You start."

"In the late spring of 1897," Wade said, "just after the snow cleared in the area, a young prospecting couple found the Grapevine Springs Valley."

Sophie loved how Bonnie and Duster and Dawn were just nodding.

"Their names were Olsen," Sophie said. "They represented some wealthy businessmen in Boise who sold lots and helped finance the construction of the main part of Grapevine Springs."

"They ran the general store for decades until the town had mostly vanished," Wade said.

"They sold off their interest to the town in 1924," Sophie said.

She could see the look of understanding finally coming over the three brilliant people in front of her.

"Grapevines Springs didn't exist when you went back months ago," Wade said.

"Because you hadn't told us about the town yet," Sophie said. "Or any of this."

"And so when you went back, we hadn't started the town yet," Wade said.

Sophie just loved the shaking heads and smiles and chuckles from the three. It made her feel like she belonged here.

And that felt great.

TWENTY-FOUR

October 18th, 2018
Boise, Idaho

AFTER ANOTHER HOUR of talking and getting used to the idea that he could jump into different timelines, Wade was floored when Director Parks came back into the big cavern and said, "We need to get these two established in 2118."

Wade had no idea what that meant at all.

"You going to do it?" Duster said.

"I just told Kerri that I would be much younger when I got home," Parks laughed.

"Six months?" Bonnie asked.

"And you think Kerri wouldn't notice?" Director Parks asked, then laughed.

"2118?" Wade asked, not having a clue as to what the director was talking about.

"We built this institute like a way station into the future," Duster said. "This timeline just keeps moving forward and crystals are stationed every hundred years for the next four hundred years."

"Someone from 2118 can only come back as far as 2018," Bonnie said.

"We have all the different areas scattered in different chambers," Duster said, waving at the cavern around them.

"We are all established in the future," Bonnie said. "Long story on how we managed that, but we are."

Wade suddenly realized what that meant. "So if something happens to you in this life, you have only actually lived for just over two minutes in the future."

"Exactly," Bonnie said.

"You are immortal," Sophie said, her voice hushed.

Wade knew she was right, but couldn't really grasp it.

"In all reality," Duster said, "we have lifespans in a future time, but in this time, we can live and then live again for as long as we like. Just as we do when we go back into the past from here. So yes, in essence we are immortal. And in a few minutes you will be as well."

Wade just opened his mouth, but nothing came out.

The idea of living forever had never crossed his mind. He had a lot he wanted to get done and had always seemed to be in a hurry because of limited time. But now he was being offered unlimited time.

That was a dream he flat couldn't grasp.

"Painless," Director Parks said, smiling at Sophie and Wade. "I promise. Come with me."

"Might as well jump them to 2218," Duster said. "Just to be safe and give them a real tour."

Parks laughed. "I'm going to be nine months younger now. Kerri's going to have to catch up now. You know how she feels about younger men."

Duster and Bonnie both laughed at that.

Wade had a hunch there was a story behind that.

Wade and Sophie both stood and Sophie took his hand, holding on tight.

"We'll be back in about twenty minutes," Parks said. "Then we can talk about heading to Grapevine Springs."

Wade saw that Bonnie and Duster and Dawn were all nodding.

"We'll be getting ready," Bonnie said.

Wade decided to just ignore that until they finished what they were doing at the moment.

One major life event at a time was more than enough.

Director Parks led them in the opposite direction across the large living room area and through a door there, down a long carved-out-of-stone tunnel, and then down two flights of stairs.

When he reached the bottom and opened a door there into a massive cavern, the lights came up.

Wade was shocked. The cavern looked like someone had bought out an entire Walmart store. Maybe two or three. Everything anyone could need in this time, all sorted for easy access.

"How do you maintain all this if only the twenty-two of you know about this cavern?" Sophie asked as they headed through the large cavern to a row of doors on the other side.

"We do a lot of shopping," Director Parks said, nodding. "Take turns, actually. Some of us like it more than others. But from where we are going, there are just about sixty who know about this part of the institute and travel back to this time and places along the way. They help keep this stocked as well by buying and leaving things here when they leave."

Wade was stunned.

"Who runs the institute in 2118?" Sophie asked.

"I do," Director Parks said. "Remember, to be back here for a lifetime, I am only gone for a few minutes at a time in the future, although I do go back and forth far more often."

"Oh, yeah," Sophie said.

"And you run it in 2218 as well?" Wade asked.

"I do," Parks said. "Same reason. I am actually established and aging in 2318, but with all the work here and in the next few hundred years, I spend very little time in 2318."

"How many years have you actually lived?" Sophie asked.

Parks laughed. "Kerri and I gave up counting past five thousand years. Bonnie and Duster are far, far older than that."

Wade just flat wanted to sit down, but by that point they were at the row of doors in the wall. Parks opened the first one and went in.

The long room looked exactly as the other long room had looked that took them back to 1885. Wooden tables with wooden boxes on them, wire fences down both sides, and glowing crystals tucked into the stone walls.

"No one can go farther back with these crystals than this moment," Director Parks said. "Bonnie and Duster figured out a way to limit the range to exactly one hundred years on these and no farther back than 1882 from the first chamber we were in."

"Where is the other chamber to jump the next hundred years?" Sophie asked.

"It's in another area," Director Parks said as he led them down the line to a crystal that was already hooked up to a machine. "But at this point in time, it has no crystals in it."

Wade nodded. If the traveling was limited to only one hundred year jumps, there would be no reason to stock that chamber. So this place was like a train station. You had to change trains to go farther back or forward.

"How many researchers are authorized to go back into the 1880s?" Wade asked as Director Parks put on a leather glove.

"Counting you two," Director Parks said, "twenty-four. The twenty-four researchers who started in this time period so far."

"So no one from 2118 can access that other chamber?"

"They cannot," Parks said, standing next to the wooden machine. "Come over and hold onto me tightly as well as each other."

"That's this timeline?" Sophie asked, pointing to the crystal in the wall."

"It is," Director Parks said.

"That's the timeline we were born in?" Wade asked.

Director Parks chuckled. "Actually, you were born in every crystal in this room and every crystal in the entire complex and an infinite number of more crystals in the nexus caverns."

Wade suddenly realized what Parks was saying. If the universes were basically the same, then they were in all of them. Doing the same thing in each one.

"Come in close now," the director said.

Wade, holding Sophie's hand, put his other arm around Director Parks. Sophie reached around and took Wade's other hand so they had the director wrapped up in a giant hug, Wade on his right, Sophie on his left.

This was not a position Wade would have ever imagined himself being in with Director Parks.

Director Parks put his uncovered hand on their hands and then moved all three of their hands down to touch the wooden box. Then, holding on tight, he pulled the wire off the machine with his gloved hand.

Nothing happened.

"You can let go now," Director Parks said, laughing. "Welcome to January 6th, 2118."

TWENTY-FIVE

January 6th, 2118
Boise, Idaho

SOPHIE DIDN'T FEEL like she was a hundred years in the future. In fact, she didn't know exactly what she was feeling.

Director Parks left the one wire on the ground with the other still attached to the machine and the other end attached to the crystal on the other side of the fence.

He led them out of the room and through a very different warehouse room now. Some stuff looked the same, but there was a bunch of stuff that Sophie didn't recognize.

Director Parks offered no explanation, but just led them out, locking the door behind him. Then they headed through a long rock tunnel that seemed to bend and curve to the left.

"We are going around under the big living room area two floors up," Parks said. "No point in being distracted up

there at the moment since we are jumping forward again."

At that point he reached another locked door and went in.

"Wow," Wade said and Sophie had to agree. It was another massive room full of clothing, merchandise, and equipment of all sorts. Much of it she didn't recognize at all.

They went quickly through the room to the far wall that was again covered in a line of doors. And again, Director Parks opened the first one.

He went down the line to a machine that was hooked up to a crystal. Sophie could see other machines hooked to other crystals, which meant someone was in the past from here.

"Same routine," Director Parks said as he put on a glove.

"Didn't update the wooden boxes?" Wade asked.

"When something works," the director said, "why mess with it?"

Sophie nodded to that as she and Wade again gave the director a large hug.

Once again the director took their hands and touched the box while pulling the wire.

Then they all stepped back. "Welcome to 2218. Would you like to go take a look or just head back? But this is now where you are grounded. Anything in the past now is only taking two minutes and fifteen seconds of your life here."

Sophie wanted to take a look at the world, but at the same time, she didn't.

"Not yet," she said. "I think I would like to understand things a little more before I do, and maybe study a little of the two hundred years of history we just jumped over."

Wade nodded. "I feel the same way. And to be honest, I would be scared to death to go up there and look out that front door like we did in 1885."

Director Parks laughed. "All you would see would be other homes and an elevated magnetic transit. And some new trees. But I sure do understand."

"So we are based here now because we came forward with you?"

"That's correct. You have a lot of time to understand this time period. But before you do come to this time, you must come to me and we will jump you forward another hundred in case something happens here."

"So we can't be killed?" Sophie asked, still no sure about how all this was working.

"Oh, you can be killed in any past," Parks said. "I would try to avoid it, actually. But say you were killed in an auto accident in 2018, you would wake up in 2118 with only two minutes past."

"And if we jumped back before the accident?"

"You would jump back into a timeline where you had not jumped back in before. Infinite timelines," Parks said. "You can't be in the same time with yourself in any timeline. If it happens, time splits you to a new timeline where you are not there for some reason or another. Try to avoid doing that when you can."

Sophie nodded.

"Let's head back," Parks said, moving to a door in the cage and going in, "so Bonnie and Duster, as mathematicians, can explain more of this far better than I can."

Sophie watched as Parks wrote a note under a new crystal, then with gloves on, he hooked the wires to the crystal.

Then he came back out, closed the gate, and hooked one wire to a machine just down the table from the one his

wire was hooked to. Then he went over to the machine they had come through and checked the exact date it had been set for, then came back and set the new box.

"January 6th, 2118," he said, pointing to the timer. "About five minutes after we left so we don't fire up another timeline by crossing over."

Sophie nodded.

Director Parks handed Wade a glove and Wade put it on his right hand.

Sophie took his left hand.

"Hook the wire to the box," Director Parks said.

Wade did as instructed with the gloved hand and Parks looked at it to make sure it was right.

Then Parks nodded. "Both of you touch the box with your bare hands at the same time. Then step back and wait for me."

Wade glanced at Sophie and she could see the worry in his eyes that she was feeling.

"On three," he said. "One, two, three."

They both touched the box. Then stepped back.

Director Parks was gone. Just flat gone.

"Oh, shit," Wade said as they turned to stare at the box they had touched the first time. "How scary is this?"

Sophie laughed, her voice sounding strained. "Too damn scary."

At that moment Director Parks appeared without a sound, and the wire that had been disconnected from his box was now connected.

Sophie couldn't remember feeling so relieved before.

"How long was the difference?" the director asked.

"About thirty seconds," Wade said.

"Perfect," Director Parks said, smiling.

He moved over and went through the gate again to the crystal Sophie and Wade had come through.

He marked under the crystal on the tablet there.

"I wrote your two first names," Parks said, "and the word "full" meaning you jumped the entire time possible."

He pointed to the crystal he was using. "I already have that marked on that one."

"So we just did this in an infinite number of timelines," Sophie asked, staring at the two crystals. "That's why we can be in a different timeline than you and still be having the same conversation?"

"That's correct," Parks said. "And if something happened to you in this 2118 timeline, like an accident or death, only two minutes will have expired a hundred years in the future."

At that, he turned and led them out of the narrow crystal room, back through all the supplies that looked both familiar and very alien to Sophie, and then down the tunnel again to the door that would lead them back to 2018.

Sophie just followed, holding Wade's hand, feeling numb.

Ten minutes later, in 2018, they made it to the large living room area where Bonnie, Duster, and Dawn still sat talking.

It was going to take Sophie a very long time to understand completely what had just happened.

A very long time.

But it seems that she and Wade now had exactly that.

They basically had forever.

But she honestly had no idea what that really meant.

All she really hoped was that Wade wanted to spend that forever with her.

Not having him beside her was starting to scare her more than anything she had seen so far.

TWENTY-SIX

May 9th, 1902
Boise, Idaho

SOPHIE SAT on a chair in the top floor suite of the Idanha Hotel in Boise Idaho, looking out over the hard-packed dirt of Main Street below. She had noticed this old historical building a couple times when in the downtown area, but had given it no thought, since it had a restaurant and a bar and apartments in it in 2018. Nothing she was interested in.

But now, in 1902, she and Wade, traveling under the names Sophie and Wade Olsen, had a top floor suite and were getting ready to go down for dinner with Duster and Bonnie and Dawn.

The suite was wonderful, with a living room of overstuffed furniture and a large stone fireplace. Hardwood floors were polished to a shine and in places covered by tan area rugs. The trim was all painted a dark brown and a round area on one corner with a table in it gave them a wide range of vision over the growing city.

The bedroom had a massive feather bed, two dressers, and a closet. And the bathroom had running water and an actual toilet with the tank about six feet in the air.

Stunning luxury for 1902 as far as Sophie knew from her research. She had liked the hotel instantly, from the first moment walking into the high-ceilinged lobby to the wonderful smells of fresh bread coming from the restaurant.

For two days, after getting established in 2218 and returning to 2018, she and Wade had talked and trained with Bonnie and Duster and Dawn. Sophie could have never imagined herself riding a horse. Just not something she had ever thought of doing in New Jersey. But they had taught her how to ride on a saddle from the 1880s. And ride like a woman of the time would ride.

And they had gotten both of them a wardrobe. She would be allowed to wear her own underwear, and the pants and dresses they had made for her used modern materials, even though they looked authentic to 1885. They were about as comfortable as possible, considering the fashions and constraints of the time on women of means.

By the morning of the second day, both she and Ward were so nervous, they couldn't even eat breakfast. With every passing minute she had come to love him and depend on him more and more.

And he said he felt the same way, that without her beside him, he never would be doing any of this.

They had walked hand-in-hand from their condos to the institute along the river walk, both carrying small bags of personal stuff. They both knew they would only be gone from here for a few minutes, that later today they would make this walk back along the river, but there was no telling how long they would live in the past before that.

Bonnie had told them a story about how she and Duster, when they first started going into the past, had taken so many trips, done so many lifetimes one after another, that when they finally had decided to stop going back and actually go home, neither of them could remember how to drive.

They had laughed at that, but the idea of that had scared Sophie more than she wanted to admit, and that night, both she and Wade had talked and agreed to only a few trips into the past at a time before coming back to grounding and their work in this time.

But even with that, Sophie had no doubt she would be a different person the next time she walked this sidewalk.

And Wade would be different as well.

"Do you love me?" she had asked Wade right before they got to the institute.

He had stopped and faced her and taken her in his arms. "I love you more than anything."

"So you want to spend a lot of time with me?"

He had smiled and kissed her.

Then he said while holding her, "I can't imagine not being with you. In any time."

That had been what she had needed to hear.

Exactly what she had needed.

They had jumped to 1902 instead of all the way back to 1887 for more training.

For Sophie, the ride into Boise along the wagon trail that was Warm Springs Avenue was amazing and scary at the same time.

Sophie had spent her entire adult life researching the past she now was in, trying to imagine it, trying to imagine how women felt living in it.

For the moment, all she felt was total fear combined with a feeling of awe that she was actually here, in 1902.

Wade asked her at one point how she was doing and she had said, "Scared to death."

He had asked of what.

"Riding into an unknown situation and falling off the horse," she had said. "Take your pick."

For the entire ride she couldn't decide which fear trumped the other.

Besides that, the leather and cloth riding clothes of the time pinched her in places she didn't realize could be pinched.

She wore her wide-brimmed hat to keep the sun off her fair skin. She had brought suntan lotion in a bottle from the time, but not a lot and Bonnie suggested she not use it unless in an emergency.

Beside her on the ride, handsome on his horse, Wade looked both worried and fascinated and seemed to be taking in everything with his wonderful green eyes. He had on dark jeans, a wide black belt, a light blue dress shirt, a long oilcloth coat, and a black cowboy hat.

He hadn't ridden a horse either before, but had taken to it faster than Sophie had. He almost seemed at ease. She hoped she got to that state.

The plan was to spend a week or two in Boise in 1902, keep up their training, before jumping back to 1887. As Bonnie had said, the difference in Boise of 1887 and Boise of 1902 was stunning. Clearly she and Duster loved 1902.

Duster had jumped back a few seconds ahead of them from a different crystal, but about six months ahead of them in historical time, to get details ready such as making sure they all had horses and equipment for their short stay in 1902. Bonnie and Dawn had also used a different crystal and gone together.

They would all be gone only just over two minutes, but by taking different crystals, they could leave 1902 when they wanted.

So when they all reached the Idanha Hotel's beautiful stone and mahogany lobby, Duster had made sure they had room reservations

Now, after checking into the hotel and going to their suite on the 4th floor, Sophie was staring to relax and see the charms of being rich in the Old West. Especially with a wonderful room like this one.

But living in those mining camps was going to test her and Wade more than she could imagine at the moment. She wasn't sure she was up for it. She had never done any camping as a child and still hadn't spent a night in a tent. All of this was totally new, but she sure wasn't going to back out now.

She had studied the past most of her adult life. Now she got to be a part of the past, to actually start a western mining town. Fear of making a fool of herself or falling off a horse wasn't going to stop her.

Besides, this was where Wade was and being beside him, having him as her partner, just felt perfect.

She could have never imagined loving one person as much as she did Wade.

Ever.

TWENTY-SEVEN

May 23rd, 1887
Central Idaho Mountains

WADE HAD BEEN surprised at how much he had enjoyed the two weeks in Boise in 1902. During that time, both he and Sophie had gotten much more comfortable on horses and learned how to

Now Available
from all your favorite booksellers in trade paper and electronic editions.

DEAN WESLEY
SMITH

USA Today BESTSELLING AUTHOR

WARM
SPRINGS

A THUNDER MOUNTAIN NOVEL

care for them and saddle them and brush and feed them.

They both had also learned to shoot their saddle rifles and both had learned how to act as a married couple of money in 1902.

The last part had been the hardest for Wade. Sophie caught on quickly to that since she said she grew up with a lot of rules in New Jersey. She had also been a natural with a rifle, something that seemed to even surprise her.

Duster had spent a few hours teaching them how to pan for gold, the hardest work that a human should ever be allowed to do. If it wasn't for some lotion that Bonnie had brought along, Wade was convinced his hands would not have recovered quickly.

Now, after two weeks, it was just Duster with the two of them headed into the tall mountains of central Idaho. Around them the mountains towered impossibly high into the crisp blue sky. The pine trees smelled wonderful under the warming sun, and the snow on the mountains seemed to shine like a beacon of brightness.

Both Wade and Sophie had one packhorse each. They carried enough supplies to last for a month without problem. It would allow them to set up a camp in the future home of Grapevine Springs they could leave to go back into Boise in a month.

During the three-day ride into the mountains, they had seen a number of bear and more deer than Wade could count. Duster had taught them how to catch trout and how to cook them over an open campfire so that they tasted like a chef in San Francisco had done the job.

Both Sophie and Wade had decided that cooked like that, they wouldn't get tired of fresh-caught trout.

Duster had laughed and said that he never did. Considering how many thousands of years Duster had lived in the past, that was amazing to Wade.

Duster wasn't going all the way with them into the valley. He was going to show them the entrance to the drainage for Grapevine Springs valley and then head back to Boise.

The stream that flowed through the town site and down the valley was called Shannon Creek. None of them could figure out how the stream got its name. More than likely, Wade decided, it hadn't been named yet.

They had about a two-day ride to the future town site up the drainage from where he was going to leave them. Duster warned them about a few areas along the rough game trail. No trail in there was cut.

At one point, when describing the two-day ride they had into the future site of Grapevine Springs, Duster had said, "Some real rough stuff, so go slow."

Wade hadn't liked the sound of that in the slightest. And having Duster leave them scared Wade and Sophie more than either of them wanted to admit. Being alone in a wilderness was one thing, being alone in a wilderness well over a hundred years in the past was downright terrifying.

Duster just radiated confidence and considering the vast amount of years he had spent in the wilderness and in western towns, his knowledge seemed to be like a light to Wade in the darkness.

But now he and Sophie needed to go it alone. And into a valley that Duster, a man completely comfortable in the wilderness, thought was "Some rough stuff."

But history said they went in alone. The great Duster Kendal had not been with them when they entered the valley the first time.

The plan was that Sophie and Wade were to set up a camp and then pan for gold in the valley. They were to stake out a placer claim along the most open and flat part of the valley where the future mining town of Grapevine Springs would be, then head back to Boise with their gold and detailed, hand-drawn maps of the area.

That part would take about a month total, Duster had figured.

In Boise, Duster would help them through the process, be a secret investor, and they would file the claims as well as a plat for a proposed town mostly on their claims.

Then, with Duster with them, they would go back in and stay and work the placer and build a general store until just before winter set in, then go back to Boise to live in the institute until the spring.

Duster had suggested at that point that they might want to winter in the valley if they could get a house built before the snow started, but both Sophie and Wade had decided to hold that decision until later.

Wade was convinced it was a great plan, following what all of them knew from history of what Sophie and Wade Olsen had done.

But reading about it in history was one thing, riding along a streambed on a narrow game trail with snow-capped mountains towering over him was another thing completely.

Duster got Sophie and Wade both squared away the last night he was with them around the fire as they finished dinner. They had camped on a flat area above Shannon Creek.

The stream was wide at this area and high, running fast over rocks. To Wade it looked dangerous from all the spring run-off of the snow. Duster had told them they wouldn't need to cross the stream until just below the town site where the stream would be much smaller.

Duster had assured them that the stream wouldn't be like that at all up at the town site. "Good fishing there," he had said.

Wade and Sophie had pitched their tent, but Duster said he wanted to sleep out under the stars, even though the night was cold and the air still damp.

At first light of the sun coloring the tops of the nearby mountains, Wade left Sophie snuggled down in their bedding and climbed out of the tent.

Duster was gone.

They were alone.

In the most rugged and dangerous wilderness on the continent.

In 1887.

Terrified didn't begin to describe how he felt.

Somehow, he managed to not just crawl back into the bedding with the woman he loved.

Somehow, he managed to start the day.

Somehow.

TWENTY-EIGHT

May 24th, 1887
Central Idaho Mountains

SOPHIE TRIED to keep up a cheerful attitude as they made themselves breakfast in the cold, morning air. The sun was still hours from finding the steep valley floor, but it shone bright on the snow on the mountain tops above them.

She found it funny that neither of them talked about the sheer terror of being alone she knew they were both feeling. Her attitude was that if humans could survive in this country hundreds of years before them, then she and Wade could as well.

She just didn't say that out loud, and the thought honestly didn't help much at all. Her problem was too much research into this time in history. She knew how really hard it was on the people of this time. That very difficulty was what had fascinated her and how women had dealt with it.

Now she was dealing with it.

She just never expected to be one of the people from her own research.

They repacked their saddlebags, saddled their horses and the two packhorses. Both of them double-checked everything.

Then both got saddled and he said, "Here we go."

"I love you," she said to Wade.

He smiled at her, even though she could see the worry in his eyes.

"I love you as well."

"Together," she said.

"Together," he said, nodding.

At first the going was easy.

Wade led the way, followed by one of the packhorses. Sophie followed a safe distance back as Duster had taught them to do, letting her packhorse follow without much effort.

The pine trees around them seemed to tower into the sky, often blocking most of the sunlight off the mountains and making it feel almost gloomy in the bottom of the valley.

The rushing sound of the high, angry water of Shannon Creek seemed to fill every sense she had as the sound was often trapped under the trees with them. It was far, far too loud for them to talk.

There was very little underbrush since no sun seemed to reach much of the steep valley floor and Sophie only caught glimpse of the snowcapped peaks above them through the branches.

The path they picked along the river seemed to constantly climb upward and at times they had to dismount and lead the horses around rough areas or up steep slopes.

There was also still a lot of mud and some snow hadn't melted yet under a lot of the trees. Twice she had slipped in the mud, but otherwise she had done fine.

They rested after an hour in a very gloomy small rock shelf above the raging stream, each snacking on some nuts and getting a good drink of water.

Duster had warned them that at this attitude, they needed to make sure they were drinking regularly and taking in salt. He had laughed and said, "The last thing you two need on your first time out would be altitude sickness."

The next two hours just repeated the first and it wasn't until starting the fourth hour, after a short lunch break, that they broke into the daylight. The sun was now almost high enough in the sky to hit the bottom of the valley and it had warmed up enough that Sophie had shed her heavy coat.

She couldn't believe how good the warmth felt after being hours in those dark, damp trees.

The game trail they were on went up away from the edge of the stream and through some lower brush. It was easy going until they broke out of the other side of the brush.

Ahead of them was a talus slope.

The game trail sort of vanished out into the small rocks and nothing at all grew on the slope. The slope seemed to start at rock cliffs a good thousand feet above them and ended only in the angry water.

To Sophie the slope looked like an impossible river of rock wider than any football field. She couldn't even believe that rocks could stay on that steep slope without just tumbling on down into the water.

They both dismounted and just stared.

"How are we supposed to get across that?" she asked, knowing Wade had no more idea than she had. They were about fifty yards above the fast-moving water. One slip and they would be in the water faster than they could react, of that she had no doubt.

"Duster said to just go slow across it," Wade said. "Or we could stop and just camp and spend a week digging a trail and securing the trail across."

"He suggested that?" Sophie asked, glancing at Wade, then back at the slope blocking them. She had no idea how they would even begin to build a trail across that. But she had a hunch if she had asked Duster, he would have said, "One rock at a time."

He often had answers like that.

And she knew that the people who lived in this time period had the attitude of "You did what you had to do." Especially the pioneers into the west, which was, in essence what she and Wade were at the moment.

"He said that's what many do on slopes like this," Wade said nodding. "But he said he made it across and back without a trail and it is possible if we go slowly."

Possible?

She looked down at the raging water of the creek below. Going into that snow-melt water wouldn't be survivable.

She just couldn't believe that literally on their first morning alone, they were facing death.

Very, very clear death.

TWENTY-NINE

May 24th, 1887
Central Idaho Mountains

WADE DIDN'T FEEL like he was in a hurry and before they risked their lives, he wanted to stop and think. So they took a break, pulling out a map of the Grapevine Springs valley.

They had both studied the map many times before, and both of them knew this was the only way in and out of this valley. When the town got started, a wagon road was built into the town along this stream. And even though the town was remote, very few were ever killed trying to get to the town once that wagon road was dug out.

The mountains were so steep on both sides of the valley around the town that they made some of the best downhill skiing in the world. And the valley ended just above the town site in a rock cliff.

On the map he could see exactly where they were located.

"So say we get across this going in," Sophie said. "We have to cross it coming out as well."

Wade nodded. He had been thinking the same thing.

He went back to the edge of the slope and studied the area above them. If anything, it got steeper and snow still clung to the massive cliff that fed this scree slope. Nothing about it looked stable.

131

"We have no good options here," he said.

Sophie nodded. "And even if we do get across twice, we have to come back in here in a month or so with even more supplies."

Wade nodded to that.

"So we stop and build the trail now?" he asked.

She shrugged. "We build it now or on the way out or on the way in. One way or another, we have to build it."

He agreed. "Let's see if we can find a decent camp close by."

They found one just about twenty yards to the side of the talus slope. It had an area that was flat enough for their tent and a place in the brush to tie up the horses and feed them.

"Know anything about building a trail?" Wade asked her, smiling.

"I know we start first thing in the morning," she said, kissing him.

Wade liked that idea more than he could imagine. After just a few hours on this game trail in this valley, he felt exhausted. And what did it matter that they were late getting back to Boise for a week or so. Duster would wait for them.

They spent the rest of the afternoon enjoying the brief time the sun was hitting the camp and then eating a light dinner.

As the sun still hit the rock cliff above them, they fed the horses and got ready to call it a night. The air already had a chill to it and they had both put on their coats again.

Suddenly, the horses seemed very restless.

Wade instantly looked around for a snake nearby as Sophie worked to calm one of them.

But it did no good.

Then, over the sound of the water below them came a rumbling that sounded more like a massive piece of equipment moving.

The horses bolted, knocking Sophie to the ground.

Wade went to her and pulled her to her feet as the ground around them shook.

What was happening?

He had no idea.

"Slide!" Sophie shouted over the intense noise.

He instantly realized she was right.

And a moment later a twenty-foot wave of rock hit them.

Neither of them even felt a thing.

They were both dead instantly.

PART FIVE
The Brutal West

THIRTY

July 8th, 1887
Central Idaho Mountains

AFTER SIX WEEKS, Duster had a hunch something had gone horribly wrong. He had expected Sophie and Wade to maybe take five weeks, since they were new and would go slowly. But six weeks worried him.

Bonnie and Dawn had gone to San Francisco and he doubted he would see them again in this timeline. What those two found interesting about San Francisco was beyond him. He liked the more rugged, growing towns.

And, of course, the great poker games in Denver. He planned on heading that way once he had Sophie and Wade settled in for the summer in Grapevine Springs.

He checked the institute's weather records for the next few days for the central Idaho mountains just to make sure that this year there wouldn't be a freak summer storm up there.

Nothing.

So he packed up and headed out, following the trail that he knew they would take coming back, just in case.

The days were warm and he kept drinking and chewing on jerky as he climbed up into the mountains, a habit that he had gotten used to over the many years.

Making far better time alone, two nights later he camped at the same place that he had left Sophie and Wade over six weeks before.

The next morning he got an early start up the game trail along the stream, looking for anything unusual.

Shannon Creek was now nothing more than a regular creek, nothing like the raging torrent it had been six weeks before.

It was an hour into his ride that he saw the remains of one of the packhorses. No saddlebags were attached and wildlife had chewed at it, leaving mostly only a skeleton and a head, half-in the water.

He kept going, spotting two more horse carcasses along the way, but no sign of Sophie or Wade.

After three hours he reached the talus slope. He had warned them that this would be their first really dangerous place along the trail in.

Another horse carcass was tangled up in the rock along the edge of the talus slope just above the river and he could see the remains of a tent and some camping gear twisted in the rocks as well.

Skirting along the side of the loose talus rock, he went down toward the stream until he finally spotted what he now knew he would find. Sophie's body, half-buried under rock, right at the edge of the slope.

Below her, just above the water line he could see a part of Wade's hand. He didn't need to get any closer.

He turned and studied the slope above him. They must have camped very near the edge of the slope, more than likely to build a trail, and a slide had caught them in the middle of the night.

He shook his head.

He had learned early on to camp back away from talus slopes because of the regular nature of slides.

He climbed back up the slope to his horse and turned and headed back down the trail to Boise.

It looked like he was going to find out if the institute had picked well with Sophie and Wade a little sooner than expected.

There was just no way of telling how a person would handle and recover from sudden death.

THIRTY-ONE

May 23rd, 1902
Boise, Idaho

SOPHIE FOUND herself standing beside Wade in the narrow rock crystal room, touching one of the wooden boxes. They were both dressed as they had been on the way into Grapevine Springs.

Then Sophie remembered the terror.

There had been a rockslide.

They had been hit by a rockslide.

"What just happened?" Wade asked, glancing around.

"You died," Duster said behind them.

Both of them spun around to look at Duster as he came up and unhooked one wire from the box.

He had been touching another box to go back into the timeline just ahead of them.

"They did what?" Bonnie and Dawn both asked at the same exact moment from another box behind Duster.

"What time are we?" Sophie asked. "This still 1902?"

"It is," Duster said, "because this is where we all jumped from originally to 1887. Let's go out into the main room and talk about what we all did in those last two minutes."

Dawn giggled.

Bonnie said, "Hush."

Dawn giggled again.

Sophie was still trying to understand the terror of one moment knowing they were going to get hit with a rockslide and the next moment standing here in the cavern.

"You all right?" Wade asked her, taking her into his arms and holding her.

"Physically I feel fine," she said. "But very confused."

"Yeah," Wade said.

He kissed her and she kissed him back. That helped her more than she wanted to admit.

They were both here. That was what mattered.

Her mind was not wrapping around any of this, even though she had understood the concept of being established in another time and being able to die or live a long time and not have more than two minutes go by.

She just hadn't expected to have to test the idea that quickly.

Especially with the death part.

Beside her, Wade looked as shocked as she felt as they turned and followed Duster out of the narrow crystal room and went across the large supply room.

In the main living room area, the kitchen looked like it belonged in 1902 as did the furniture, but Sophie knew that there was ice water and a good supply of food stored in hidden rooms behind the kitchen area. And running hot water in the bathrooms.

"I'm headed for the shower first," Duster said. He looked at Sophie and Wade. "Get something to drink and then take a shower and we'll explain more shortly. Then maybe head into the hotel for a late lunch there."

Sophie nodded as Duster walked off.

"So what happened?" Dawn asked Sophie as Bonnie also headed behind the kitchen to take a shower.

"Rock slide," Wade said.

Dawn nodded. "Talus slope in the spring melt, right?"

"I think it killed us both instantly," Sophie said, glancing at Wade, who just slowly nodded.

"Yeah, got injured real bad in a slide like that myself," Dawn said, moving to get them something cold to drink as both Sophie and Wade sat at the wooden-topped counter. "Killed Madison and all but one of our horses. Took me ten more days to die from internal bleeding as I tried to make it back to the big cavern. That was before we built the institute here."

Sophie watched as Dawn shook her head. "I didn't make it."

"So how long were you and Bonnie in the past this time?" Wade asked.

"About forty years," Bonnie said, not even blinking. "We both love San Francisco."

"Oh," was all Sophie managed to say.

She and Wade had only made it less than a week, clearly Duster had waited for them and then went and found their bodies, more than likely taking many weeks, and Bonnie and Dawn had been gone forty years. All of them had arrived back here at the same point.

She leaned against Wade and he put his arm around her, giving her strength.

They needed to face that talus slope again. It had killed her once. It would not a second time.

She would learn how to be as tough as the women she studied.

A second time she would win.

THIRTY-TWO

May 24th, 1887
Central Idaho Mountains

WADE AND SOPHIE had gotten back to the talus slope above Shannon Creek one day ahead of the slide. This time they had camped back in the trees after Duster explained to them that often the reason there were no trees close to a talus slope was because of rock slides like the one that had killed them the first time.

They both had on their heavy coats and had the four horses tied securely a distance back in the trees to make sure they didn't bolt with the rumbling.

Duster also taught them a few tricks to building a decent trail across the slope once the slide passed. Wade was scared to death to face that slope again, but these kinds of slopes were normal in the steep mountains of the west, so he and Sophie both decided they needed to just get past their fear and get through it.

Now, they were standing off to one side, in the tree line, with a decent vantage spot for the coming slide. By Wade's best guess, it would happen at any moment.

Once again the sun was on the rock face above them, but the valley around them was in shade. Under the trees the air had a thick dampness to it and below them the raging waters of Shannon Creek filled the valley with a loud rumbling all its own.

"You find this sort of creepy?" Sophie asked, squeezing Wade's hand as they both stared up at the rock face.

"What?" Wade said. "Watching a landslide that killed us in another time-line happen? Nah, nothing creepy about that."

She laughed.

He let go of her hand and put his arm around her, pulling her close to him.

At that moment, on the rock face far up the hill, a large section seemed to just break away and fall, almost in slow motion.

He held Sophie tight as they watched the massive slide of rock gain speed, coming down the thousand feet faster and faster.

The sound just kept growing and growing until they could no longer hear Shannon Creek below them.

The force of it going past them almost knocked them off their feet as the ground shook and the wind felt more like standing in a hurricane.

Wade had never felt anything like that before.

Ever.

Nature was amazingly powerful.

Dust filled the air, swirling clouds and they both turned away to protect their faces as the clouds washed over them.

Then, after only what seemed like a few seconds, it was over.

The sound of Shannon Creek below seemed to stop, and only the sounds of an occasional bouncing rock echoed through the valley.

Through the settling dust, they could see that the landslide had filled in across the creek and water was quickly backing up behind it. And as they watched, the intense pressure of the water pushed through, carving a channel without seeming to even stop.

The sound of Shannon Creek returned with the added sound of rocks being tumbled along with the water.

Before the slide, there had been maybe a hundred paces of brush between the tree line and the main talus slope. Now most of that brush was gone, wiped out or stripped of all leaves and branches.

"Tomorrow we start the trail," Wade said, hugging Sophie.

"So what are we supposed to do between now and then?" Sophie asked, looking up at him.

He smiled at her. "Warm tent, warm blankets, two warm bodies. Both very much alive. I have a few ideas."

She laughed and moved around in front of him and kissed him.

Then she stopped and looked at him directly, her dark eyes trying to be serious but he knew she wasn't.

"So getting killed makes you hot?"

"No," Wade said, trying to keep a straight face while looking into her wonderful dark eyes. "Not getting killed makes me hot. That and your wonderful brain and fantastic body."

"Well, Doctor," she said, smiling. "You know all the right things to say to make a girl feel better."

"Wait until we get to the tent," he said, smiling at her. "I'll show you feeling better."

She laughed and then took his hand and started back into the trees toward their camp.

They were both alive and for the moment, they were going to celebrate that.

THIRTY-THREE

May 28th, 1887
Central Idaho Mountains

IT HAD TAKEN them three days to build the trail across the talus slope, as Duster had told them, "One rock at a time."

Sophie had been terrified the entire time, but Wade had insisted that they rope themselves together and also tie the rope to a large rock near the edge of the slope. That had helped the fear some.

And they had built the trail to last until professionals got in and built a real wagon road.

She had worn heavy gloves to pick up the sharp-edged stones, but after two days her hands were bruised and hurting and she had really smashed one thumb which caused her to use swear words Wade said he had never heard before or imagined.

He had looked at it and said it wasn't broken, just badly bruised. He had her ice it in cold stream water for an hour before he would let her think of going back to work.

By the time they finished the trail to the other side right before sundown on the third day, all she wanted to do was soak both her hands and then sleep.

Back in the camp they had both done just that and both had slept soundly.

By the time the sun was hitting the tops of the snow above them the next morning, they had crossed the slope. But her hands were so sore, she could barely hold onto the horse's reins.

In all of her studies about the women in the past, she had never run across a mention of sore and aching hands. Anywhere. It seemed that there was a lot of stuff about the women of the early west that hadn't been written about and she had a hunch she was just starting to discover them.

They took breaks every hour, continuing to follow game trails along the creek, often finding themselves a couple hundred feet above the water and often having to walk and lead their horses up tough spots.

There were two smaller talus slopes they had to cross, but both were so narrow, they figured out another way to cross them without spending the time to build a trail.

Wade roped himself to a tree, then went across first leading his horse. Then he came back and did the same thing again, this time leading his packhorse, and then a third time leading Sophie's pack horse.

She had objected that she could lead her own packhorse and he shook his head and reached out to take her hands. When he touched them, she jerked in pain.

"I can hold the reins better," he said. "We're a team, remember? This isn't me being macho, trust me, this is me being a team member."

She kissed him and let him take her packhorse across and then come back and take her horse across.

Then Wade tied his end of the rope to another tree on the other side and Sophie tied herself to the rope and went across as Wade took up the slack. That method worked for both small slopes and they both felt as safe as possible considering.

They found a nice rock shelf in the trees above the creek to make camp for the night on the other side of the last talus slope. They were just a few hours ride from Grapevine Springs future town site, but they both wanted to ride into the valley with the sun overhead instead of the dim of the evening.

Plus, they had one more problem area Duster had warned them about. They had to cross Shannon Creek just below the future site of the town.

Sophie was not looking forward to that at all. And when she had said that to Wade, he had smiled. "I got a couple ideas on that. Depends on how the crossing looks."

She just smiled at him and let it go because she was starting to realize quickly that Wade was very good at improvising ways to keep them safe. It seemed that dying during the last attempt at this valley had really gotten to him.

It hadn't exactly helped her confidence, either. But what it had done was given her a very healthy respect for how dangerous these mountains really were.

And how the pioneers into these areas never got a "Do Over" chance like they had gotten.

THIRTY-FOUR

May 29th, 1887
Central Idaho Mountains

JUST AS THE sun was filling the narrow canyon below the town site of Grapevine Springs, they reached the second problem area that Duster had warned them about.

The steep walls on their side of the valley pinched down to rock cliffs and there was no way for them to go forward without crossing to the other side of the valley, over Shannon Creek.

Duster had assured them that the creek wouldn't be running as high in this area, and that he crossed about a hundred paces below the cliff.

But from what Wade could tell, the drop in elevation and tightness of the streambed and the volume of water made the creek even rougher here.

"That's not possible," Sophie said, standing beside him and staring at the raging water twenty feet below them, right about the point where Duster had said he crossed.

Wade laughed. "No wonder no one found this valley before now. It's damn near impossible to get to."

"Got that right," Sophie said.

Wade couldn't even begin to see any way they could get themselves and horses across. The other side of the valley from where they stood seemed almost shallow and would be easy riding if they could get over there.

"When do the history books say we found this valley?" Sophie asked. "I've lost track of the days."

"Tomorrow," Wade said. "But we might just have to camp and wait for the water to go down and change history."

"I honestly don't mind the sound of that," she said.

Wade nodded. "I don't either."

The stood there for a moment together, watching the crashing water below them.

Finally Wade said, "Let's back up and find a spot to camp, then explore along the creek to see if there is any place that

might be possible to cross at this high-water level."

He had just trusted Duster to be right about the flow being smaller the higher up they went. It might be, but nowhere near small enough. That water was a nasty death to them or any of their horses. He had no doubt about that.

The went back for about ten minutes until they found a flat area sheltered in some trees, took care of the horses, set up camp, got some lunch, and then went for a hike.

"So what are we looking for exactly?" Sophie asked.

"First off," Wade said, "we look for any place that has calm flow, that water isn't crashing over rocks like an out-of-control washing machine."

She laughed. "Had one of those once. Not fun."

They walked upstream, stopping and checking the creek below them just about every hundred paces.

Nothing.

Every time they looked, the water was churning and tumbling over rocks. But about five hundred paces upstream, Sophie pointed to the other side. "Look at the high water mark there. It's still wet."

"That means the water is dropping fast," Wade said, feeling encouraged.

"So how about tomorrow we go back to the cliff area, climb up a little to see into the valley, and that way we won't be lying about when we saw it for the first time."

Wade liked that idea a lot. "Then we camp right where we are and wait."

She nodded. "That seems like what true pioneers with only one life to spend would do."

He laughed. She had that right. And he had no intention of spending another of either of their lives on this craziness. Patience was something he had to learn.

Being in a hurry in the Old West would get them killed. He had no doubt about that.

THIRTY-FIVE

May 30th, 1887
Central Idaho Mountains

THE SCRAMBLED up the steep slope the next day high enough to see beyond the cliff and into part of the valley beyond. Sophie instantly knew she would love it. She could feel that.

"That's a beautiful place," Wade said, standing just below her and staring into the meadows and trees of the valley beyond.

"Want to live some lifetimes with me there?" Sophie asked, looking down at him, something she seldom did since he was a lot taller than she was.

He looked up at her with those wonderful green eyes. "I'm looking forward to every lifetime with you."

Damn he sure knew the right thing to say at exactly the right time.

They stood there for a few moments staring at their future home, then started back down the steep, rocky slow.

That's when things turned sour once again.

Wade was looking up at her more than he was watching his own footing and suddenly there was a rattling.

Nasty, angry rattling that could be heard over the sounds of the water.

She froze.

Wade froze.

He slowly turned to look down at where his boot was within a half foot of a rattlesnake on a wide, flat rock.

The snake was curled and clearly angry.

Sophie was stunned that Wade hadn't stepped on the snake.

She wasn't that afraid of snakes and they had killed a couple of snakes already on this trip. But on the steep slope, there was nowhere for Wade to go quickly.

Her only thought was that the snake would strike at his boot. She knew rattlesnake bites were not deadly, but they sure made a person sick.

Wade slowly tried to move his boot away.

Slowly.

But the snake lunged and struck his pant leg, right above the top of the boot.

"Shit!" Wade said, jumping backward.

And when he did, he lost his footing on the steep rock slope.

He went over backwards before he had a chance to even try to catch himself.

Sophie watched, frozen, with nothing she could do to help him.

It was like a nightmare movie in slow motion.

He tumbled and tumbled.

Head over heels, going backwards.

He tried to grab anything he could to slow his momentum.

Nothing helped.

Then he smashed his back and head into a rock so hard, she heard the crack over the sounds of the stream.

He went limp at that point.

With three more tumbles, he hit the rough, angry water.

"Wade!" she screamed, moving as quickly as she could around the snake and down the hill.

By the time she got down to the game trail, his body was only flashing bits of blue color of his coat in the bouncing water.

A moment later he vanished downstream.

He didn't seem to be moving at all.

Or fighting to get out of the water.

As fast as she dared, she ran along beside the stream, checking every hundred paces for any sign of him.

She did that for the next two hours, all the way back to one of the small talus slopes before she gave up and turned back toward where they had camped, still checking the banks along the way.

By the time she got back to their camp she knew one fact for certain.

Wade was dead.

There was no doubt at all.

Wade was dead.

In this timeline.

At this point in history.

But she had to believe that he wouldn't be dead, that he would be standing beside her in the cavern in 1902.

And that when she went back and unhooked that wire from the box they had been touching, she could hold him and kiss him again.

She had to know that.

She had to believe that. She couldn't allow herself to believe anything else.

He was only dead in this timeline.

Just as they had both died in the other timeline.

She refused to let herself even grieve. They had talked about something like this happening to one or the other. The only plan they had was to get back to the institute.

Now she was alone in a wilderness that had already killed her once as well.

She had wanted to know how women of the west handled hardship. It seemed she was about to get a very real lesson.

THIRTY-SIX

May 31st, 1887
Central Idaho Mountains

SOPHIE TRIED to sleep, but without Wade beside her in their bedding and their tent, every time she closed her eyes she heard noises.

And if she actually did manage to drift off, all she saw was Wade tumbling down that slope, frantically trying to catch himself.

That vision would haunt her for the rest of her life, she had no doubt.

Finally, in the middle of the night, she got up, made sure her fire was stoked full so that it illuminated the trees and underbrush around her. She then sat there with her saddle rifle across her lap and had a little talk with herself and with Wade.

"So what would you suggest I do next, Doctor?" she asked into the air, her voice carried away in the sounds of the stream below her and the crackling of the fire. "Besides get some sleep?"

She laughed. She knew Wade would tell her to just sleep.

"Not doing that," she said, "until I have a plan."

The moment she said that, she knew exactly what she had to do. She had to get back to Boise, back to the institute, and pull the plug on this timeline for her and Wade.

She had to get him at her side again.

She couldn't believe how much she had come to love him in just their short months together. She felt empty without him.

For a woman who had prided herself on her independence, it was startling how much she had come to love having Wade as her partner.

Together they were stronger.

She knew that Bonnie and Duster and Dawn and Madison spent years and decades apart, but she wasn't ready for that yet. She wanted to spend some decades with Wade first.

It was strange how they had talked about one of them getting injured or killed. If that happened, the other was to just head to Boise and pull the plug, hit the do-over switch.

But when they had that conversation, she figured she would be the one killed or hurt, not Wade.

They had made it sound so simple.

"So I know the goal," she said out loud into the dark, cold night air.

The steam from her breath mixed with the smoke from the fire.

She glanced around in the direction of the four horses. She couldn't just leave three of them or two of them here. They wouldn't survive for long at all.

So she had to take them with her as far as she could. But leading a train of packhorses she knew was a skill.

Especially over the rough terrain.

"Jersey girl, looks like you had better learn that skill quickly," she said into the darkness.

For the next hour she sat there, watching the fire, listening to the sounds of the creek below and the creaks and moans of the forest around her.

Finally, she felt like she might be able to sleep.

She crawled into the tent and the bedding inside, putting her rifle where she could reach it quickly.

Then she said out loud, "I love you Wade."

Two hours later, at the first hint of light at the tops of the peaks above her, she was packing the tent and the bedding and leaving all of the provisions she didn't think she would need to take along.

She saddled up her horse and put a light load on the packhorse she had led, then got the other two horses ready, leaving Wade's saddle and gear behind.

It was going to be everything she could do to get out of this valley.

Everything a girl raised in modern New Jersey could imagine.

She loved researching the Old West and how women of this time dealt with the hardships. It seemed she might just have a chapter in a book if she made it out of here.

She looked around at the steep mountains still in blackness above her, the dark raging water below her, and the four horses. Scared didn't even come close to describing how she felt.

Not even close.

Terrified would be more like it.

THIRTY-SEVEN

May 31st, 1887
Central Idaho Mountains

SOPHIE, WITH SOME adjustments on the lead lines to the three packhorses, managed to get back down the steep valley to the first small talus slope. It took her two hours with only one break.

The sun still wasn't anywhere near the valley floor, but it was a beautiful day with bright blue sky overhead and she had a hunch it would be fairly warm eventually.

She tied the horses on one side of the forty-paces-wide rock slope, then worked her way across the loose rock slope with coils of rope over her shoulder.

On the other side of the slope, she tied the rope off around a tree trunk about thirty paces up the hill, then tied another end around her waist and went back across the slope, keeping the rope tight.

If she fell, the rope would keep her from going into the whitewater below the slope. She felt better having that safety line on.

She took her horse, made sure she had some supplies on the second horse in case her horse went down, and then went across the slope, going slowly, not allowing herself to hurry.

Then she went back three more times and eventually she had all four horses across safely.

From that point onward, she watched the banks of the water for Wade's body as she moved forward and did the same routine with the second small talus slope.

She really didn't want to see Wade's body, but she knew it would help her if she found it.

She forced herself to rest finally and have a large lunch and extra water and some salty jerky to make sure she kept her head clear.

The sun had now hit the valley floor and the day was warming up so much, she could shed her heavy coat.

At the large slope that they had built the trail across, she simply led each horse across one at a time.

Then on the other side, she rested again in the shade of the trees.

She found herself thinking that she was proving to herself that this valley could be beat.

But she still was a ways from the mouth of the valley, so she killed that thought and focused on two things.

First, she had to be careful and keep the horses moving slowly, but steadily over the rough ground.

Second, she needed to watch the banks of the stream for any sign of Wade's body.

She reached the original camping site at the mouth of the valley just as the light was vanishing from the tops of the peaks around her and the darkness was closing in.

There had been no sign of Wade's body at all.

She quickly got a fire started and the horses taken care of for the night.

Then, in the light of the fire, she set up her tent and bedding.

Every bone in her body ached, and she felt more exhausted than she could ever remember feeling before.

But she had beaten the valley, alone, and on her own terms.

She made herself eat a little, then crawled into the bedding and with the rifle near her, she said into the night, "I hope you'll be proud of me, Wade."

She was very proud of herself, that was for sure.

And a moment later, she was asleep.

THIRTY-EIGHT

June 3rd, 1887
Boise, Idaho

SOPHIE HAD MANAGED to get all four horses down out of the mountains and sold three of them to a rancher and his wife near the small town of Grangeville for a very cheap price. The rancher had wanted to give her more, but she had insisted that she didn't need the money, she just wanted to get the horses taken care of.

In exchange, the rancher and his wife fed her a solid meal and gave her some fresh jerky.

The days were warm and the lower she got out of the mountains, the warmer they got.

She had camped the second night near the ranch, then she had managed to make pretty good time along the wagon road for the next two days going south toward Boise. It was amazing how fast she could travel without having to deal with three other horses.

She had decided to go around the main area of Boise to get out to Warm Springs Avenue and the institute buildings. Duster and Bonnie had showed her and Wade how and she was surprised that she remembered the path.

She put her horse in the barn and gave her horse a good brushing and food and water and thanked her. She had been a wonderful horse and Sophie was surprised at that moment that she hadn't even bothered to name her horse.

She went through the secret passage from the barn into the cavern under the main house, carrying her saddlebags.

There was no one there. And no fire going in the large fireplace.

She had to get a message to Duster who would be waiting for them in town. But she honestly didn't know enough about the staff working this time period.

If she didn't get word to Duster, he would travel up into the mountains looking for them again and she didn't want that.

She decided to take a shower first and change into clean riding clothes and get something to eat.

She knew, had to believe, that Wade was only a few steps away through a cavern and would be there when she unplugged that wire, but she just couldn't let Duster worry about them again.

And she wasn't sure if Duster was sleeping here at the institute each night, or in one of the other buildings, or in town somewhere. Neither she nor Wade had thought to ask him.

Or if Duster was even in Boise at this point. He didn't expect them back for a month, so he might have headed off somewhere for the month.

So after cleaning up, putting on clean clothes appropriate for a woman of the age who was riding, and finishing a beef sandwich, she headed upstairs into the secret room behind the main room where she had first seen Wade.

No one was in the main room from what she could tell through the peephole, so she went out and made sure the secret panel shut behind her.

The living room hadn't changed in the slightest. Same furniture, heavy curtains open to let in the warm spring light, but no fire in the fireplace. The day was going to be too warm for that.

She went to the stairs and climbed them, making sure she made enough noise to let someone know she was coming.

As she reached the top of the stairs, Director Parks stuck his head out of a door and frowned.

Then Sophie could tell he realized who she was.

He came to her and hugged her.

And she hugged him back, feeling the immense relief that now she was no longer alone.

"I sent a rider for Duster yesterday," the director said, turning her toward a hidden door that would take them back to the cavern. "He's up in Idaho City playing poker. He should be back shortly."

Sophie looked up at the director, trying to keep her composure from the relief of not being alone.

"How did you know?"

"You told me the story in 2018," he said. "You had to wait around for Duster for almost twenty days. I figured I could help with that."

"I don't understand," she said. "If I waited the first time, how can you change that?"

"Just ran some longer cables to the same crystal you and Wade are hooked into," the director said. "Bonnie and Duster and I had wanted to test that and we figured this would be the perfect time to do just that."

Sophie was so tired, she wasn't completely sure she understood, but she was very glad she hadn't had to wait for Duster.

They had just gotten to the long counter and Director Parks was working on fixing them both a milkshake when Duster strode in from the entrance to the stable.

So after she hugged him, she told Duster what had happened, with Director Parks nodding.

And then the director told Duster what he was doing there.

Duster just shook his head and laughed, then he turned to Sophie.

"Well done getting yourself and those horses out of there. It's turning out that valley is very, very dangerous."

Sophie nodded, then she looked at Duster and said, "I think we have it tamed."

"It would seem so," Duster said, smiling.

"So can we now go retrieve Wade and tell him what happened as well?" Sophie asked. "I kind of miss him."

Both Duster and Director Parks laughed, but both of them went with her.

Back to 1902.

Wade appeared next to her, then grabbed her and hugged her and apologized for being so clumsy before kissing her in a way she would never forget.

In love with Wade didn't begin to explain how she felt.

She now knew, without a doubt, she wanted to spend lifetimes with Wade.

Lifetimes.

He was worth every hardship she had to face, of that she had no doubt.

THIRTY-NINE

June 8th, 1887
Boise, Idaho

THE THIRD TRY into the valley really did turn out to be the charm. Wade and Sophie went slowly and started a week later to allow the landslide to already have happened and the water level to drop where they needed to cross.

Wade felt even more challenged, since this valley had cost him his life twice already. And yet, he felt as if the valley no longer threatened him.

And Sophie seemed almost completely at ease with it. She had managed, on her own, to get herself, her horse, and three packhorses out alive. As she had laughed about later, "No one from 2018 New Jersey would recognize me now."

The two of them seemed to not want to let the other out of their sight. And Wade didn't mind that at all. They worked so well as a team; he wanted her with him.

They slept in each other's arms every night, something he could never imagine doing with any person before Sophie.

Finally, on June 8th, they made it across the stream and then up and into the wide valley that would be the site for the mining town of Grapevine Springs. It was as beautiful as it looked as a ski resort in the future, only very, very peaceful.

Wade loved it instantly. And he could tell Sophie did as well.

He felt like he was home. A very strange feeling he had never experienced before in his life.

They set up camp, found a perfect spot to build a home at some point, and then worked at panning gold. Both of them hated the process, but they needed to get enough gold to file the claims they needed back in Boise. So they panned until their hands went numb, warmed them up and put lotion on them, then went back at it.

Using that system, they managed three hours a day and found more gold than Wade could imagine them finding.

After just over three weeks of wonderful trout dinners and chapped hands, they reluctantly stored a lot of their equipment and headed back down the valley.

Wade was surprised how much he didn't want to leave the valley.

And Sophie said the same thing.

Back in Boise six days later, they filed the claims and got Duster to help them with filing the plats for the town site.

That took two weeks. Then with Duster and others with them, they headed back in.

Duster had a foreman who rounded up a crew in the Grangeville area to build the wagon road into the valley and another crew to come in and start building a general store and other structures along the main street, including the town's first saloon, The Daisy.

It took them just under two months to build the road in, including the bridge over the creek.

As the summer wore on and more and more miners came in and filed claims, the sounds of construction filled the once peaceful mountain valley.

Three Cold Poker Gang Novels
Available at your favorite booksellers.

Also, in August, the first piano arrived for The Daisy and from that point forward the valley was filled with music.

The plan they followed was taken directly from their research, and at some point Wade decided he would need to ask Duster what came first, the plan, the research, or what? It just gave Wade a headache trying to puzzle that out.

The summer seemed to flash past as more and more supplies arrived for their general store and more and more miners needed the supplies.

And from everything Wade heard, the gold being taken from the placer claims was high grade and a dozen tunnel claims had been filed and would be starting next spring as soon as the snow cleared.

He and Sophie had hired two men to work their claim for a very high percentage. Neither Wade nor Sophie had any desire to stick their hands back in that freezing cold water.

Wade was surprised how much he loved their store. He never expected to love working a general store, but he sure did. He loved talking with the people, learning a little about their lives and what they loved and didn't love.

And he helped out with the medical emergencies as well around the valley.

It was the best summer he could have ever imagined. And that was because Sophie was beside him the entire time.

FORTY

September 19th, 1887
Grapevine Springs, Idaho

SOPHIE COULDN'T remember being so happy for a summer before. She worked until her legs and back and hands hurt, then spent one hour each night detailing out the events of the day in her research journal.

By the end of the first two months, three women besides her were living in the valley and from her and Wade's best guess, a good two hundred miners and support people were also there. Tents dotted the landscape as far as they could see now.

The weather during the summer held nice and even a few days of rain seemed welcome.

In late August, Duster and another crew of men arrived to build her and Wade a home. Duster had laid out the plan for them and it looked wonderful, but the day Duster showed them the house plan had been one of those days where people were lined up in the store and Wade was needed in an emergency a half-mile above the town site.

So as their home went up very quickly, they both tried to pay attention, but they just knew it looked beautiful, tucked onto a flat shelf about forty feet above the valley floor.

It wasn't until Bonnie and Dawn arrived with two wagons full of furniture that Sophie actually made herself stop work and go look.

She and Wade left a friend in charge of the store and went to their new home.

It was only a ten-minute walk from the store up the valley, but as she took the walk, holding Wade's hand, she got more and more excited seeing the beautiful log home sitting there majestically.

All of the furniture, including a massive feather bed, had been unloaded from the wagons by the time they arrived and the wagons and horses were headed back toward the stables.

Bonnie, Duster, and Dawn stood in front of the house, smiling, waiting for them to arrive.

The house was made of logs, tightly fitted, with shakes on the roof. A large porch wrapped around the front, looking out over the valley, and a large window was cut into the front wall.

She had no idea how that glass window had made it up here, but it had.

She walked along the porch with Wade, listening to the sounds of the valley and the piano from the downtown area. She could easily imagine herself sitting out here in the evenings.

It was wonderful.

As they entered through the front door, a large living room with furniture and a large couch was on the right in front of a large stone fireplace.

On the left was a wonderful kitchen with a wood stove, a sink, and what looked like an icebox. And on one side of the kitchen was a large wooden table.

She had no doubt she and Wade would spend a lot of time at that table.

"The kitchen can easily add in running water," Duster said, "but a little early for that in time at the moment. Same with the bathroom plumbing."

Down a center hallway was a room on the right and two smaller rooms on the left. The large room on the right was a huge master bedroom with the large feather bed and a bathroom off of it with a huge tub and washbasin.

The other two rooms had desks in them and lots of shelves, at the moment all empty.

Sophie loved the place. Just loved it.

Wade hugged her. He was smiling as wide as she must have been.

"I think we have a home," Wade said.

"I know we do," Sophie said, hugging him back. "This is heaven."

"Got some special features," Duster said, indicating that they should follow him to the end of the hall and out back. There was a covered area out back that was for firewood to stay out of the rain and snow on the left and an outhouse tucked against the right and built like it was part of the building.

Directly across from the back on a wood walkway was a large door that went into what looked like a building dug into the hillside.

Duster pointed off to the right. "We brought you in water to a pool there from upstream. But until you can dig a well, make sure you boil the water."

Sophie nodded. That pool would be a lot easier to get water from than buckets down at the stream. And in the winter they could use snow melt just fine.

"This would be a standard meat and fruit cellar," Bonnie said, opening the door that went into the building dug into the hill.

Sophie was impressed. There was more than enough shelving to hold supplies for a very long time.

Duster moved over and clicked a hidden latch on one shelf and it swung inward, showing another room behind the shelf.

"Anything from the future you bring in needs to be kept back here," he said. "The two rooms on the left have no windows and have some pretty secure locks, and a generator could be set up in here to charge batteries for laptops and such to work on in those two rooms."

"Wow, just wow," Sophie said.

Wade shook Duster's hand and Sophie hugged first Bonnie, then Dawn.

"How can we ever thank you," Sophie asked.

"We built it for you in this timeline," Duster said. "In other timelines, it will be up to you."

Sophie loved the sound of that.

Other timelines, other lifetimes.

That sounded wonderful, just wonderful.

So that evening, she and Dawn cooked the five of them a wonderful venison steak dinner with grilled potatoes and fresh corn brought in from a Grangeville area farm.

And the next morning Bonnie, Duster, and Dawn headed down the valley. Duster had left them weather data for the next ten years and in three days the first snow would hit.

And in a week that wagon trail into Grapevine Springs would be rough going.

Sophie and Wade were about to live their first winter in their new home town.

In their new home.

And Sophie was excited.

As long as she could do it with Wade at her side, that was all that mattered. They would face the future together.

Face all of the futures, actually.

EPILOGUE

August 12th, 1892
Grapevine Springs, Idaho

DUSTER AND BONNIE and Dawn and Madison had decided on the fifth summer of Grapevine Springs existence, to go visit Sophie and Wade and see how Grapevine Springs was doing.

Duster had spent the last five years in Denver, playing cards, and then helping out a small town in Northern Nevada with some law issues.

Bonnie and Dawn had been in San Francisco for the five years, and Madison had spent his time in a mining town in Montana doing research for his next book.

Duster was impressed at Grapevine Springs from the moment they crossed the main bridge on the road in. It now had three saloons and law offices and two large stables. The main street of town had boarded sidewalks on both sides and a good half-dozen bridges that he could see spanned the creek up the valley.

Many, many log homes dotted the edge of the hills, with very few tents left in evidence. Sophie and Wade's home looked huge sitting above the hill and it clearly had been added on to in the last five years.

The feeling of the town as they left their horses in the stable and moved up the walkway was of energy, but controlled energy.

And when the four of them went into the front door of the general store, Duster was even more shocked. The place was fully stocked and smelled like fresh cookies. It was, without a doubt, one of the nicest general stores he had ever been in.

Sophie was behind the counter and looked up and beamed.

She shouted for Wade in the back room and when she came around the counter to hug them, Duster got an even larger shock.

Sophie was pregnant.

Very pregnant.

Like any day pregnant.

And when Wade came out of the back room, he was walking a two-year-old boy.

Duster just stood there, staring.

Dawn and Madison instantly shouted for joy and went to them. Dawn and Madison had raised many families in the past in the Monumental Lodge that they wouldn't even build yet in this timeline for another ten years, so they instantly understood.

Bonnie came over and hugged Duster, then whispered in his ear. "Your kids need to grow up. Don't be shocked when they do."

Duster just laughed at that. He wasn't certain why he was so shocked. It just wasn't what he had expected. But since Wade was an MD, they clearly knew what they were doing.

No wonder their home on the hill looked like it had additions added.

Duster learned later that Sophie and Wade had gone back to 2018, in the summer of 1888, leaving the timelines

plugged in, gotten computer and other supplies they would need for their research, including many medical supplies, and come back to 1888 just one day after they left.

They did that every summer since, being gone from their store for less than a week. Wade had gone alone this summer since Sophie was pregnant and the summer when she was pregnant with their son.

Sophie and Wade got some help to run the store and watch their son for them for the day and then gave Duster, Bonnie, Dawn, and Madison a tour of their town.

Duster was impressed. The town had no marshal but seemed to run itself. The lawyer by the name of Bryce was the

This book is serialized in this issue and the last issue. If you would like a copy in book form or to give to a writer friend, the book is

Now Available
from all your favorite booksellers
in trade paper
and electronic editions.

With more than a hundred published novels and more than seventeen million copies of his books in print, USA Today bestselling author Dean Wesley Smith knows how to outline. And he knows how to write a novel without an outline.

In this WMG Writer's Guide, Dean takes you step-by-step through the process of writing without an outline and explains why not having an outline boosts your creative voice and keeps you more interested in your writing.

Want to enjoy your writing more and entertain yourself? Then toss away your outline and Write into the Dark.

mayor and major decisions about the town were dealt with by a committee of business owners.

In all his travels around the west, Duster had never seen a town so well run and calm, especially a mining town.

Later that day, they were out in front of the general store, standing in the warm sun, talking about how the town had developed and who was here for the summer, when Duster glanced around just in time to see a man take their picture.

He started laughing and got them all to look around as the man waved and smiled at them.

"He just took the picture of us, didn't he?" Wade asked. "That's Bryce, our resident lawyer, mayor, and photographer."

"That's the picture you found the day we told you about timeline travel," Duster said. "Don't you just love this traveling in timelines?"

"I do," Wade said. "Everything goes around and comes around."

"So do I," Sophie said, hugging Wade as best she could with her large stomach. "I'm just glad I had my back to the camera when he took that shot. Imagine if I had been pregnant in that photo?"

"You were pregnant in that photo," Duster said, smiling. "You just couldn't tell."

"Told you that you looked good," Wade said, smiling at Sophie.

"Don't even try," Madison said. "I gave up trying to tell Dawn she looked good pregnant about forty kids ago."

"I still appreciated it," Dawn said, kissing her husband.

With that, Duster followed the others up the street and then along the wagon road to the large house on the side of the hill.

Around them, Grapevine Springs hummed along, the sounds of construction filling the air mixing with the music from the pianos in the saloons.

He had thought this valley beautiful when he found it uninhabited. But now he found it even more beautiful.

It seemed the mystery of Grapevine Springs has been solved.

He liked that.

He had hated the idea that history could be cheated by simply being planted for the sake of money. That had bothered him more than he wanted to admit.

To him, history was everything.

He loved history, he loved supporting the research into history. He loved the researchers who worked to get history correct, no matter how politically wrong or inconvenient that might be.

And more than anything, he loved living in the history.

He loved the people and the way of life and everything about it.

Even after thousands of years of living in the past, it just never got old.

Available at Your Favorite Bookstore

Now Available
from all your favorite booksellers
in trade paper and electronic editions.

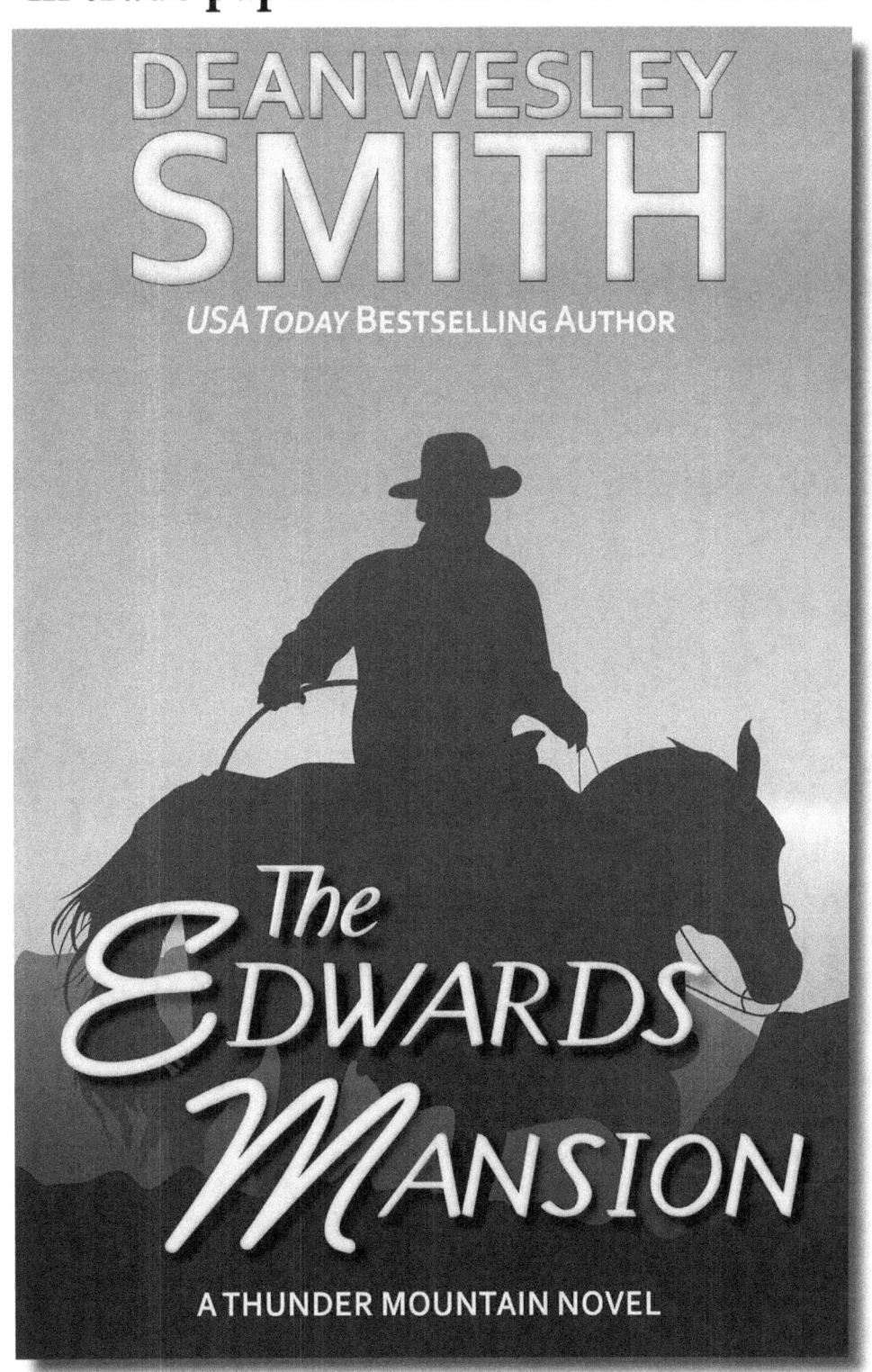

#1... October 2013

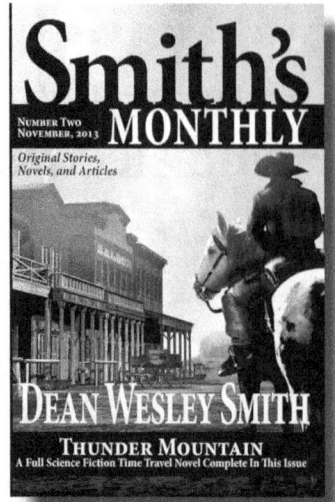

#2... November 2013

#3... December 2013

#4... January 2014

#5... February 2014

#6... March 2014

#7... April 2014

#8... May 2014

#9... June 2014

#10... July 2014

#11... August 2014

#12...September 2014

#13...October 2014

#14...November 2014

#15...December 2014

#16...January 2015

#17...February 2015

#18...March 2015

#19... April 2015

#20... May 2015

#21...June 2015

#22...July 2015

#23...August 2015

#24...September 2015

Don't Miss an Issue!

Subscribe

Electronic Subscription:

6 Issues... $29.99

12 Issues... $49.99

Paper Subscription:

6 Issues... $59.99

12 Issues... $99.99

For Full Subscription Information Go To:

www.SmithsMonthly.com

All Issue Also Available at Your Favorite Bookstore

Now Available
from all your favorite booksellers
in trade paper and electronic editions.

Thank You!!

I would like to thank the following wonderful people who support my blog and my work through Patreon. Your support is very important to me. Thanks!

Betsy Wilcox -
Irette Y. Patterson -
Kathryn Rooney -
Wendy Lee Maddox -
Jamie Curierre -
Chris Cousino -
Jane Lawson -
Shantnu Tiwari -
Miguel Angel Alonso Pulido -
Nancy Hendrickson -
Ryan M. Williams -
Jacob Proffitt -
Marian Goldeen -
Gary Speer -
Megan Bryce -
Michelle Tatam -
Ann Tucker
Kari Wolfe -
Albert Lemke -
Stacey Larson -
Diane Darcy-
Krystle Jones -
Kari Gallagher -
T. Thorn Coyle -
Tasha Turner Lennhoff -

Erick Lindman -
Christopher Ridge -
Terry Mixon -
James Husun -
Sherman Cox -
Chong Go -
Maria Grace -
Grondpom -
Fen -
Robin Brande -
J.R. Murdock -
Kathleen McClure -
Gunnar Gunderson -
F.I. Goldhaber -
Mary Jo Rabe -
John Kilgallon -
Dave Hendrickson -
Jabberwocky -
Eric Goebelbecker -
Marsha Kessler -
Scott Gordon -
Martyn Folkes -
John -
Cj Lehi-
Brenda Smith -

www.ingramcontent.com/pod-product-compliance
Lightning Source LLC
Chambersburg PA
CBHW081151170626
46813CB00009B/3150